THERE'S NO WAY I'D DIE FIRST

THERE'S NO WAY I'D DIE FIRST

LISA SPRINGER

DELACORTE PRESS

Text copyright © 2023 by Lisa Springer
Jacket art copyright © 2023 by Betsy Cola
Dark black textured background by YENI/stock.adobe.com
Umbrella art by Мария Запеченко/stock.adobe.com
Blood drops and splatters art by tiena/stock.adobe.com
Vomit emoji by Vladymstock/stock.adobe.com
Claw marks art by Nataliia/stock.adobe.com
Film reel icon art by Comauthor/stock.adobe.com

All rights reserved. Published in the United States by Delacorte Press, an imprint of Random House Children's Books, a division of Penguin Random House LLC, New York.

Delacorte Press is a registered trademark and the colophon is a trademark of Penguin Random House LLC.

Visit us on the Web! GetUnderlined.com

Educators and librarians, for a variety of teaching tools, visit us at RHTeachersLibrarians.com

Library of Congress Cataloging-in-Publication Data is available upon request.
ISBN 978-0-593-64317-4 (trade) — ISBN 978-0-593-64319-8 (ebook)

The text of this book is set in 11-point Warnock Pro Light.
Interior design by Cathy Bobak

Printed in the United States of America
10 9 8 7 6 5 4 3 2 1
First Edition

To my sister, for sharing your horror books even
though you knew I was afraid of the dark

When the people have no more to eat,
they will eat the rich!

—Jean-Jacques Rousseau

THE GUEST LIST

Noelle Layne   Host of Jump Scares horror movie club
                          and aspiring film critic.

Archer Mitchell   Singer. Songwriter. Hitmaker.

Demario Rollins   Star swimmer. All-around good guy.

Elise Thomas   Makeup guru and designer darling.

Kelsi Crankenshaw   Model. Jet-setting heiress.

Dylan Hansen   Lacrosse captain. Thrives on big moments.

Josh Sullivan   Award-winning host of *A Lot to Unpack*
                          podcast.

Taylor Kissick   Low-key world traveler and animal lover.

Mariana Martinez   Broadway fanatic. Randomly breaks into
                          Hamilton songs.

Hailey Daniel   Social activist on a mission to change the
                          world.

Vivek Bhatia   Internet entrepreneur poised to take over
                          the metaverse.

Maddie Xu   Fashion influencer. Too busy shopping to
                          care.

Charlie Huang   Finance bro. Trusted crypto expert.

PROLOGUE

Two weeks before Fright Night

Josh Sullivan: Welcome to *A Lot to Unpack with Josh Sullivan,* the culture podcast where no topic is off-limits. We're talking to the one and only Noelle Layne, who's making quite a splash—or should I say slash—with Jump Scares, a movie club for all things horror. Her watch parties are bringing over a thousand viewers every month, with thousands more following on social. What's going on, Noelle?

Noelle Layne: I'm great. Thanks for having me.

Josh Sullivan: So, let's start at the beginning. Why horror? I pegged you more as a rom-com kinda girl.

Noelle Layne: [*laughs*] Listen, rom-coms and horror have a lot in common. There's sacrifice, loss, and a light at the end of the tunnel. Both genres take us on an emotional journey. It's like holding a mirror up to yourself and asking, "What are you afraid of?" The mirror is just bloody in horror.

Josh Sullivan: And what's different about Jump Scares is that you feature a lot of Black horror in your watch parties. Gotta admit I'd never heard of *Blacula* before I signed up. Man, that movie's wild!

Noelle Layne: I love everything about the genre, but I have a special spot in my heart for Black cinema. And I'm not just talking about horror movies with Black people in them. I'm talking about Black horror movies made by Black people. I don't want to feature movies that focus on racial terror for entertainment, but movies where Black experiences are at the forefront and where we explore the things that scare us, ya know? And where we even make it out alive!

Josh Sullivan: [*laughs*] And that fear of what will happen next is universal. I mean, I'm a massive fan of *Get Out.*

Noelle Layne: Me too. It was the first Black horror movie where I really saw my fears on-screen.

Josh Sullivan: Plus, you and I bonded over *Get Out* because for the first time, I was able to tap into the universal fear that comes with loss of agency and control of one's body.

Noelle Layne: Exactly. But the canon is so much more than one movie. Black horror has such a rich film history, despite Hollywood ignoring us for years and years and years. We want escapism with characters who look like us, but what exists now rarely gets mainstream recognition and that's why I started Jump Scares.

Josh Sullivan: Nice. And I hear you're planning something exclusive for the club's first anniversary.

Noelle Layne: Yeah, yeah. I've got a special movie lined up, and I'm hosting a private Fright Night party.

Josh Sullivan: Love a Fright Night. What more can you tell us about this party?

Noelle Layne: I've invited twelve of the top influencers from Salford Prep who are also Jump Scares members for some fun and games. No spoilers, but people will be talking about this night for a long time. I'm hoping that with their individual connections, they'll also bring lots of new followers to the Jump Scares community, and it'll be the perfect launching pad for a podcast.

Josh Sullivan: Exclusive Halloween parties and a podcast about horror movies. I'm ready for all of it! If you had to rate your Fright Night on a scale from twisty to sinister, what's it gonna be?

Noelle Layne: Absolutely diabolical.

Josh Sullivan: My invitation better be in the mail, then.

Noelle Layne: [*laughs*] Careful what you wish for.

CHAPTER 1

**"It's Halloween, I guess everyone's
entitled to one good scare."**
—Halloween **(1978)**

I'm not one to seek attention, but I don't mind having all eyes on me today. It's the first anniversary of my horror movie club and the day of what will be the most epic party Salford Prep's senior class has ever seen. Hopefully.

I hop out of my car, my best friends Elise and Demario following a moment later. They popped out at lunchtime with me to help grab last-minute goody bag items.

A year ago, I never would have expected my mini rant on Insta about Black people being offed first in horror movies to go viral. Or that hundreds would log on when I threw out a random invitation to watch a horror movie with me online, one where the Black person actually makes it to the closing credits. That's one of many reasons why I think *Get Out* is the greatest movie ever made. And my obsession with the film is why each of the twelve invitations to my anniversary party was accompanied by a vintage Tiffany silver spoon, a nod to the movie's legendary hypnosis moment. With all the spooky activities I've got planned, everyone's going to the Sunken Place.

A gust of wind swirls through the parking lot of the Glen Cove strip mall, located a few miles away from New York City, scattering a raked pile of burgundy leaves. I tighten the belt of my coat. Like every other beach town in the Northeast, it gets pretty cold this time of year.

"We're gonna be late getting back to school," Demario grumbles. "You're really doing this?" He rubs his hand over his head, tousling his short locs. He's got rich dark-brown skin, and broad shoulders from competitive swimming.

"Yes, we are," I say, making a beeline to the antiques shop. The window display is overdone, with a mix of skulls, hanging bats, and spiders.

I glance at Demario, unable to contain my excitement or laughter. Going to see a tarot reader on Halloween is the perfect content for building buzz.

I've got about forty thousand followers across both my Tik-Tok and Instagram accounts. After tonight, I'm hoping to hit fifty. The magic number where I follow through with my plan of expanding my Jump Scares brand into a podcast.

"Need help with your makeup for the party?" Elise asks. She tucks a handful of unruly hair behind her ear. It's a combination of loose coils and tight springy curls, from her Black and Filipino ancestry. Elise plans to follow in her mom's footsteps as a Broadway makeup artist, and she's my go-to when it comes to glam.

"Yes, prom makeup, but make it dark," I say. My costume is top-secret. Not even these two know what I'm wearing.

Witchy bells chime overhead as the door swings open.

"Did you see Archer liked your last post?" Elise says, showing me her phone. "Then again, he likes *all* your posts."

The cheesiest grin spreads across my face. "Stop." Yesterday, I posted a teaser about going to a tarot reader and asked followers to drop questions I should ask in the comments.

Archer Mitchell might be a big-deal musician now, but when I first started crushing on him, back in middle school, he was just a scrawny kid with spiky blond hair and a nose ring, making music and posting videos online. Then, last summer, one of his songs blew up on TikTok and he landed a record deal, and now *Billboard* calls him a "hitmaker." But to me, he's still just Archer, the nice guy who sits next to me in AP English.

Smoke swirls from a stick of incense burning in a wooden boat holder that produces an overwhelming smell of lavender. The midday sun glints off a set of silver trinkets displayed on the countertop along with a clutter of collectible plates and shiny polished candlesticks and other knickknacks. There's a sign near the doorway: PSYCHIC READINGS BY ADELINA.

Demario gets his phone ready. He films most of my reels and other social media stuff and gets a real kick out of me being awkward on camera. Since I launched Jump Scares a year ago, people are taking notice, and the response to my poll on whether I should start a podcast was an overwhelming yes. My escape room event last spring with a *Haunting of Hill House* theme was a success, and the summer outdoor horror movie in the park had a huge turnout. But Halloween is my favorite time of the year. Aside from the entertainment, it's cozy, the temperature is cooling everything down, and pumpkin spice season has begun.

A girl appears from down a narrow aisle and introduces

herself as Adelina. I first notice the contrast between her pale skin and ombré blue hair. She's dressed in baby blue and pink from head to toe. And with the black lipstick, her outfit's giving serious pastel goth.

Adelina leads me to a geometric patterned table behind a tangerine-colored Moroccan-inspired curtain. I smile at Demario's phone camera, masking the anxiety that threatens to rise to the surface.

Listen, I'm pumped about this party. Hella stressed too, though, because what if it flops? My nerves are buzzing—not only is this a huge milestone for the club, but it's also the launch of something much bigger. Instead of me just uploading cult classics to a streaming platform for my monthly watch party, people are actually coming over to my house. Everyone thinks I'm renting a place by Crescent Beach like I did for the escape room, so when I drop the location pin, they're going to freak. No one passes up an invitation to Castle Hill, thanks to Mom being a legend for the epic parties she throws.

Everything's ready—the house is decorated with nightmare-inducing black and orange decorations. I've got a mouthwatering catering menu to die for. Plus, my parents have taken off for an anniversary weekend in the Adirondacks.

So, if not now, when?

I get comfy in the chair as an electronic dance version of "I Put a Spell on You" plays at a low volume from a speaker.

"Do you want to ask the deck a question?" Adelina asks, handing it to me. "Handling the cards will help you tap into your intuition."

"Right," I say, fanning out the cards like in a poker game.

I bite back laughter. Tarot cards are fun and the perfect vibe for Halloween, but it's not like I take them seriously. I clear my throat and ask the question that got the most likes on my poll. "Is starting a podcast the best move for me right now?"

Weirdly, posing the question out loud brings out all my insecurities. There are tons of horror-related podcasts out there. I'm trying to build credibility as a film critic, but on a podcast I'll be just another voice echoing in the wind. *Why would anyone be interested in what I have to say?* has been a persistent thought.

Adelina shuffles the cards and cuts the deck by dividing it, then combining them into one again. She pulls three cards and sets them facedown on the table.

She flips the first card. Her glossy lips part in the tiniest *O*. There's an image of a hand coming out of the clouds holding a coin.

"Oh shit, is that a pentagram?" Demario asks from behind the camera.

I lean over for a better look. Um, yep, that's a pentagram. *Ominous.*

"Ace of Pentacles," Adelina says, nodding. "It's about growth and prosperity. A new beginning or venture will bring along great opportunities."

"Ha!" I pop my fingers into a V sign for the camera. "Okay, next card."

Adelina turns it over and her lips flatten into a thin line. The lady on the card is sitting up in bed with her head in her hand as if jolted awake from a nightmare.

"What's wrong?"

"The Nine of Swords," Adelina says. She lets out a wispy sigh.

"Pain. You're carrying worry or guilt. Something's weighing on you."

"I do have an AP Chemistry test on Monday that I haven't started studying for," I say. It's my senior year, I'm beyond worried. Besides the fact that college application and internship deadlines are coming up, Salford Prep's biggest influencers are coming to my house because I promised a standout party and my parents think I'm just having a few friends over for movie night. Luckily, Dad's personal assistant, who never asks any questions, pays the credit card bill, and she'll assume Mom had an event. Mom stopped checking my socials after I uploaded a gory video clip from *The Human Centipede 2,* so she has no clue that it's about to be party central at our place in Long Island in a few hours. I also blocked her from viewing my stories, just in case.

"Could be time for introspection. Examining how you really feel," Adelina continues.

I lean forward, curious. Maybe that's about my love life and relationships. Is Archer noticing me, or am I imagining it? I've loved that boy my entire high school life. Archer's always been cool and friendly with everyone, even after becoming famous. Elise says I should tell him how I feel, but that's . . . not happening. What's worse than being shut down and friend-zoned? Being labeled a groupie.

"Okay, last one."

Adelina's manicured nails hover above the card for a few seconds before she flips it. And when she does, her entire body jerks. Mine does too.

There's a guy lying facedown with ten swords sticking out of his back. Based on every cheesy, witchy teen movie, it's a card no one wants to see at a tarot reading. Ever.

"What in the—" I start to say.

"Ten of Swords. Don't be alarmed," Adelina interrupts.

Demario whistles.

"At least it's not the death card," Elise pipes in.

"This shouldn't be taken literally," Adelina says. Her nostrils flare as she sucks in a breath. I relax into my seat, watching her. The way she alternates between running her fingers through her hair and tugging on her shirt buttons is textbook ventilating behavior. I read an article about this in one of my psychology journals. After watching so many horror movies and true crime shows, I started reading up on human behavior. It said that there are over two hundred behaviors linked to psychological discomfort and most of them aren't facial expressions. It's also one of the main behaviors that investigators use to sniff out a liar.

"This guy looks pretty dead," I say, staring at the card.

Adelina fidgets. "It's about picking yourself up and moving forward after a major change or betrayal." She taps the card, on the sun rising in the background. "Think renewed hope and opportunity."

"Will do. Well," I say, slapping my hands against my thighs before standing, "thanks for the reading, Adelina." Checking this off my seasonal to-do list.

"Happy Halloween," she says.

Demario cuts the video.

"Noelle, I still can't believe your ass is throwing a party," Demario says as we walk through the school's main doors minutes before lunch ends. The hallway is already packed with students jostling to get to their next class.

"Hey, I've had parties before," I say, weaving through the crowd. Okay, so maybe my murder mystery parties with the film club never really became a thing at school, but I'm ushering in a new era with Fright Night.

Some people are on their phones, checking out the video I just posted to my socials. Engagement is good. A few kids come up to tell me how much they enjoyed the reading.

I tuck my chemistry textbook under my arm just as Salford's power couple round the corner. Kelsi, the socialite turned Insta model, and Dylan Hansen, the star lacrosse player, were among the first to join Jump Scares. At first I thought Kelsi joined to mess with me because she's always so snarky. But, as it turns out, she's a huge horror fan.

"S'up, Scribbler?" Dylan says, grinning at me.

Elise rolls her eyes and rushes off to her locker. I actually don't mind the nickname. I have been known to jot down notes in the back row of a dark movie theater once or twice.

"Who else is coming to this Fright Night again?" Kelsi asks, coyly. "You know, Wolfie Marlow is having a big bash, too."

A bubble in my stomach bursts. Wolfie throws the wildest parties. It's why I had to step up my game with basically everything, but especially the promise of exclusivity, and it worked. Rich people love feeling special—I'd know. The entire senior year's been buzzing ever since I had the invites delivered by courier. The guest list isn't that much of a mystery because Salford's influencers aren't that much of a mystery, and most of them are in my movie club, *but* no one knows which celebrity is making a virtual cameo appearance. And if Fright Night goes according to plan, Wolfie's party will be a blip in people's memory.

"Guess you'll find out when you get there," I say, hugging the textbook to my chest. "And don't forget the dress code. Or your phones." Who needs a marketing budget when these twelve invitees have millions of followers combined?

Kelsi says, "I'm sure we can throw a cute Halloween costume together, right, Dylan?"

"Sure," he says, shrugging.

Throw something together? I almost laugh out loud. Kelsi and Dylan *really* love matching. They're known for it. I'm talking perfect Megan Fox–and–MGK outfit synchronization. There's no way they don't already have their looks planned out.

"And what's with this not-sharing-the-address-until-one-hour-before thing?" Kelsi asks, exasperated.

"Party crashers. I don't want people from Wolfie's party getting any ideas. It's an *exclusive* event, after all." I had to slip in the buzzword, had to. I can't have anyone backing out last minute.

"Guess I'll see you there," Kelsi says. She smiles, then flips her dark hair, links arms with Dylan, and continues up the hall.

To hit fifty thousand followers so I can leverage my audience to find a popular podcast sponsor, I've got to throw the ultimate Halloween party. My friend Josh Sullivan runs a culture podcast called *A Lot to Unpack with Josh Sullivan.* His guests are a mix of students from Salford, teens making strides in all kinds of activities, and well-known industry experts. Rumor is, he recently landed a megadeal with Spotify, but he's not allowed to talk about it until the contract is finalized. Josh's podcast is basically an extension of himself. He says whatever he thinks and feels with his whole chest, even if he doesn't know what he's talking about. For one-percenters like Josh, it's easy to conflate overconfidence with intelligence and much easier to get every-one to think he's the real deal. I'm not trying to copy Josh, but a podcast would really help me carve out my own niche as a horror film critic.

It's the next logical step for Jump Scares. I could have *actual* guests talking about all things horror, and solid sponsorship could draw traffic and really boost my audience base. My phone dings with more notifications—the video of the tarot reading is gaining traction. Archer reposted my video and in less than twenty minutes, I've gotten over two thousand views and over a hundred new followers. I resist the urge to shimmy the rest of the way to my locker. Fright Night is going to be a scream-ing success.

CHAPTER 2

"Get her prepared. Tonight is yours, tomorrow is mine."
—The Invitation (2022)

"You invited Kelsi Crankenshaw? You don't even like her," Demario says, calling me out.

"Kelsi's got four million followers on Insta refreshing their feed to get a clue of what she's doing at all times. Jump Scares is about to level up," I say. "And"—I pause for emphasis—"now that Dylan's signed his student-athlete endorsement deal, he's blowing up, too."

Kelsi and I have a complicated friendship. She's allergic to boundaries and the queen of non-apologies. So, why is she on the guest list other than for her social media presence? Because our parents play golf together, and I don't need her as an enemy, not when I have to totally focus my energy on building my brand and getting into the cinema studies program at NYU. It's really competitive, but landing a film internship is the boost that could get me in with the film snobs in the program *once* I'm accepted.

I can't count on the teachers at Salford to build me up.

Especially not Mr. Wagner, who rejected my paper on "Analyzing Societal Fears in the Horror Genre" because he wanted me to "broaden my scope." I focused heavily on Black womanhood and survival in horror films, and with the empirical research to back it up. Trust, I understood the assignment. But is talking about the need for greater diversity and representation in film criticism, specifically in horror, enough to make my internship application stand out? What if they don't take me seriously?

What skills can you bring to the position? I have excellent communication and problem-solving skills, and I'm a team player. Textbook-perfect response, but it's also generic and dry as a sand dune. What I need is a competitive advantage. A response that shines with personality and insight that will make the selection panel sit up and take notice.

"Okay, Noe, I know what this is about," Demario says as we're walking to chemistry class.

"Turning down the summer job at my mom's store has nothing to do with this," I say, reading his mind.

Demario was the only Black kid in the neighborhood when my family moved out to Long Island from Queens years ago, and he was as relieved to see me as I was to see him. As six-year-olds, we were inseparable, and we've been riding together ever since.

He knows me better than anyone, and he's absolutely right. Mom was looking forward to me working with her this summer. Thankfully, Dad is backing me up on the podcast idea, but that's just him celebrating me for wanting to grow Jump Scares into a full-fledged business.

"Internship application's in?" Demario asks, tailing me.

"Kind of. Now I have to submit a video," I admit with a sigh. "They want to know about a movie that has had a big impact on me and why. Sounds easy enough. But what if I pick a movie they don't like?"

He purses his lips. "Just go with something that really resonated with you. You and I both know it's going to be one of Jordan Peele's."

"We *are* watching *Us* tonight. It's a film that can be interpreted in a lot of different ways," I say. My mind goes into overdrive thinking about the doppelgängers and the rage the Tethered felt about everyone else having a better life. "Maybe we can go live after the credits to talk about the themes. Our discussion—led by you, of course—could really show off what Jump Scares is all about."

"I'll shoot some B-roll reaction footage while we're watching, maybe you can use that," he says.

I nod, feeling a lump in my throat. Demario always has my back. We look out for each other like siblings, and I don't know what I'd do without him.

My notifications keep going off. There are so many comments about the card reader's pastel vibes and even the spooky antique shop itself. The place was better than our initial plan, which was to hop on the train from our quiet Long Island suburb to Manhattan and find a rando in the East Village. But it takes over an hour to get to the city by train, and learning my future would have cost twice as much.

"Ready for Halloween, I see," a voice says behind me.

"Hey, Archer!" I say, whirling around to face him. He's in his off-duty-singer look: gray sweatpants and a green bomber jacket and white sneakers. We all thought Archer wouldn't return to school after his music career took off, but his parents insisted he finish high school. His hair is messy, sticking out in all directions, but AP History will do that to anyone. He shows me his phone and I realize that he's watching my story. Butterflies in my stomach take flight.

"Thanks for sharing the video," I say.

Demario peaces out and heads into the classroom next door.

"Course. For the record, I think you'll do great on a podcast," Archer says.

I let his words sink in. Archer Mitchell thinks I should do the podcast. My feet do an imaginary happy dance. We've always been cool, but after volunteering to work at the school's ice cream social, we started getting closer.

"The more I think about it, the more ideas I get," I say. "I even have a list of potential episodes." I'm babbling, which is my default behavior whenever Archer's around. "Like, what if I invited you on as a guest?"

"I'm down. Just say the word," Archer says. There's a slight smirk on his face as he gives me his full attention. I look away first and glance down at my phone. Insta is still open. A new comment appears under my latest post.

Forget the podcast and stick to watching Buffy, loser.

It's from @DisturbingJester. Again. The profile picture is a joker playing card. A troll. A real nuisance.

"Noelle, everything okay?" Archer asks.

I hold up the phone for him to read the comment and his brows pinch together.

"You get messages like that a lot?" he asks, serious.

I shrug. "There's always a hater or two or twenty in the comments." I tell Archer about the last one, who felt the need to discredit my analysis of the Blaxploitation era as a legitimate, noteworthy American film movement. I wonder why movies made by Black filmmakers, with Black actors, for Black audiences would be questioned.

"Can you believe this?" I say to Archer. My fingers reach for the Block button like an old friend. "Like, sir, nobody asked your ashy self to come into *my* mentions talking about 'go watch *Buffy.*' Honestly, Archer, I don't know how you deal with all the attention and naysayers." I've seen a lot of the mess people post about Archer, and it's hella toxic.

Archer chuckles. "It's a balancing act, popularity and social media."

"I know I shouldn't feed the trolls, but if they keep it up, I could make time," I say. I don't tell him about some of the worst messages, steeped in hate and misogynoir. The ones that think a seventeen-year-old Black girl couldn't possibly know anything about film. Others are just mad that I dare to exist in a public space.

"Silence is strategic," he says thoughtfully.

"But it makes me feel complicit," I say.

"I see how you handle the Jump Scares chat," Archer says. "I think it's cool that you stick up for others online. You're so sure about yourself and your voice and I love that you want to fight back, but trust me, never engage."

My shoulders sag. "Yeah, I get it. But you know what?" I say, perking up.

Archer cocks his head, and a slow smile spreads across his face. "What?"

"Maybe next month, I *will* stream *Buffy the Vampire Slayer*. Even though the movie was a huge letdown compared to the TV series. And maybe I'll talk about how the monsters are an allegorical threat to contemporary social order. And maybe I'll discuss Buffy being a progressive, feminist show that was way ahead of its time. And @Disturbing whatever his name is can beat it."

Archer grins. "I like it." He leans forward and I pick up a scent of green apple and mint. When the bell rings, he says in a low, husky voice, "I've got AP Music Theory next, but I'm really looking forward to seeing you later tonight." Then he brushes my arm.

Goose bumps break out all over me. When he steps back, there are two pink dots on his cheeks. Did I just make Archer Mitchell blush?

"Can't wait!"

He walks away and I release a shaky breath before heading to Chemistry. We're in for one hell of a Halloween.

CHAPTER 3

**"There'll be food and drink and ghosts . . .
and perhaps even a few murders.
You're all invited."**
—*House on Haunted Hill* (1959)

Dark clouds take over, with bluish-white streaks opening like cracks across the sky. The treetops are naked, leaves stripped away by an early cold snap, brown branches twisting in the wind. A fat raindrop lands on my windshield as I turn off the main street and onto the remote mile-long stretch to Castle Hill, my family's estate marked by a small, easy-to-miss metal address plaque. The tall iron gates slide open slowly, the red sensor at the top flashing like a warning beacon in the late afternoon.

"Weather's acting up," Demario mumbles. Rowboats rock on the river that runs behind the house.

"Thirty percent chance of rain," I say. I've been obsessively refreshing my weather app since I heard about a possible storm, but it's heading east and well out of our way.

I coast up a stretch of road, the asphalt ribboning through the tree-lined avenue, past the fenced paddocks and stables, all painted sleek gray and trimmed in picture-perfect haint blue, a nod to Mom's low-country roots and deep superstitions about evil spirits and boo-hags. Wind gusts through the stripped tree branches and the raindrops tumble faster, landing hard and splattering wide across the windshield. So much for thirty percent.

I've got two voice messages from Mom. The first message is about her taking an earlier flight out to the Adirondacks. No surprise there. As a sports agent, Dad has high-profile clients, and Mom tends to make last-minute travel changes in case the paparazzi catch wind and ambush Dad about an athlete. The second message is a bunch of reminders: *Don't forget to pick up the dry cleaning; electrician coming at nine tomorrow to change pool lights; ask Gloria to work on red-wine carpet stain.*

The lawn is littered with foam tombstones featuring lifted skulls and crawling zombie decorations with flashing red LED eyes that look as if they're literally crawling up out of the ground. Mom calls this time just as I'm approaching the small bronze fountain in front of the house.

"Hey, Mom," I say, shifting my Tiguan into park and taking the call off speaker.

"All set for tonight?" she asks, excited.

"Almost," I say. My parents think I spend too much time watching horror movies, either alone or with my "little internet friends." As far as they're concerned, having real people over is a good thing. It reassures them that I'm not an antisocial hermit crab holed up in my room in front of the TV or computer or on my phone.

I glance up at my house, at all the dark empty windows. *Why is it so dark?* Usually Mom or Dad leaves at least the porch light on. Dad probably forgot to set the switch timer again.

Mom hesitates. "Did you make another appointment with Dr. Dillard?"

"No, um . . . not yet," I say. I like Dr. Dillard and I've been to see him a few times, even with his reputation as "the rich-kid therapist," but I haven't been back since I had a meltdown in his office, stressing over getting into NYU or any good college. "I'll set something up. Promise."

"Okay, honey. If you need anything, I can always ask Lauren to—"

"Nah, I'm straight. I've got everything covered," I say, cutting her off. Last thing I need is our nosy neighbor driving over here. Our houses aren't that close, so at least she won't hear anything from the party. I know Mom is worried after a small fringe group calling themselves the Liberation Bloc made the evening news a few nights ago for vandalizing the homes of prominent local businessmen, but Dad already has a top security system in place. There's absolutely nothing to worry about.

If Mom picks up on my frostiness, she doesn't let on. Her dream for me is that I go to Spelman College, her alma mater, and then fast-track to a senior role in either Dad's talent management empire or her stationery business, Miss Paperie. Even though they're supportive of me pursuing cinema studies, their disappointment over me fighting against nepotism drips like a leaky faucet.

"Before I forget, I have news: Kennedy's joining Miss Paperie as a junior executive, so we've finally got more family blood in the business," Mom tells me, light and airy like she's socializing at one of her charity events.

Here we go. "Sounds great, Mom. Hey, the rain's letting up now, so I should head inside. Have a great weekend! Happy anniversary!" I disconnect the call before she can say anything else. I feel like trash for cutting her off like that, but she knows I can't stand my cousin Kennedy, and even though I have zero interest in taking over either family business, Kennedy and my know-it-all Uncle Cedric, who works with Dad, are super annoying.

Demario gives me a questioning look as he unfastens his seat belt.

"Don't ask," I say before hopping out of the Tiguan. A gust of wind whips my hood off. Glass crunches under my feet. I take a giant step backward, startled. A security camera lies broken on the ground. I glance up, and sure enough, the bracket bolted to the side of the house is broken. Sheesh, the wind is strong this evening. I set a reminder in my phone to mention it to the electrician in the morning.

Demario follows me inside, both of us now safe from the rain. His wet Gucci loafers squeak against the foyer's white marble floor. The mansion is a few degrees cooler than usual, as if there's a draft leaking through a cracked window.

"What are you doing with Quilly?" he asks.

Quilly is my pet porcupine. I've had her since she was a bottle-fed baby. Mom is completely fine with a rodent living under her roof but somehow me wanting a hairless cat is *extreme*.

"She'll stay in the den. It's soundproof, so she's good," I say. Quilly's not keen on loud noises.

Demario gives the creepy mannequin family positioned near the door a once-over as he joins me in the kitchen.

Mom's caterer came through with the food and premixed cocktails. The charcuterie boards with imported Alpine cheeses and fig and cherry jams look delicious. Demario and I organize the food and cutlery until Elise shows up to help me get ready. I pop back outside to move my SUV from the driveway to the garage. Exactly one hour before the party kicks off, I drop the location pin with my address to all the guests. Besides Demario and Elise, I rarely have people over. Even before my parents moved here, Castle Hill used to be a well-known party house and was even featured in a few movies. That's partly why my mom wanted to make an offer on it.

Now the wait begins.

"I think we're set," I tell Demario, almost an hour later. He's changed into his costume: Joel Jones, the cameraman on assignment with Gale Weathers (Courteney Cox) in *Scream 2*, in a blue tee and black utility vest with khakis. In the movie, when the bodies started dropping, Joel knew what was up and got the hell out. Fun fact: in the original *Scream* franchise, Joel is the only Black person to survive a *Scream* movie.

My outfit is a nod to the cult classic *Carrie*. I'm in a light-pink tiered tulle minidress with a plunging V-neck. Layered tulle embellishments on my shoulders add to the whimsical look. At the right moment, I'll activate the blood squib device embedded in the bodice, releasing a packet of fake blood that I made myself. I'll transform from prom princess to a blood-drenched horror. A glittering crystal tiara and Mom's metallic silver Prada boots complete the outfit perfectly.

I've transformed my luscious curls into a sleek, straight silk press, keeping most of my makeup light except for my lips, which are painted with a navy Fenty lipstick called Clapback. Thanks to Elise taking me on a quick train ride to Manhattan a few days ago, I'm also batting a full-volume set of eyelashes.

Heels click as Elise descends the stairs. She's dressed as Elphaba, the witch from *Wicked*, with emerald-green skin and a plum-colored wig. She's rocking a black crop top with matching high-waisted skirt under her black witch's robe.

"You look gorgeous," Elise says, taking me in. She catches the flicker of doubt as I glance around the room, reassuring myself everything's in place. "The party's going to be great. We gon' be all right." She breaks into the chorus of Kendrick Lamar's "Alright" and I join in, singing off-key. Elise always knows how to defuse my brain whenever I start overanalyzing; that's partly why we've been close since middle school.

I fuss with the white tablecloth on the welcome table, which is draped with black netting with tiny plastic spiders clinging to it. Bowls of misting dry-ice cocktails with festive names like Black Widow, Witches' Curse, Zombie Brain, Green Apple Poison, and Vampire Kiss are arranged on top of the netting. If that's not enough to set the mood, I've curated a five-hour playlist to keep the haunted vibes going all night.

The doorbell rings and my phone lights up. On the screen, Josh grins and waves at the Ring door cam.

"You're early," I say as I welcome him inside.

"I didn't want to miss a minute of this party," Josh says. He holds up the vintage silver spoon I sent with the invitation. "Loved the detail. Glad it didn't get lost in the mail."

Josh's idea of a costume is a white T-shirt with the words THE LIBERAL ELITE and ripped jeans. Very on-brand.

"Ah! Figured you'd be on the guest list. What's up, man?" Demario says.

"Cute shirt," I say.

Josh grins. "Late-stage capitalism. I paid $450 for jeans full of holes, that's where we are right now."

Such a Josh answer. My phone vibrates with a text from an unknown number.

"Hold on a second." I check my messages.

Don't turn off the lights

"Ha ha, very funny." I flash my screen. "Which one of you sent this?" I say, then read the message out loud. I get a bunch of scrunched-up faces. It's probably Mariana, president of the drama club, messing with me. The girl lives for pranks. We've teamed up a few times for class plays in English literature, and she's tons of fun. I wouldn't be surprised to find her lurking around outside in a Jason Voorhees hockey mask. But sending cryptic shit from an unknown number? Eerie even for her.

"Hey, Elise," Josh says when they finally make eye contact. Before she can respond, he steps into the other room to take a call.

"You invited Josh?" Elise murmurs once he's out of earshot. Something's up with them. Elise insists she and Josh are cool, but the way she dips out whenever Josh shows up or vice versa tells me they're anything but.

23

Josh returns with a bowl of pretzels, popcorn, and candy corn.

"Stop eating all the snack mix," I say, taking the bowl from him.

"Quality control testing," he tells me, winking. He picks up a white pumpkin dressed in black lace up off the floor. "What's this?"

"This," I say, gently taking the pumpkin from him and setting it back on the floor, "was special ordered from a designer with Fendi Casa." I smooth out the wrinkles in the pumpkin's black satin ribbon bow.

"Looks like a lumpy butt," Demario says, laughing.

I shove him, then give Josh a quick rundown of tonight's plan. "We'll mostly be in the living room, shift to the dining room to eat, and then head to the home theater for the movie. I've converted the guesthouse for tonight and put in some cool fun-house mirrors."

Ten minutes later, the appetizers are ready. Cheers ring out each time the doorbell rings, with everyone placing bets on who the guest is. Hailey Daniel, head of Girls Forward, a girls' empowerment club at school, arrives with her Broadway-fanatic girlfriend Mariana Martinez, and they gag over the decorations. The twelve-foot skeleton with light-up eyes and a flaming pumpkin head is a smash. I pose for the obligatory welcome pics. Hailey's most recent cause is reproductive rights, and her costume is an extra-chunky red sweater with a picture of a womb and the phrase I'M NOT OVARY-ACTING above a pair of silver bedazzled ovaries. Mariana's nineteenth-century Victorian gothic-style black-and-peach dress is all ruffles, lace, and intricate embroidery.

"It's Aminta's dress from *Phantom of the Opera*," she explains, doing a quick twirl.

"As in Aminta's *actual* dress," Mariana continues, "from the Museum of Broadway."

My mouth falls open. "No way! For real?"

"If Kim Kardashian can rock Marilyn Monroe's gown at the Met Gala, then why can't I get Aminta's? This is the place to be, right?" she says, shrugging.

"Right." Her family is that connected. Mariana's play *Amor en Spanglish* was a huge success during its limited off-Broadway run last year. There's even talk about taking *Amor* to the big screen. She's making high-level movie connections that could put Jump Scares on a lot of people's radars.

"Well, thanks for coming!" I usher them over to the appetizer table, where my lab partner, Vivek Bhatia, is giving Freddy Krueger in a red-and-black-striped sweater, black pants, and black hat. A thick ponytail hangs down his back. He's aiming for a ten-inch ponytail that he plans to donate to a nonprofit that makes wigs for cancer patients. Vivek is a tech geek and the developer of Simmer, a social networking site that's gotten so much hype, he's undoubtedly heading to Harvard on a full ride. He's already given me tons of ideas about how I can use Simmer to create a more interactive space for the Jump Scares community.

The rest of the guests arrive within minutes of each other. Charlie Huang and his girlfriend, Maddie Xu. Charlie is the resident "finance bro" at Salford Prep. He's always watching markets and analyzing stock ratings. He'll pop half a Xanax while tracking crypto and remind everyone how stressed he is. Maddie's

Insta bio reads "Pampered Princess." She's never lived in one country for more than two years and is known to drop mega chunks at Dior and Saks.

"Noelle, I'm crowdsourcing a flight to Miami next weekend. You interested?" Charlie asks. He's in typical finance bro attire: pastel button-down, khakis, and brown loafers. I'm sure there's a horror theme in there somewhere. Numbers are terrifying. Meanwhile, Maddie is dressed like her favorite anime character, No-Face, in a feathery black dress and smoky makeup, and she looks amazing.

"Uh, no, got things to do," I say. As much as I'd love to jump on a chartered flight for some fun under the Florida sun, I really need to work. Competition for this internship is tight, so my video needs to be solid.

Premiere Critic is a top review website for film and TV, and a subsidiary of a major broadcasting company. For three months over summer after graduation, I'll get to work with well-known industry critics, doing administrative tasks and even reading early-draft reviews. Getting a spot would be a huge deal.

"You have horses?" Maddie asks me, staring out the door in the direction of the stables.

"Yeah, two," I say.

Maddie purses her lips as if she wants to say something, but Mariana tugs her away to play Halloween Tic-Tac-Toe with small pumpkins marked with X's and O's.

I wait at the door while my friend Taylor Kissick parks their pickup. Its sides are mud-splattered from off-roading, and two large kennels are packed into the cargo bed. Taylor and I have been friends since we paired up on a precalc project; and like Kelsi, they are one of the first members of Jump Scares.

"Taylor!" I squeal when they reach the door. I wasn't sure if they were going to make it. Taylor had a bad breakup a few weeks ago, so I'm happy to see things moving in the right direction for them. Their ex, Silas, turned out to be a jerkwad and now the two of them don't talk.

"Hang on." I take a step back and try to guess their costume: the nineties-fashion jean jacket, black jeans, and motorcycle boots. "Sidney Prescott from *Scream*," I say, clapping my hands.

"Ding, ding. Noelle, this place looks amazing," they say, gawking. They nudge me in the ribs, whispering into my ear, "I don't see Archer's car. Is he here?"

I make a face. Taylor has a way of sensing people's emotions without them saying anything, thus they can probably feel my twinge of disappointment. I'd been secretly hoping that Archer would be one of the first to arrive so we could have a little alone time, but I'm definitely *not* going to stress.

Taylor sees through my bravado. "He'll be here. Archer's not the type to ghost."

True, and he did seem super flirty earlier.

The doorbell rings and Kelsi's face pops up on the doorbell cam. She blows me a kiss before she swishes inside. Her judgy eyes take everything in at once: the mansion, the decorations, and, most importantly, the guests. She flashes an extra-white smile and practically shoves her phone into my hand.

"Get one of me here," she says, hopping in front of the twelve-foot skeleton.

I take a bunch of shots with Burst mode and hand the phone back to her. "Can you use #JumpScaresPodcast and #Horror-Podcast in your photos?"

"You got it," she says, swiping through the images.

I'm not sure what her costume is—black Bardot dress with twenty-inch black wig—until Dylan shuffles through the front door with a case of craft beer. He's wearing a dark-gray pin-striped suit and I put it together—Morticia and Gomez Addams. Technically, not horror, but spooky enough.

My notifications for Jump Scares are already buzzing non-stop from being tagged in photos. I've got two hundred new followers from a handful of story posts and the party's barely started. Am I a genius?

Comments are flooding in.

> Can't wait for the #JumpScaresPodcast!!
> Love #Horror!

A new notification pops up from @DisturbingJester with the same joker playing card profile picture. Acid fills my mouth.

> World's most annoying voice #LoserPodcast
> #JumpScaresSucks 🤮🤮

Didn't I block this person? I hit the Block button. Not to-night, troll. I square my shoulders and put an extra swing in my hips on my way to the kitchen.

I gather the crowd as I make everyone Zombie Brain shots, for the experience.

"Schnapps goes in first and then some menthe for color," I say, adding a few drops of the green liquid. When I pour the Irish cream into the glass, there's a loud gasp as diffusion occurs and the cream curdles, separating into cloudy shapes that resemble brain matter.

Maddie downs two shots before I finish explaining how the alcohol in the cream interacts with the schnapps and syrup to create the zombie-brain effect. She's noticeably quiet. I've heard rumors that her dad got a new job and her entire family might be moving to Beijing, disrupting her senior year at Salford. She needs this night.

No one besides Vivek is interested in the chemistry behind the drink, but they're taking shots back-to-back. Kelsi disappears into one of the haunted-house-themed rooms with Elise, presumably to take more selfies. I kindly suggest they hype me up.

"Shots! Shots! Shots! Shots!" The chant grows louder, and Dylan takes over, adding his own vodka spin to the drink.

Through the floor-to-ceiling windows at the front of the house, I spot a matte black Porsche coasting up the road. Thankfully, our driveway is long enough for me to get my heart rate into normal range before Archer Mitchell swaggers up to the front door.

"You made it," I say, all breathy. I ran to the door a little faster than I care to admit.

Archer meets my gaze and flashes the kind of smile that makes all the lights in my head come on.

"How could I miss the biggest party of the year?" he says. His eyes travel up my *Carrie* costume, and from the widening smile on his face, he approves. He looks ridiculously good in a

Squid Game jumpsuit. But because he's *the* Archer Mitchell, his jumpsuit is metallic red and covered with red sequins and zippers. He's wearing platform boots that add at least another two inches to his six-foot frame. His hair is extra gelled up and spiky.

"Sorry I'm late. I brought you a little something," he says, holding out a giant white pastry box. It's from a bakery two towns over.

Inside are the most decadent mini chocolate cheesecakes ever made. *Jump Scares* is written on top of each one in orange buttercream.

"Thank you! But you didn't have to bring anything," I say, hugging him.

"No biggie," he says, though his cheeks are almost as red as his jumpsuit.

"Look who it is!" Demario shouts when he spots Archer. I try not to laugh when they do their convoluted fist-bumping, handshaking thing from middle school that they still think is cool.

Spoiler alert: it's not.

"Okay, who wants to win some free stuff?" I shout.

With zero objections, we all head into the living room and launch right into a trivia game with a giant cardboard prize wheel that features things like gift cards, makeup, and liqueur chocolates. Mariana cleans up at the game. I swear her brain is a machine. Trivia is quickly followed by Halloween Shazam (guessing the spooky songs as they play). Archer nails most of the songs at the first chord, leaving us all in the dust. He walks away with two concert tickets to Doja Cat, one of my favorites.

"I think we need more cups," Mariana says from the kitchen.

"Really? I left a huge stack right there," I say, pointing at the corner table with the tableware. The spot where I left the cups is empty. "Never mind, I'll grab more."

On the way to the pantry, my phone vibrates with another text from the same unknown number:

Scatter. Run. Hide.

I snort at the ghost and skull emojis in the message and climb up onto a small stepladder. Being five foot two and a half has its drawbacks. I'm rummaging through a mountain of holiday plates and cutlery when I hear a loud rustling, flapping noise like fabric being ripped coming from the back of the house. I pause, listening. Probably patio furniture or something Mom left outside. I grab as many of the orange Solo cups that are stuffed into the corner at the back of the cupboard as I can carry.

Thump.

Thump.

What the hell is that?

The pantry door swings shut and rattles in its frame. *Great.* I climb down the stepladder slowly in my boots, shifting the stacks of cups under my arm and balancing them against my body. My fingers curl around the doorknob and I open the door, just as a shadow shrinks away to my left.

The roar of a chain saw explodes in my eardrums, and I scream. Orange cups go flying in all directions. The pungent scent of diesel descends around me. I'm halfway up the hallway when I hear it. Laughter. The rumble of the chain saw cuts off. Josh steps into my path, his phone held high in the midst of recording.

"Happy anniversary!" he yells. He circles me, zooming in on my stunned expression. Cheers of "happy anniversary" go up. Archer gives me an empathetic pat on the shoulder, but everyone else is laughing their asses off. Demario squeezes me in a tight hug.

"What the hell?" I say, out loud this time.

"Yo, she's shaking. Like legit shaking," Demario says. He frowns at Josh. "I told y'all this was too much. Noelle, let me get you some water."

"Get her a real drink!" Charlie yells. He slips a small speaker out from a shelf in the corner and passes it to Hailey. It was a recording . . . of a chain saw.

"But why does it smell like a gas station?" I ask, sniffing the air.

Josh picks up a burning candle with a Blue Collar Organics label and blows out the wick. "A fuel-scented candle. Diesel is one of the brand's most popular."

I'm still clutching my chest, but now I'm laughing. "Guys, I almost twisted my damn ankle!"

"You handled that shit like a trouper, though, Noe," Demario says, shoving a cup of soda into my hands. "My girl was flying!"

"The way I screamed," I say, laughing as I watch the replay on my phone. It's as good as any stock scream a movie director could find in a database. I'm actually glad they recorded it.

I repost a clip of the moment the cups go flying as a Boomerang and post it to my socials with the caption *They got me ghoul #JumpScaresPodcast #Comingsoon #FrightNight #Halloween #NewPodcastAlert.*

CHAPTER 4

"It's not too late to flee, you know."
—*Ready or Not* (2019)

The party heads back to the living room while I pick up the cups scattered throughout the hallway. Archer, Demario, and Elise help, and we're just about done when a flapping sound echoes from the back of the house again.

We follow the noise down to the lounge near the patio. The temperature has dropped. I rub my arms, the fall chill sending goose bumps across my skin.

Clang!

Low light from the wall sconces bathes the space in dark shadows. Hazy moonlight filters through the wall of large windows, and the long pier that leads out to a floating dock is shrouded in fog. Dad's small rowboat bobs at the end of the pier. All the windows are open. Did Mom forget to close them in her rush for an earlier flight again?

One corner of the patio awning dips at an odd angle. There's a giant rip in the fabric and part of the steel arm has broken away from the wall, causing the awning to slam against the window with every gust of wind.

"Uh-uh, it's too cold," Elise says. She ducks back inside, leaving us to sort it out. We have to strap it somehow.

Archer takes over. He knows exactly what to do. We manually retract and secure the broken awning the best we can, enough to stop the racket.

"Not bad," I say.

Archer holds up both hands and waggles his fingers. "Not just for piano playing. I'm pretty handy too."

"Apparently," I say, double-checking the awning's stability.

"I helped out a lot at the store with maintenance stuff with my dad," he says, referring to his family's flagship marine supply store. "I work in the storeroom now, though."

I imagine the legions of fans that would descend on Mitchell Marine for an autograph or a glimpse of Archer if they knew about his side job. I'm about to tease him when I notice muddy footprints, trailing up from the pier and stopping right under the window.

"Hey, D, did you see anyone come back here, by chance?"

Demario shakes his head. "I don't think so."

A knot tightens in my stomach. Something isn't right. "Maybe your dad had some workers out here," Demario says.

Maybe? The mud is dry, possibly hours or days old, and the prints stop outside the window. There are no visible ones inside the house. Demario starts up the firepit, and flames dance across the blue crystals. Leaving the others, I head inside, toward the lounge, still feeling off because of the footprints. *It's just leftover jitters from their prank.* I search for more traces of mud, but there's nothing. The music is pumping, and my shoulders relax. Maybe Mom is onto something; all this horror and true crime stuff could be making me paranoid. I shake off the nerves.

I have a party to host.

Josh has ventured into the dining room to show Mariana and Hailey something on his phone. He's laughing, and I'm glad he's having a good time. I know he's been stressing about his dad being sick, and we've all been tiptoeing around the subject, giving him more space than we have with Taylor and Maddie until he's ready to talk.

Charlie raises his cup, toasting to fun parties and something about hyperinflation, spilling his drink on Mom's imported Turkish rug in the process. I'll have to add that to the list of stains for our cleaning lady Gloria tomorrow.

"Are we watching the movie now?" Kelsi shouts over the music.

"Not yet. I've got a special message from a very special guest up next," I reply, cutting the music and switching on the TV.

Queen Robyn Rihanna Fenty fills the TV screen, and we all go nuts. She's laughing and waving, and even I'm in awe. I could have peeked at the recording when the email landed in my inbox, but I wanted to share the moment with everyone here.

"Happy first anniversary, Jump Scares!" Rihanna says. She's wearing a ball cap that reads *Teenage Fantasy* and I'm already mentally adding it to my shopping cart.

"Y'all know I love horror, so shout-out to Noelle and her

crew. Have a good time tonight!" she says. She blows kisses at the screen and the video ends, and I am not okay. Mentally, I flash back to Rihanna's scene in the *Bates Motel* episode and how she turned the genre on its head. Iconic.

"Omigosh, do you *know* Rihanna?" Kelsi says, circling me like a vulture spotting prey.

"My dad called in a favor," I admit. As much as I'd love to stunt, I'm just as blown away.

Still on a high, I dim the lights for the next portion of the night and hand out grab bags to the group. Elise squeals when she pulls out a fluorescent jelly wig and custom Glow headphones.

"A silent dance party?" Elise guesses, turning the headphones on. She toggles through the channels, listening to the range of music, from EDM to hip-hop to pop.

"This is awesome," Archer says, checking out his own headphones.

"Let's go!" Demario shouts to the crowd. Loud cheers go up as he switches on the strobe lights and we fan out on the dance floor, aka the cleared-out family room, drinks in hand and headphones flashing.

"Wanna dance?" Archer asks, leaning in. His breath brushes my ear. I shiver. If he notices, he doesn't let on.

"Sure," I say. Blame the Vampire Kiss for melting away my nerves or the dimmed lights camouflaging how excited I really am, but I feel pretty confident.

I switch my headphones to the pop channel, and they light up in blue, and Archer does the same. He holds out his hand and

I take it, my heart rate ratcheting all the way up. Thankfully, my sweat glands get the memo to stay cool.

"Nightmare" by Halsey is playing. Heavy base notes flow through me and I move to the bouncy beat. Archer's eyes lock with mine and a smile forms on my lips. In the dark, his eyes are intense navy pools, and I don't imagine the way he sucks in a breath. I spin around so that he's dancing behind me, and I get a chance to let out a shaky breath without him noticing. One of his hands lands on my hips and suddenly it's too hot in here. Dancing is so much better than talking. We dance for two more songs before Archer slips off his headphones. When I follow suit, I hear everyone belting out lyrics off-key of whatever's playing on their channel. Demario shouts *"Tuuune"* each time a new song comes on.

"I'm glad you came," I say to Archer. "Demario said you might have a gig."

"I rearranged some things. I wouldn't miss this," he says, his gaze heated.

Butterflies have moved up into my chest, hosting their own party.

"So, about those Doja Cat tickets," I say, leaning in.

A burst of laughter to my left distracts me. Archer and I break apart when we see that Demario, the little blocker, has chosen this exact time to lead the others in a fun choreographed dance routine to Michael Jackson's "Thriller," re-creating an iconic scene from the music video. By the time I film and post the clip to my Insta Stories, I'm already halfway to meeting my follower count goal for the night.

Castle Hill is a rollicking mess of laughter and high-pitched screams, and I'm living for it.

And there's not a neighbor around for miles to hear a single thing.

We're all packed in a tight circle and dancing freely when every light in the house suddenly switches on. After dancing in the dark, the light hits us like a solar flare. Dad must have set the light timers wrong. Again. I yank off my headphones and head over to the control panel, a cloud of funk threatening to burst my good mood. Before I can reach the panel, the TV comes on at full volume.

An '80s sci-fi horror movie, *Killer Klowns from Outer Space*, is on, but it wasn't on the playlist. *Who's messing with me now?*

"Ha ha, funny. Where's the remote?" I shout.

We're all running around searching for the remote in neon jelly wigs flipping sofa cushions and checking under furniture while on-screen the actors investigate a green glob in a cocoon. Now that I think about it, the remote might've gotten pitched somewhere when we lost our collective shit over Rihanna.

Josh finds the remote tucked into a spot on a bookshelf. I push down the anxiety flaring up. I guess it's all part of Fright Night done right. Right?

CHAPTER 5

"It's a long, fucked-up story and you probably won't believe it anyway."
—*I Still Know What You Did Last Summer* (1998)

The dinner table is set for thirteen. Heavy black drapes cover the windows and the chandelier bulbs have been replaced with flicker ones for the perfect mood lighting. Mom's contemporary artwork has been swapped out for vintage movie posters like the striking close-up of Drew Barrymore, hand covering her mouth, from *Scream;* the "Here's Johnny!" moment from *The Shining* with Jack Nicholson, teeth bared; and *Nope* with the iconic Daniel Kaluuya, large eyes wide open.

Kelsi's scrolling through her socials and sipping a cup of Green Apple Poison.

Instead of taking a seat like the rest of us, Archer heads over to my piano and starts playing a few scales, then launches into the opening notes to his hit song "Pursuit." My legs move on their own until I'm in front of him and leaning on the baby grand. He delivers the kind of unique magic his shows are famous for.

Archer is classically trained, and while I've heard him tinkering on the piano at school before, this is the first time I've seen him play in person.

I'm mesmerized as his fingers fly over the keys, and he begins to sing, his eyes locked with mine the entire time. It's as if Archer's singing to me, as though he sees right through me. This is a *way* different vibe from Archer jumping around onstage to hype the crowd.

We're all crowded around the piano now and belting out the lyrics. Elise blames our chaotic emotions on Mercury being in retrograde. Apparently, Earth is moving backward for the third time this year, throwing the world out of whack. Maybe it's the song or my hormones, but I'm feeling an irrational desire to confess my feelings to Archer.

Ever since that time in ninth grade when he brought me lozenges when I thought I was coming down with strep, I've wondered if maybe he had a teeny-tiny crush on me. If it was more than just flirty banter. This kind of thinking could leave me with a charred hole in my chest, Googling *how to get over a broken heart.* But Adelina had used the word *introspection.* So, tonight, I take the risk and let his raspy voice wash over me like a warm beach wave and try not to raise the dead with my singing.

Archer finishes the song with a dramatic chord progression, earning applause and whistles. Kelsi throws her arm around my shoulder, suffocating me in the spicy scent of Tom Ford's Fucking Fabulous.

"I can't believe you like his music," she whisper-shouts. "I thought you were just into Cardi B and stuff."

And stuff. I inhale and count backward from ten, debating a snippy response. Then I decide to be the bigger person. Ignoring her, I head over to the snack spread and nibble a kebab of orange slices and marshmallows, resisting the urge to skewer Kelsi. Yes, I love Cardi, but I like other artists too.

A flash of lightning pours through an opening in the drapes and suddenly I'm heading to the window, phone in hand.

"Is it raining?" Hailey asks.

"Not yet," I say, peeking outside. I launch the storm app and suppress a sigh.

"Remember that bad weather that was headed east?" I say, scrolling. "Well, some of it's heading this way."

No one seems bothered enough by the forecast to leave, so I pour myself a Black Widow cocktail and chill. I dig into the food and try to ignore the whistling wind. The lights above us dim and brighten again and I'm not sure if it's just the flicker bulbs acting up or the impending bad weather.

"Hey, Dylan!" Josh shouts, even though he's right across the table. "Can I borrow your apartment in Manhattan for a few hours tomorrow night? I have a date."

Dylan grins, wide and sleazy. "Not a problem."

"Gross," I say to Josh. "We're eating here."

Dylan's dad has an apartment in Manhattan's Billionaires' Row, a bunch of ridiculously overpriced apartments in some of the city's newest, tallest buildings. He's a real estate mogul, and last I heard, Josh's parents were in discussions to get Josh a place in the same area.

"Hey, so I'm planning next month's Jump Scares watch party list. What movies do you think I should add?" I ask the group.

"*American Psycho,*" Josh says right away. "Patrick Bateman

doesn't hold anything back." He reaches for his third cupcake, and Taylor swats his hand away. "Remember how he killed that homeless Black dude right in the beginning? Brutal."

Normally, I'd launch into a diatribe about how Hollywood gets off on inflicting violence on the homeless and setting up minority characters as murder bait in horror movies, *but* I'm not going there. Nor will I attack the misconception that Black people always die first. Because if you really check the statistics, like I did for my research paper, the white woman actually gets offed first, fifty-two percent of the time. Maybe if Mr. Wagner knew this, he would have taken my essay more seriously. Anyway, like I said, I'm resisting. Tonight is supposed to be fun.

"You could do either of the *It* movies," Archer suggests. "Pennywise gave me nightmares!"

"Same!" Taylor adds.

"A Black horror flick that doesn't take place in the hood," Demario quips.

I watch the range of quizzical expressions as everyone tries to think of a movie that fits the criteria. The few titles thrown out are all relatively new. Demario glances at me and cracks up, because how many times have I ranted about filmmakers' utter lack of originality about Black horror? And don't get me started on Black horror movie titles with extra *z*'s and *s*'s. *Zombiez* and *Vampiyaz*? Hard pass.

"You know," Josh says, "if I had to wager, I think Demario would make it to the end of *American Psycho,* or any horror movie really." He waves a celery stick in my direction. "But, Noelle? You wouldn't make it past midnight."

I glance over my shoulder because Josh is obviously talking

to another girl named Noelle. "Pshh, you're looking at a Final Girl," I say. "I'd be the last one standing, telling everybody and their mama how shit went down. Like Freddie Harris setting Michael on fire in *Halloween: Resurrection*." Let's be honest, Busta needs to be confronted about that acting, but at least he made it to the closing credits.

"My point," I say, repositioning a dark floral arrangement of purple artichoke and wine-colored roses, "is there's no way I'd die first. Or at all, for that matter. Ask Demario, I've got a go bag in my room, prepped and ready." A few light laughs break out, but I'm not finished. "D, remember how my mom wasn't a fan of the TikTok challenge where we timed each other to see how fast we could escape in a murder scenario? I topped my personal best time just last week."

"She stay ready," Demario confirms. Everyone laughs, but no lie was told.

My go bag has everything. Water and toiletries to stay hydrated and fresh, flashlights and chargers, and a demolition hammer and multi-tool to break myself out of sticky situations. I've also got a stealth pen and waterproof notepad—I'm always writing film reviews—and a cute poncho to stay dry.

Jokes aside, Hollywood tells us over and over again that girls like me and Elise don't get to be Final Girls. The first *Scream* movie, as much as I love it, has no Black people. Nada. I talked about this in the live chat during one of the movie club's first meetings. *Scream 2* addressed the issue, but then we got to watch Jada Pinkett Smith and Omar Epps, with all their star power, die spectacular deaths before the opening credits.

Slasher films never show the Black girl stepping over all the dead bodies on the way to the finish line like a badass. Progress has been made, but there's still no shortage of movies where I'd be the loyal sidekick, the one who screams for everyone to run and save themselves, while I end up on the killer's meat hook. Brandy in *I Still Know What You Did Last Summer* is the exception, but I'm guessing being famous kept her alive in that one.

"Bury a Friend" by Billie Eilish filters through the speaker system, shaking me out of film critic mode. Elise nudges me to ask Archer for a selfie. He's loading up a plate from the charcuterie board, occasionally popping blackberries into his mouth. He's tall and skinny, but his presence fills up the entire room.

"He hasn't taken his eyes off you since he walked in here," Elise says.

Elise and Taylor are the only ones who know about my feelings for Archer. I've tried talking about it with Demario, but each time I bring up Archer's name, he drowns me out with really bad mumble rap because he knows it irritates the heck out of me. I gather my wits and head over to Archer, butterflies in tow. *Okay, Noelle. Keep it light and flirty.*

"Selfie?" I ask.

"Sure, yeah," he says, giving me a grin that takes over his entire face. He puts down his plate and steps into the photo frame. We "cheese" for the camera.

"Cute," he says, reviewing the photos I snapped. His gaze lingers on me for a moment, and I find myself leaning on the banquet table for support.

"Text them to me?" Archer asks.

"Yeah, it's cool," I say. Elise watches us from across the room and gives me a thumbs-up. Should I text Archer right away or play it cool and wait a few minutes? I'm not good at this shit. *How long is too long?*

"I hope you're not planning to post these on your socials," I say, half joking.

Archer shakes his head. "Nope. Posting for others kind of makes it not as real, you know. I like to keep special moments just for me."

His honesty takes me aback and I immediately start obsessing over all the things it could mean. Like, am I special to him?

"Party's great," he says, leaning against the wall.

"Thanks. I was nervous for a hot minute," I admit.

"You? No way," he says, laughing. "You're always cool under pressure."

Right now, my armpits are the opposite of cool. My mouth goes dry, and I start nodding slowly. Taylor sees me silently flailing and comes over. Archer asks how they're doing. I scroll through the photos in my gallery to give my hands something to do. Taylor tucks a few wild strands of hair behind their ear and examines the bread cauldron, trying to make out the seams where the dough was kneaded together.

"I've decided to take a gap year to travel," they say.

"Me too," Maddie says softly. She's come over to help herself to a few olives. She glances in Charlie's direction, but he's on a call ranting. Why can't he shut it down for one night?

A clap of thunder rumbles and light rain splatters against the window. I check the weather app again. The radar colors on the map are now a solid mass of yellow, orange, and red, which translates into rain, rain, and more rain.

"Travel to where?" I ask Taylor.

"Good for you, Taylor. Put that privilege to use," Josh interrupts.

Kelsi rolls her eyes. "Save the wokeness for your podcast, Joshy," she says. She reaches for Dylan's plate and takes a tiny bite of gluten-free focaccia.

Taylor's cheeks turn pink. To me and Archer, they say, "I'm thinking about community work in South America. Something with animals."

Josh, still going, twists the cap off a beer and asks, "Are you taking what's-his-face with you?"

"Silas and I are over," Taylor says, grimly. They stare down into their cup, and I see them shutting down.

"Maybe you should take a gap year from dating, too," Josh says, smirking.

Taylor's terrible luck with guys is unprecedented. They're drawn to boys who always need saving. Nonetheless, I gesture for Josh to shut the hell up.

"What about you?" I ask Archer. "Are you taking a gap year to work on your music?"

There's no way my folks would approve a gap year. Not that I want one. I don't need time to figure out anything. I've always loved movies and writing, and cinema studies is literally the best of both worlds.

"No," he answers right away. "I'm on tour this summer, then college in the fall. I want to study music composition at Julliard."

I'm surprised. "I thought you were going full-time professional entertainer."

"Yeah, everyone does," Archer says. From the way his smile

dips, I know I've said the wrong thing. I'm making assumptions about him like everyone else.

"So, what's your audition piece going to be? Something from your next album?" I joke, hoping to steer us back into comfortable waters.

Archer laughs. "No, Juilliard's audition process is more rigorous than that. I'm playing a Mozart sonata. But it's an upbeat one," he adds quickly. "I can play a bit for you later . . . if you're interested."

"Yeah, I'd love to hear it," I say, feeling my face heat up.

We lapse into a brief silence, the tension a wire pulled tight between us. I take another sip of my Vampire punch.

I clear my throat. "Okay! Movie time." I usher everyone into the home theater. "Then a clown is coming to play a game with us later."

"A clown? Are we twelve?" Kelsi asks.

"It's an evil *It* clown," I say. "Trust me, in about ninety minutes, he'll have us screaming."

CHAPTER 6

"Welcome to Fright Night . . . for real."
—*Fright Night* **(1985)**

Ambient lighting warms the cozy theater, and we settle into the plush armchairs and recliners arranged around the room. Archer and I get comfy on a sofa in the last row, in front of an artsy accent wall covered in damask and tufted velvet.

Josh grabs a handful of snacks from the stocked wet bar and takes a seat in front of the large screen. "What's happening with this clown?"

"After the movie, we're playing a game of hide-and-seek tag. The adult version," I announce, getting everyone's attention.

"How do we play?" Dylan asks. He's already wearing his game face, ready to destroy the competition.

"We hide and the clown tries to find us. If you're tagged, you're dead and you have to wait here, in the theater, and watch *Gingerdead Man vs. Evil Bong* until the game is over."

Vivek cackles. "Sounds great. I think I wanna lose on purpose."

"What does the winner get?" Elise asks.

"To live?" I say, laughing. "Nah. Winner gets two platinum VIP tickets to Horrorpalooza in San Francisco. Tickets have been sold out for months. You wouldn't believe how hard it was to get these."

It's one of the biggest horror conventions in the country: celebrity appearances, autograph signings, film screenings, and exclusive parties.

Archer's arm is stretched behind me on the sofa. Technically it's not around me, but if I shift a few inches to the right, I'll be tucked right into him. My phone lights up with another notification, a welcome distraction from the fluttery feeling in my stomach. I lean away from this not-cuddling position and open the text.

> Super rich kids with nothing but loose ends

> Super rich kids with nothing but fake friends

"Who's sending me Frank Ocean lyrics?" I ask the room. "The movie's about to start."

"What?" Archer leans over and I tilt my phone, showing him the message.

"Somebody's been sending me messages all night," I say. I get a mix of blank and puzzled expressions. A chill burrows into my neck. Shit is getting creepy. Is someone really messing with me tonight?

"Okay, *okaaay*," Hailey says. She flicks a few tortilla chip crumbs off her red womb sweater. "It was Mariana's idea. She gave me a SIM card to swap out with my normal one," she says, exchanging looks with her girlfriend. "But we didn't send any Frank Ocean lyrics. Pinky swear."

"Y'all are so corny," I say, rolling my eyes. The last text is from a different number, so Hailey's telling the truth. But if she and Mariana didn't send it, who did?

Before I can consider it any longer, Kelsi pulls out a small black lacquered box with a gold Libra zodiac symbol on top. "Whatever. Let's get back to the fun stuff. I've got edibles! Orange Creamsicle and candy corn."

She passes the box to me. I'm already buzzed from the drinks, so I hesitate for a moment before popping one into my mouth. I don't normally mix weed and alcohol, but it is Halloween after all. The edibles make their way around the room and the movie starts with everyone happily chewing. I can totally see us all hanging out again.

Nearly two hours pass in a blur. Archer and I latch onto each other during all the "scary" moments. When we laugh together, I can't help but think, *What if we had more moments like this?*

As the credits of *Us* roll, some people clap. When Demario asks about going live, I don't bother. I'm way too buzzed to be recording anything for part two of my internship application. Instead, we file out of the theater and into the kitchen to grab some more snacks before the clown arrives.

"Guess who I saw when I picked up my sister from swim practice?" Charlie says. As always, his face lights up whenever he talks about his younger sister. I swear this six-year-old is the only proof that Charlie has a soft side.

"Who?" Elise asks.

"Jack Hudson." Charlie leans back against the kitchen island as the name detonates like a bomb around us. "He was getting physio."

Dylan's throat bobs. Jack and Dylan were the top two players on the lacrosse team, up until last year. Jack was slated to get a lucrative endorsement from a major sports brand, but after an on-field accident took him out of contention, the scouts focused their attention on Dylan. The record-breaking deal was announced shortly after.

I glance at Dylan again, whose jaw is tensed. We were all at the game when Dylan collided with Jack, when Jack went down and didn't get up. It was an accident, but I can see by Dylan's reaction that he still carries guilt over it. That hard hit was followed by getting caught in an illegal-gambling raid at a noodle shop in downtown Manhattan. Dylan insisted he was only there for the ramen, and nothing came of it. Did his new endorsers put in a good word for him? I mean, who can (yes!) say?

The lights flicker on and off again, and Charlie somehow manages to steer everyone's attention to Koro coin and how it's already rebounded forty percent since its most recent crash. I go to nudge Elise, only to discover that she and Josh are glaring at each other across the table. *What's up with those two?*

I unwrap a pan of enchiladas and reach for an oven mitt. Archer uses the other one to grab a second pan and slide it into the oven.

"Thanks," I say. It dawns on me how little I know about Archer outside of school. His socials are all professional, strictly about music, with pics of him in his studio or performing at a gig. From time to time, an occasional selfie with Oscar, his rescue chocolate Labrador. No pics of family or friends, no personal introspective posts. I know he has an older brother, but that's about it. Archer flips open the cooler at the end of the island and reaches for a Blood Bag, which is really a cranberry juice concoction in an IV bag.

"Of course. So, Noelle, fill me in on your life. Still applying to schools?" he asks, lifting the bag to his lips.

"Almost finished," I say, ignoring the tug I feel in my stomach whenever I think about college and leaving home. This is exactly why this crush needs to go away. It's our first and last Halloween together before we head off into uncharted territory. By this time next year, hopefully I'll be enrolled in a top cinema studies program, and Archer will be done with his European summer tour, and in college, too.

"Need me anywhere else?" he asks.

I can think of a lot of places where Archer could be, but I just shake my head and start filling up the slots in the middle of the serving tray with various sauces.

As Archer helps me, I think back to his impromptu performance on the piano earlier. "Pursuit" and "Wildflower" are the most popular songs on his album. I've watched videos online of all his performances. Our eyes lock for a moment over the serving tray, until I realize that I'm splashing blue cheese dressing everywhere.

"Shit!" I yelp, just as the doorbell rings. I glance up at the Ring door cam and swear. The clown is here. He's half an hour early.

Archer nods at the door. "Don't worry, I'll clean up here."

I speed-walk to the door. "Gage the Clown" stands on the other side under a rainbow umbrella in the pouring rain, and even though I *am* expecting a clown, the white painted face and shock of red hair put me on edge. Curved red lines arch from the corners of his downturned mouth, and he peers at me with heavily kohled brown eyes.

"Gage?" I say for confirmation. He nods and hands me a business card that reads GAGE "THE CLOWN" DERRY, JACKASS OF ALL TRADES, OLD BROOKVILLE ENTERTAINMENT, but he doesn't speak. I gulp. His white ruffled high collar is dotted with yellow age spots and one of the red pom-poms dangles from his flouncy shirt. Even his wig is lopsided and in dire need of styling. He looks as if he has literally just rolled out of the sewer. Definitely not the officially licensed *It* clown I was expecting. I quickly compose myself, though. In one hand he has a battered brown leather trunk with thick brass buckles and rivets. It looks kinda heavy.

What kind of props does he have in there? I wonder.

Chill. It's just an evil clown, Noelle. That's what you wanted.

Yeah, I answer. *But he's kind of too weird, though.*

I knew I should've ordered the premium clown package. Berating myself, I step aside and invite Gage in. He smiles then, revealing a mouthful of pointy yellow fake teeth that look like jagged tombstones. He takes a giant, confident step over the threshold with his oversized yellow shoes, like a vampire accepting an invitation inside. A clap of thunder sends a flock of birds flying from a low ridge on the roof.

All heads turn the minute Gage walks into the living room. The playlist is still going, albeit at a low volume. The drum-heavy beat of an Evanescence song comes on.

"This is Gage. He's here for the game," I explain to the room of wary faces. "Gage is 'It,' get it?"

Only two people laugh. I guess a pun about a demented clown and a kids' game hits different when there's an actual creepy clown in the room. Or maybe the Orange Creamsicle edibles are kicking in and no one cares. My own head feels a bit light, as if I'm floating. No more drinks for me tonight.

Gage nods again. Okay, he's doing the silent thing. Got it. He turns to drop his dripping umbrella into the stand but steps on what can only be described as an imaginary banana peel and goes ass over head, landing with a loud thud on the floor. He lets out a moan and rolls over, slowly pushing up to his knees.

Everyone gasps. The clown struggles to stand and I'm not sure if he's a good actor or a plain klutz.

"Oh my God, are you okay?" I ask, concerned. Last thing I need is to get sued if this guy cracks his back in my house.

Gage groans and eases a metal horn out of his back pocket and massages his ass. "Just a bit half-assed." His eyes land on Vivek and he flashes a leering smile. "So how 'bout it?" he says in a freakishly perfect Pennywise voice. "Kiss me, fat boy."

We laugh out loud at the iconic line that made it into both *It* movies, especially because Vivek is fit. Many of us have still not gotten over his shirtless thirst trap display on the school tennis courts last summer. Gage makes his way to the entry table and examines the decorative pumpkin mounted there, the one from Fendi. I head back to the buffet, where everyone's got a serious case of the munchies. They all ate a second edible, although I warned them not to. When it finally kicks in, Taylor might be high for days.

Gage hefts the pumpkin, throwing off the black lace, and turns it around in his hands as if trying to guess its weight. Then he pulls out a long knife with a bone handle and drives it into the pumpkin. My hand flies to my mouth but doesn't cover the squeal that rips out of me. Then he does it again, slowly. And that's when I see the blade disappearing up into the handle when it hits the pumpkin and springing out when he pulls the knife back.

"It's a prop knife," I say, trying to catch my breath. Holy shit. This guy *is* terrifying.

"A prop knife?" Demario repeats. He's standing several feet from where he was before. I never even saw him move.

Now it's the clown's turn to laugh. A harsh, barking cackle that turns my nerves into a frayed, frazzled mess. His voice is distorted and gravelly, and I notice a small circular device attached to his neck. Demario had a *Transformers* voice changer just like it when we were kids.

Gage tilts his head back, taking in the mansion. His gaze pans slowly like one of those old-time handheld video recorders and his lips flatten, his jaw clenched.

"This guy's a bit sus, Noelle," Archer murmurs.

"If you're feeling freaked out, then he's nailing the gig," I whisper back. Maybe he's doing too good a job, because he's got me antsy too. Did I get what I paid for?

Nervous energy charges through the room, and a low-level hum fills my ears, waxing and waning. Even Dylan rouses from his stoner slumber and lowers his vape pen to take note of the clown's faded gray jumpsuit with frilly bell sleeves and pants that hit too high on the ankles. Janky.

"Um, Gage, we're just finishing up a quick snack and then we'll start the game," I say.

The clown doesn't respond. He's moved over to a standing vase and is sniffing a bunch of clearly fake—Mom's allergic—long-stem red winter jasmine. *What in the world?*

"I need to check on the enchiladas," I say to Archer, and drag him into the kitchen.

"Seriously, that clown is hella creepy," he whispers.

"It's Halloween. He's supposed to be," I say.

Demario and Josh pop into the kitchen. Demario jabs his thumb over his shoulder and shakes his head. "Nah, this guy's off."

"What happened?" I ask.

"Come see for yourself," he says.

When I venture into the living room, Gage is slowly twisting the head off the last of the family of mannequins and filling its neck cavity with the long-stem flowers, creating the appearance of blood spatter against the off-white walls. He takes a step back and admires his handiwork.

Elise cocks her head. "I don't know, it's kinda creative."

I smile gratefully at her. While we finish the snacks, the clown roams the room, rearranging the Halloween displays. He takes an unsmiling selfie under the black foil balloons that spell out HAUNTED and he seems to get a special kick out of the zombie fisherman mannequin trapped in its own net. Gage disentangles the fisherman's conch shell from the net and blows into it, releasing an eerie and disorienting series of notes.

"Okay, I think we can start the game now," I say, mustering up some late-night energy.

Assembling the group, I hand out a map of the house to each person. The plans are printed on black postcards with the letters *CH* for Castle Hill and my family emblem in gold foil in one corner.

"Hide wherever you want inside the house," I say, and pick up a wicker basket from the floor. "To make things more interesting, I'm going to need your phones. Can't have you texting each other with all the good hiding spots." I drop my phone into the basket before collecting the others'. Charlie swears and blasts off one last text before dropping his phone in.

Demario goes to the window and pulls back the curtain. His expression turns grim. Heavy rain pelts the window with no sign of letting up. Like most of the county, my neighborhood is located in a flood zone and the intersection closest to my house usually ends up underwater in heavy rain. Another crack of thunder rips the sky and I try not to think about how bad it might get.

"Guys, we might get flooded in," I say.

Charlie and Maddie look way too excited about the possibility of getting to spend the night. Elise raises her brows at me— earlier, she texted that she had caught them making out inside the fun house. I'm guessing they have unfinished business.

Kelsi leaps off the sofa and struts on her model legs in ridiculously high heels over to Gage.

"So, how do we know when you catch someone?" she asks, impatient.

Gage holds up his index finger and turns away to open his trunk. Inside, there's a plaid-covered compartment with all kinds of gadgets and buttons. He grabs a silver clown horn and squeezes the black rubber bulb at the end a few times, producing a loud air horn blast. He then reaches back into the trunk and pulls out a metal timer with a pair of bells on top. He taps the clock and holds up two fingers, then turns to face the wall.

"Two minutes to hide. Remember there's a prize on the line," I announce to the room. This is going to be fun.

Gage faces the door and starts the timer, and we scamper like bloodthirsty shoppers at a SoHo sample sale. Another clap of thunder rips the sky and someone yips. Mariana and Hailey run off together; Demario and Elise head in the opposite direction, with Josh not far behind. Everyone else rushes for the staircase.

Archer is just standing there, practically begging to be tagged first. "Come on," I whisper, urging him along. "Do you *want* to suffer through *Gingerdead Man vs. Evil Bong* or hide with me?"

"Lead the way," he says, smirking. He follows me to the staircase, but instead of going up, we slip into a hidden storage nook under the stairs.

Archer stares at the shelves, all bare except for a folded blanket and a throw pillow.

"*This* is the best hiding spot?" he asks dubiously, glancing around the small space.

"One of many. My house. Home court advantage. I spent a lot of time hiding when my parents had networking events," I say.

I position myself in the sliver of space between the door and the wall. A shard of light filters into the tight, dark space. The *tick-tick-tick* of Gage's clock echoes through the house as if coming from a microphone. Footsteps thump against the wooden steps as people rush up and down the stairs, searching for a hiding place. The timer goes off, loud enough to wake the dead. Behind me, Archer's breathing gets heavier. We wait.

One minute.

Two.

The house is silent except for the theme song from *Ghostbusters*. It's starting to get warm under the stairs.

"Noelle, I didn't wear Alexander McQueen to hide in a closet!" Kelsi yells from nearby. A moment later, she swishes by our hiding space. I can hear the rustle of her floor-length dress and her five-inch heels click-clacking across the floor.

Archer shrugs.

I have no idea what's crawled up her butt. The invitation clearly said there would be "hair-raising games."

"C'mon, Dylan," she barks.

Dylan doesn't answer. He's probably dashed off to hide by himself because he's obsessed with winning.

Another minute goes by. Archer's cologne smells like wood and citrus. At least it's dark enough that he can't see the goofy look on my face. *Footsteps.* Gage clomps by and stops right in front of the hidden door. Archer stills. Neither of us takes a single breath. Kelsi's heels stop clicking. Gage links his fingers and stretches his hands out, releasing a sickening, choreographed set of knuckle pops. Then he smiles, wide and leering, zooming in on his first target.

CHAPTER 7

"Do you like scary movies?"
—*Scream* (1996)

I'm pressing my face so hard against the paneling that when I pull back, I know I'm going to have an indentation from forehead to chin. Gage lunges for Kelsi, who feints left, then sprints right, running away so fast you'd think she was wearing sneakers.

Gage slips, crashing into the heirloom-style credenza with an "Oof."

"Sounds like this dude's wrecking your place," Archer whispers each time the clown collides with something.

I'm stressing. The clown is doing the most. I'm going to have to hire a tasker from TaskRabbit to clean before Gloria gets here. I *did* tell him to make it "fun and messy," but this is a bit much. Mom will freak out if the furniture gets damaged.

Gage slips the clown horn into his back pocket, freeing up both his hands. I can't see Kelsi anymore, but from the way Gage sinks into a low crouch, she can't be far. Next to me, Archer fidgets and coughs, loud enough for all of Long Island to hear. I pluck him.

Gage's head swivels our way. *Shit.* I squeeze my eyes shut. *Don't come over here.* I chant the words like a morning affirmation. Lightning splits the sky, and the entire room is filled with a flash of white light. Kelsi shrieks, going past the staircase. Gage is close behind her, and they both disappear.

The intercom in the hallway clicks on, and my gaze flicks over to Archer. Kelsi's voice filters through. Then I hear Josh's voice, and I realize it's a recording. My hand reaches out to push open the door. I need to go out there and figure out what's going on. Archer motions for me to chill, and my hand freezes on the latch.

An episode of Josh's podcast, the one with Kelsi, is playing through the house intercom. I turn to Archer, confused. *What's happening? Who's doing this?* Hailey better not be playing around again.

The recording echoes through the intercom as Kelsi talks about what motivated her to live stream her cooking attempts on social media. The family chef had to leave for an emergency one day, so she decided to bake something . . . while the whole internet watched. Kelsi in the kitchen is like watching a cat in an ice-skating rink. Horrifying and hilarious at the same time.

Josh Sullivan: Tell me about the apple cake.

Kelsi Crankenshaw: [*laughs*] Oh, we're going there?

Josh Sullivan: Hell yeah. My seat belt's fastened, so take me to Fruit Sticker Town.

The recording of the infamous episode continues, with Kelsi giving her side of her most controversial Instagram Live, where she couldn't be bothered to peel off the bar code stickers on the organic apples before tossing them into the food processor for an apple cake.

> **Kelsi Crankenshaw:** Like I said a bajillion times already, fruit stickers are edible, Josh.
>
> **Josh Sullivan:** Actually, they're not, Kelsi. I know you were trying to do damage control by sending that giant apology sheet cake to a nursing home after someone posted a video of you stealing a parking spot from an old lady. But those poor grannies were munching on microplastics and glue. [*laughs*]
>
> **Kelsi Crankenshaw:** At least the caramel drip made it taste good. [*laughs*] Besides, those fruit stickers are annoying, like, who has the time?
>
> **Josh Sullivan:** Everyone but you. A few people actually got sick from eating your cake. What if the nursing home sues you?
>
> **Kelsi Crankenshaw:** Gosh, I hope not. Lawsuits are expensive and you know how much I like my winter trips to Telluride.

I'm just about to storm out and tell whoever's hijacked the intercom to quit it, hide-and-seek be damned, when the power goes off. Castle Hill is plunged into darkness.

"You've gotta be kidding me," I mumble.

Loud beeping comes from Dad's server room down the hallway, confirming the loss of power. Our hiding space is now a pitch-black void. Gage could be standing right outside the door, ready to eliminate Archer and me from the game. The high-pitched beeping burrows into my ears, dulling my other senses.

"What now?" Archer asks.

"We wait for the backup generator to kick in," I say. A minute ticks by, and then another. Spoiler alert: it doesn't kick in.

Inside the nook, the walls are closing in. I listen for any sound of movement, but I can't hear anything through the incessant beeping.

"I need to check the breaker," I say. "That noise won't stop until the power comes back on or the generator starts working."

I ease open the door an inch at a time, bracing for a creak any minute. My faithful playlist is still going from the Bluetooth speakers, with "Disturbia" haunting the entire house. I can barely make out my hand in front of my face, but memory leads me around the furniture toward the foyer. Moonlight filters thinly through the windows, but it's hardly enough to pierce the shadows around me.

Archer taps my arm and I nearly jump out of my skin. I didn't realize he'd followed me. "I thought we were going to the server room?" he whispers.

"I need to get my phone," I whisper back. I head over to where I left the wicker basket filled with everyone's cells. "I have to ask Dad about how to work the generator."

"I can help," Archer says, his voice calm and steady. The exact opposite of everything I'm feeling right now because the basket is gone. Along with Gage's trunk.

Where's my damn phone? If that clown just wanted to rip off a bunch of rich kids . . .

I take a breath, a cry strangling my throat. First the podcast nonsense, and now this? I'm tempted to call off the game, but how would that make me look, tapping out like a punk?

I pivot toward the kitchen, the beeping jackhammering in my head. I don't know how Archer stays so calm. The hallway is pitch-black and freezing. *Ugh.* Somebody must have opened a window again. I glance over my shoulder, unable to ignore the prickling on my neck. The air is sickly sweet with traces of weed from Dylan's vape pen. I arrive at the server room, which is just across from the laundry room. I slowly turn the knob, hoping that no one's standing behind the door. The room smells like wet mop and linen air freshener.

"Breaker panel is over here," I say, feeling my way in the dark room. I reach the metal shelving bolted to the wall and run my hand along the middle shelf. "There should be a flashlight around here. One of those small ones like a Mini Maglite."

"Well, this is a first. Me in a dark room with a pretty girl . . . and we're looking for a breaker panel," Archer says, with a laugh.

My mouth falls open and then snaps shut. *He thinks I'm pretty?* For a moment, sanity is pushed from my head.

"Guess you never forget the firsts, right?" I say, hoping that I sound sufficiently flirty.

His hand slides over the shelf, feeling for the flashlight, and his fingers brush against mine. A warm tingle travels up my arm.

"Mini Maglite," I say, to refocus myself more than anything.

Archer clears his throat, stepping back. "Right." His foot connects with something, sending it skating across the tile floor.

I suck in a breath and hold it, listening for footsteps or voices.

"Can you try to keep it down?" I whisper. I can't shake the creeped-out feeling that came over me when Gage walked into the house. "I still want to win. Let's just hurry up and find this thing!"

After another two minutes of hushed conversation and clumsy rummaging on the shelf, my fingers curl around cool metal. A high beam shoots out of the flashlight and my breath whooshes out with relief. I rush over to the breaker box and pop open the cover.

"You know what you're looking at?" Archer asks.

I snort. "Horror Movie Survival 101: know how to check and reset a tripped breaker."

I flip the switch off, then on, then off and back on to reset the breaker. Nothing happens.

Archer reaches for the flashlight. "Count to twenty and try it again. I'm going to check the generator."

I follow him to the back of the server room, to the compact generator. "You know what you're looking at?" I ask, throwing his question back at him. I aim the flashlight and Archer flips open a panel.

"I know a thing or two about generators," he says, examining the equipment. "You've got fuel and soot backed up in the exhaust. It's totally busted." His expression is grim.

"Seriously? What's the point of a backup if it doesn't actually back up anything?" There's no way a repairman is coming out now. The night's not even over yet and I have a headache for the ages.

"Okay, time for another crack at the breaker," I say. I toggle the switches again, and this time the overhead light in the room comes on.

"We nailed it, baby," I say, high-fiving Archer. We laugh and things quickly get awkward again because he's staring at me as if he was about to say something and changed his mind.

He cracks open the door and peeks out. "All clear."

We're halfway down the hallway when I hear Kelsi's voice again. Not a recording this time. This is Kelsi's asking-to-speak-to-the-manager voice.

"Let me go, you moron," she snarls. A moment later, a primal scream rips from Kelsi's throat.

My blood turns to ice in my veins. I hear her heels clatter against the tiles, and then a heavy thump.

"Tag!" the clown shouts. His horn blasts a series of high-pitched honks, announcing the elimination of the first player like we're in *The Hunger Games*. I wait for Kelsi to protest, to hear her stomping her way to the home theater, but there's only silence.

CHAPTER 8

"Get out!"

—*Get Out* (2017)

Archer and I bolt to the living room.

"Kelsi?" I whisper into the darkness. She couldn't have gotten far in those ridiculous shoes.

No answer.

My fingers tremble around the flashlight and panic grips me by the throat as the light cuts through the murky shadows and I see Kelsi sprawled on the floor, dark blood pooling beneath her. I realize with sudden, horrifying clarity that Kelsi won't ever scream again.

What the actual fuck?

"Kelsi?" I say again, my voice quaking. I inch closer. Part of me expects her to jump up and yell, "Gotcha!" But she doesn't because she's dead, like dead, dead. Her eyes are wide open, her face frozen in surprise.

"Oh my God." I slap a trembling hand to my mouth. In fact, my entire body is shaking, and then I'm screaming until it feels like my vocal cords are about to rupture. Immediately, footsteps sound from the hallway, and a moment later, Demario, Elise, and Taylor come running in from wherever they've been hiding. Someone turns on the lights. Archer checks Kelsi's pulse and shakes his head, an incredulous look on his face.

"What the hell is this?" he asks. He stands and turns in a slow circle. "Where's that clown?"

Cold sweat breaks out over my face and neck. My chest contracts and my lungs collapse. I think I might be going into shock.

Demario paces back and forth, fingers laced behind his head. "Oh shit, oh shit, oh shit."

Elise and Taylor are both in tears. Maybe I am too, but my face is too numb to feel anything. Bile rushes up into my throat, and I swallow hard. I think I'm gonna puke. There's a dead body in my living room. Kelsi's body. The daughter of a federal judge. Dead at the hands of a deranged clown that *I* hired. How am I going to explain this to the cops?

Archer hugs me to him, but I untangle myself and start yelling for everyone to come out. My brain clicks off and restarts. I've spent my entire life obsessed with horror films, formulating scenarios about what I would do in a situation like this. First order of business: get the fuck out of here. With no phone, I opt for the next best thing.

"Alexa!" I shout. On the coffee table nearby, the virtual assistant device lights up in teal blue. "Call 911!"

The red ring of doom flashes. "I'm having trouble understanding right now. Please try again later," answers the robotic voice. *A server problem? Really?* I hit the reboot button, but nothing happens.

It's official. The universe hates me. Hope spontaneously combusts and escapes like atoms into the atmosphere.

Gage appears from the kitchen. He's holding a bloodstained hunting knife in one hand and his rainbow-colored umbrella in the other. He storms at us, and I scream. I grab Archer's arm and tug him backward, toward the door and away from Gage. Demario, Elise, and Taylor back up with us. My heart is a frozen lump in my throat. Kelsi's blood seeps into the joints of the hardwood floor. I can't believe this is happening.

Gage takes two steps forward and dips the pointed end of the umbrella into the jack-o'-lantern candle on the side table. The umbrella's tip ignites. A flaming arrow explodes out of it with stunning speed and embeds itself into the wooden router storage box tucked in the corner of the room, shattering the modem and half the credenza. The wood splinters into a million weaponized fragments, and we scatter. I dive to the ground, but not before I feel a slash of pain above my elbow. I belly-crawl behind the sofa, hysterical, especially when I notice the trail of smudged blood I leave on the floor from the small gash in my arm. The air stinks with acrid smoke, a mix of kerosene fumes, burned electrical wires, and melted plastic.

"Oh my God, Noelle!" Taylor shrieks from across the room, pointing right at me.

I glance down and my hands fly to my chest. A large bloodstain is spilling down my stomach and streaking toward the hem of my dress.

"Shit!" Demario yells, his gaze darting between Gage, who's still standing in the entryway, umbrella raised, and me.

"You hit?" Archer asks at the same time. He's hovering over me, but his words sound far away and garbled.

"It's the dress," I manage to say, relieved. I try to explain about the blood squib incorporated into the dress, but my throat feels like it's closing up. "It's f-fake blood. I think the clown found a way to trigger it."

I need to get it together. *Focus.* The key to surviving a scary movie is to recognize that you're living in one. And if escaping a psycho slasher clown with uncanny marksmanship isn't a horror show, I don't know what is.

Gage rounds the kitchen island and charges at Elise. For a moment, she's frozen in place until Gage raises the knife. She screams as she sprints away, the knife ripping through the black fabric of her witch's robe. Chaos has truly descended upon Castle Hill.

"Nobody moves!" Gage shouts. He has the umbrella trained on Elise and Demario, who are standing in the living room, close to the front door but yet so far away. I don't want anyone else to get hurt. Demario moves closer to Elise and nudges her behind him. He eyes Gage warily. "Noelle, where'd you find this clown?"

"Just some local website," I say, hiccuping. "Tessa recommended it to me."

Tessa who wasn't invited to the party. Tessa who also happens to be friends with Wolfie Marlow.

Archer rubs my back in slow circles, but the gesture does nothing to stop the fear gnawing its way through my insides like a subway rat. He checks out my elbow again, even though I tell him it's fine. I force myself to take deep breaths. How do I get us out of here? I'm supposed to be a Final Girl, right? I mean, all that talk earlier was just for shits and giggles. But the fact is, I've got to get away from this house. My own damn house. There's a solid orange light on the home security system that isn't supposed to be there.

Doors slam and hurried footsteps echo on the stairs as the remaining hiders come out. They've barely made it into my field of vision before the sight of Kelsi on the floor and Gage holding a bloody knife in one hand and a smoking umbrella in the other stops them in their tracks. Maddie and Charlie fall back into the unlit hallway. Vivek runs down the stairs with Josh not far behind.

"What's happening?" Josh shouts. Gage swings around and points the umbrella at him. Josh freezes midstep. The clown positions himself in the middle of the room. Vivek leans over Kelsi, his face contorting into a look of disbelief. Mariana and Hailey hang back while Elise huddles on the floor, next to Demario, her hair clinging to her wet cheeks.

"We need to do something," I whisper to Archer. "We can't just stand here doing nothing."

Archer shakes his head. "Not yet."

"All of you, get over there with the others," Gage orders. He motions with the umbrella at Josh, Vivek, Mariana, and Hailey, who are all freaking out. Hailey and Mariana come into the living room, hands raised. Archer and I slowly shuffle over to join them.

"You're fucking crazy!" I scream at the clown.

"Actually, I prefer *passionate*, but yeah, I guess you could say I'm a little wild," he says.

"I want you out of my house, right now," I say. Demario and Archer are on either side of me, ready for whatever happens. "Is this about money? Just take what you want and leave us alone."

Gage doesn't answer. He frowns at a blade-wide smear of blood on his outfit. He pulls a stain remover pen from his pocket and twists the cap off, then applies it with long, even strokes.

Get out. The voice in my head is louder this time, desperate and pleading. I need a plan. Stay ready. In all my escape-a-slasher scenarios, I'm appropriately dressed for the weather, my car keys are within reach, and I'm never a breath away from throwing up. Getting my go bag is out of the question because Horror Survival Skills 101: don't go upstairs, and keep away from basements and attics.

Taylor glances over at Kelsi and backs away, hugging themself. My car keys are hanging on a wall in the mudroom, but Gage is in the way. Even if I channeled all my Wakanda warrior badassery, he's got a knife and real arrows in that umbrella. Taking a deep breath, I repeat all that I told myself after every trial run with Demario:

I am Noelle Layne, Final Girl, the rightful Queen of Castle Hill, Escapologist, and the great serial killer Survivor of Nassau County.

My eyes zip to the table in the hallway. A crystal ashtray that my family dumps their key fobs into is gone. Taylor's eyes lock with mine, and I know we're thinking the same thing. The front door is closer. Am I willing to make a run for it and risk a knife to the back? Hell yeah. If we all run at the same time, Gage can't take all of us out. But then I'll have even more dead bodies on my hands, as in multiple dead people inside my house. I don't even know how I'm going to explain the one I've got to the police. Or to my parents.

But even if I make it outside, then what? It's forty-three degrees Fahrenheit and rainy. Hypothermia can set in in as few as five minutes with exposed skin, and I'm practically naked in this pink minidress. The boots are a pain to get on and off, and the driveway is long and flooded. I could hide in the stables and try not to die or saddle up my black Thoroughbred, Old Girl, and ride out of here like Idris Elba in *Concrete Cowboy*. That is, if my frozen fingers can hold on to the reins. I'll figure it out once I'm outside.

We're all paralyzed, unmoving, as Gage helps himself to a bite of the spinach wraps decorated to look like Frankenstein's monster from one of the snack trays and stares up at the ceiling, chewing thoughtfully. He doesn't even take out his stone dentures. Beads of sweat pop up along my hairline. Kelsi's scream plays on a loop in my head and I can't stop seeing her death stare, her lips parted in silent anguish. Every breath I take is filled with her perfume, and the taint of coppery blood hits me hard in the back of my throat. I lurch forward, dry-heaving onto a nearby potted plant.

Gage aims the umbrella in our direction as he crosses into the kitchen and fills a glass with water from the fridge dispenser.

He's ready to murder us all like mosquitoes buzzing around his ears, but by all means, hydrate!

"Slight change to the game rules," Gage says, with a chuckle. "It's simple, really. I catch, I kill."

My stomach sinks down to my toes and a mewl escapes my lips. Archer stiffens next to me as a range of tormented cries and gasps reverberate throughout the room.

I make a subtle movement with my head toward the front door, hoping that Archer picks up on what I'm thinking. It works because he slowly releases his hold on my hand.

Taylor and I bolt at the same time. They are closer to the door, so I'm hauling ass to catch up. Adrenaline surges and the noises around me fade into a buzz: the click-clacking of Gage's shoes as he runs after us, Archer and Demario yelling, and the grunt and groans of bodies colliding and slamming onto the floor. For a breathless second I let myself believe they took Gage down, but the heavy footsteps don't stop. Taylor is almost at the door, but they stumble, losing momentum. I brace for the rough clamp of a hand, when a dagger with a rainbow handle with pom-poms attached sails right by me and plunges deep into the solid oak door, inches from Taylor's head. The colorful pom-poms bounce against each other and swing from the hilt of the dagger.

I almost slam into Taylor, but then I realize that they didn't stumble at all. There's a contraption attached to the door-knob. A biometric padlock. *Are you joking?* If the front door is locked, did Gage lock the other doors too? Vivek rushes to a window, but it doesn't open. Archer and Demario are picking themselves up off the floor. Demario grips his forearm, a trickle of blood leaking between his fingers. His face is twisted with pain.

Hide-and-seek tag has turned into Castle Hill Homicide. A real-life killing buffet, Jason Voorhees–style. Gage the Clown wants all of us dead. In slasher movies, the killers always have an agenda. Freddy Krueger knew exactly who he wanted to kill: the kids of the parents who set him on fire. Jason slaughtered practically everyone he met. Ghostface had abandonment issues. So who is Gage channeling? If I can't waltz my way out the front door, then time to activate Final Girl mode. I don't know how I'm going to do it, but I'm busting my ass out of Castle Hill. One way or the other.

Vivek moves on to another window. It's stuck too. He shouts that the windows have been sealed shut with some kind of caulk. He grabs a heavy accent chair, and before I can warn him, he hurls it at the window with a yell. A loud thud echoes as the chair bounces off and smashes onto the floor.

"Was about to tell you not to waste your time," I say. "Double glazed and with enhanced security features."

Vivek stares at the intact window. "Damn."

Gage shrugs, not bothering to hide the smirk on his face. *He knew.*

A wide-eyed Josh stares down at Kelsi's lifeless body. He flinches when Gage yanks the knife out of the door and points the blade at us. Josh inches around Kelsi, carefully avoiding the widening pool of blood.

I do a quick head count. Dylan is missing. If he went down to the basement or wine cellar to hide, then he has no clue what's happening up here.

"What's up with that podcast episode?" Josh whispers to me. He swallows so hard I hear it.

"I was hoping you could tell me," I say.

"So, you didn't—" he starts.

"Nope."

All heads turn to look at the clown.

Josh pales. "We're fucked, aren't we?"

I fold my arms, tucking them tight against my ribs. I look Josh dead in the eye. "I'm not dying with you tonight."

CHAPTER 9

"Huntin' humans ain't nothin' but nothin'.
They all run like scared little rabbits.
Run, rabbit, run! Run, rabbit, run . . .
Run, rabbit, run!"
—*House of 1000 Corpses* (2003)

Gage makes an exaggerated production of clearing his throat. He whips a long dart from his pocket and throws it with precision, and we all jolt. The dart sails high above our heads and lands in the cluster of foil balloons over the entry doorway. I flinch at the loud pop and my blood turns to ice in my veins. Black shards of the *a* in the HAUNTED balloon display sink to the floor, leaving the word HUNTED bobbing in its wake.

"This can't be happening," I whisper to myself.

Hailey and Mariana cling to each other with heaving sobs. Others cry silently, with soft breaths and occasional sniffles. My cheeks are wet, but I'm hyperfocused on what's happening and understanding what awaits.

"Move," the clown says, jerking his head toward the giant prize wheel we spun earlier. We shuffle over to it while my brain processes every possible exit. Windows. Doors. Garage. We need to create the opportunity for an escape, a way to demobilize Gage long enough to get away. My train of thought is cut short. The pizza slice pieces on the wheel have all been flipped over, revealing our names beneath. The clown lifts out Kelsi's name piece and tosses it on the floor. The bastard is still smiling.

"What is wrong with you?" I ask, already knowing the answer is *a lot*.

Archer urges me closer to him, away from the clown.

"What are you doing, man?" Josh pipes up. His voice is low, with none of its usual confidence.

I scan the room for something heavy to use as a weapon, but there's nothing within reach. When I do get the chance to throw something at Gage, it's going to lay his ass out. "This is bullshit—"

Gage cocks the umbrella. The sound of the bolt pulling into the ready position silences me immediately.

"You," the clown says, pointing at Archer. "Piano . . . now."

Archer doesn't move right away.

Gage takes two giant steps forward and swings the umbrella-crossbow contraption right at me. I raise my hands defensively, but before I can speak, he pulls the trigger. I scream louder than everyone else. A high-decibel terror shriek that tops any of my horror movie practice screams. It's a solid six on the horror movie scale. A yellow flag with the word BANG drops from the tip of the umbrella.

"Jesus Christ," Archer says. He rushes over to the piano and takes a seat.

His brows pinch together as he stares at the sheet music on the desk. The clown motions with his fingers for Archer to start playing. The opening riff is melancholic but picks up into a folksy up-tempo number. It doesn't sound familiar, and Archer keeps glancing at the clown as he plays.

Without warning, the piano lid slams down, snapping against Archer's wrists with a nasty crunch. His fingers are crushed against the piano keys, creating a jarring cacophony of discordant notes. Archer doubles over and screams, his face twisted in pain.

"Who's making the hits now?" the clown asks, heading back over to the prize wheel. "Fingers are so overrated."

I rush to Archer without thinking. Demario and Josh help me push the lid up, enough for Archer to slip out his hands. When we release the lid, it slams shut again. Blood gushes from nasty gashes above Archer's wrists. The clown watches, amused, as we pad Archer's wrists with paper towels and napkins that we grabbed from a nearby snack table.

I'm piecing together a psychological profile of Gage in my mind. I've learned a lot from watching horror movies. Killers plan their attacks carefully; they have a twisted worldview and believe they're being persecuted by society or a social group. They are resentful because of perceived rejection or humiliation, even if these things never really happened. Gage has scripted every moment of this violent fantasy and now he's making a pseudo power play. I need to figure out how to get out of this mess alive.

Staring past the clown into the kitchen, I notice right away that all the knives are missing from the knife block on the counter. The fire extinguisher is gone too. Every neuron in my brain starts misfiring as I recall the open windows, the broken security camera, and coming home to all the lights off.

Gage was here. He must have slipped into the house after my parents left. But how did he breach the alarm? The mere thought of Gage snooping around the house, sifting through my things, makes me want to set everything on fire.

"He took the knives," I whisper to Archer.

"Shit," Archer says, clutching the bloody paper towels against his wrists. "It's not as bad as it looks," he says. I have a hard time believing him.

What did any of us do to deserve this? I have no idea why the clown murdered Kelsi in cold blood. Or why he made Archer play that song and then hurt him. And why is he coming for each and every one of us?

I replay the facts and my heart twinges. I planned this party. I hired the clown. There are emails from me to Gage, asking for a scary game of tag. I close my eyes and my brain jumps to the worst-case scenario. How easy would it be for Gage to tell the cops that he and I had planned this together? Police aren't exactly known for extending the benefit of the doubt to Black people. I did gather these specific people in one place on a co-incidentally dark and stormy night in my house, after all. The mere thought sends hot bile rushing up my throat.

Archer's song "Pursuit" floats through the speakers. The playlist is still streaming from my phone. Gage starts to dance when the chorus begins, then he punches his knife toward the ceiling to the beat. He reaches under the cuff of one sleeve and pulls out a long scarf with the words THIS BEAT STABS! on it.

Next to me, Archer sucks in a breath. I may not know the clown's specific motivations where each of us is concerned, but I know what Gage wants, what every slasher wants: the thrill of the hunt. He wants to feed on our fear while he stalks and terrorizes us. If he thinks we're going to queue up so we can be toppled like dominoes, he's got another think coming.

"We need to stick together," I announce. Mariana and Hailey are inching toward the door.

Gage taps the umbrella against his leg, listening silently. This clown is a cocky bastard; he isn't dumb, I'll give him that.

"We can fight our way out," I say, loud enough for Gage to hear. I've watched enough horror movies and listened to enough true crime podcasts to know he'll pick us off one by one if we split up.

Archer shakes his head. We need a better plan because what I'm suggesting is dangerous, and confrontation is reckless, but it's the only one we have right now.

Gage raises the clown horn high above his head, ready to resume his twisted game. He blasts the horn, but no one runs. We don't hide. Mom's crystal and marble chess set sits on a side table next to the sofa. With a hard swipe, I send the crystal pieces sailing to the floor in Gage's direction. Eight thousand dollars be damned. No one in my house plays chess anyway. I curl my fingers around the heavy marble chessboard.

Demario snatches up the white pumpkin from the floor and lobs it at Gage's head. Gage dodges and the pumpkin smashes into an armoire. He's not as tall as Demario, but he's slim and wiry and stronger than he looks. "Make It Bun Dem" by Skrillex and Damian Marley starts up, wild, electro background noise to the frenzy unfolding. Mariana takes a swing with a light-up broomstick, but Gage evades it with an acrobatic move. Archer and Demario both charge at him. Demario lands a punch, throwing him off-balance, and Archer rams him with his shoulder, sending him flailing to the floor.

"Tie him up!" I yell.

Vivek and Hailey run into the kitchen and start pulling open drawers, and I inch closer to the clown. Archer has his knee on the clown's back, pinning him down. Josh tugs his arms behind his back. Gage starts to laugh, cackling as if he's enjoying the takedown. With a sharp twist of his torso, the clown breaks the hold, tossing both Josh and Archer aside. Lunging, I pick up the chessboard and slam it down on Gage's head. He collapses with a groan, but as he flops over onto his back, he pulls a small black canister from his pocket and tosses it at us.

I barely understand what's happening before the flash-bang goes off, blinding us with bright light and a noise loud enough to rock Castle Hill. The closest neighbors are half a mile down the road, and with the peals of thunder from the storm raging outside, they won't hear a single thing.

CHAPTER 10

"You know the part in scary movies when somebody does something really stupid, and everybody hates them for it? This is it."

—*Jeepers Creepers* (2001)

My eardrums are vibrating, and a bitter taste fills my mouth. Everybody's on the floor, stunned. When the shock dissipates, the screaming and shouting begins. Gray smoke from the flash-bang disperses as everyone moves around disoriented. I roll over, coughing and blinking the spots away. My head's spinning so fast that I can barely sit up.

"Where'd he go?" I ask, frantic. Archer hooks one arm under me and helps me up. Elise and Taylor are begging someone to get up.

Thick swirls of smoke rise and thin out, and there's no sign of Gage. He could be anywhere in the house. A fresh wave of panic washes over me.

"Are you okay?" Archer asks.

"No!" I shriek. "There's a clown trying to kill us, Archer. I am far from okay." I pick up the mangled broomstick and chuck it back on the floor. "How did he even manage to slink out?"

"He's suited up in protective gear, Noelle," Archer says, pacing. "I felt it. And the way he grappled on the floor, he's trained in something."

"This is all kinds of fucked up," Demario says.

Archer stops pacing and holds my face in his hands, urging me to focus. "Do you have a safe room?"

I almost laugh at the irony of the question. "No. Not anymore. Mom converted it into a wine cellar."

After installing such a high-end security system, Dad didn't see the point. The safe room is now a contemporary space, all stone and glass, with rows of UV-protected glass shelves storing hundreds of bottles of highfalutin wine.

"It might still be the best spot for us to—" Archer starts.

"This entire house was supposed to be safe," I say, cutting him off. "If he can disable the entire system to get in here, he probably already knows about the wine cellar. Besides, the basement is the last place any of us needs to be. For all we know, he could be down there right now, sipping a Malbec, waiting for us."

The intercom crackles to life and I freeze. Archer's fingers, warm and steady, curl around mine.

"The game is just getting started," Gage says, his voice low and raspy like Jigsaw's from the *Saw* movie franchise. "I suggest you find a place my knife can't reach."

We scamper as he laughs over the intercom.

"Go, go, go!" I yell, sprinting toward the mudroom and beckoning for the rest of the group to follow. I can't bear to look anyone in the eye. They're stuck in this mess because of me. I could have had a normal anniversary watch party and saved us all from having starring roles in this horror movie and Kelsi wouldn't be dead on my living room floor.

Gage's voice crackles through the intercom as we run, shell-shocked and terrified. "Come back and *plaaay!*"

Bruh, gotta catch me first. The only thing I'm playing now is a game of real-life *Survivor.* "Where're we going?" Archer asks. He's so close behind me that his warm breath tickles the back of my neck. A few of the others murmur similar questions, fear evident in their voices.

I take a deep breath, ignoring the way my throat still burns from the flash-bang fumes. I push open the door to the mud-room and the tiny motion light switches on. My spare car keys are gone, along with the keys to Mom's Range Rover. The door from the mudroom to the garage is locked. It's never locked. I don't know why Gage is doing this, or why he targeted my party, but I need to come up with a plan, quick.

Archer pats his pocket. "I still have my keys."

"Might not make much of a difference," Vivek whispers. He moves away from the glass-paneled door and gestures outside. At least three cars have visibly flat tires, so chances are high that the rest were decommissioned too. I do a quick head count. Dylan, Maddie, and Charlie are missing.

My headband tiara feels tight as if my brain is swelling. "What am I going to tell the cops? What if they think I had something to do with all of this?" I ask, voicing my worries out loud.

"Just tell them the truth," Archer says.

"And you think they'll believe me? Just like that?" I ask,

crossing my arms. Must be nice living in Archer's world where cops really are the protectors and crime fighters.

Archer meets my gaze. "Noelle, I'll tell the cops exactly what went down. I got you."

I'm shaking as I exhale. Okay. An alibi goes a long way. What started as such a fun night is now a total nightmare.

And just like that, the music cuts off, mid-lyrics. The sudden silence is unsettling. The house is quieter than ever. A heavy blanket of dread settles over my shoulders and I think about all the times I spent alone here or hung out with just Demario while my parents worked. We talked about what we would do if there was an intruder. But there's no more talking—this shit is real. I can't afford to lose anyone else. I need to focus. Process. Without access to the garage, I need to find a way to escape my own damn house.

The room fills with the heavy rush of our breathing. Demario guards the entrance to the mudroom while the rest of us search for anything we can use to arm ourselves.

We don't come away with much, nothing that might do any real damage anyway: a hand-crafted vase Mom brought back from Haiti, shoes, a few curtain rods, and a canoe paddle. Mariana rips the Aminta dress up to her knees. Now she looks less *Phantom of the Opera* and more *Moulin Rouge*.

"There's a toolbox in the garage with cable ties, but a chime on the door to the garage might go off," I explain. Now that the house is shrouded in silence, if the chime is still connected, it'd be a dead giveaway to our location. We can't afford the risk.

A scratching noise comes from the other side of the door. All heads turn. Waiting. Listening. My pulse rate spikes and I back away from the door, paddle pointed at it, bracing for someone or something to come crashing through.

"We should check out that noise," Archer says, reaching for the doorknob.

"No, we shouldn't," I say, blocking his path. "How about we mind our business instead?"

"But what if someone's hurt?" he asks.

I adjust my grip on the paddle. "Then they better get right with Jesus. Don't even think about opening that door. Gage could be out there faking us out."

"Fine. So what now?" Archer asks.

I can't believe I'm about to say this, to break a cardinal rule of how to stay alive in a horror movie. "I need to go upstairs to my room," I say, lowering my voice. "For my go bag."

"What's the go bag doing upstairs?" Demario asks. He knows I normally keep it under the stairs, in the hiding spot where I took Archer earlier.

"I moved the bag so it wouldn't be in the way tonight," I say, feeling doltish. "But there's a bolt cutter in it we can use to remove the contraption on the front door."

"Okay, let's go," Archer says, heading for the stairs.

I make a quick stop in the kitchen. The knives might be gone but the cast-iron skillet could come in handy. I pass the canoe paddle to Mariana, ease open the cupboard, and slide the pan out slowly, praying not to set off an avalanche of pots and pans.

"You said this guy's all tactical, right? We need to be ready for next time we see him," I say, shuddering at the mere thought. "We can't risk tackling him again."

"Yeah, that plan sucked ass," Demario says, rubbing his ribs.

I shove down the guilt that rises up inside me like flood-water. "We are getting out of here."

"Or die trying," Demario grumbles.

Approaching footsteps echo against polished tile. We sink to the floor behind the kitchen island. I squat with the skillet in my hands like a bat, ready to come up with a right-hand swing. My heart pounds, rattling my rib cage. I peek around the corner, just in time to see a blur of stripes rushing toward the staircase. He's too far away to chance calling out.

"Dylan," I whisper. Suddenly, the wide-open plan of the house feels too vast.

We sneak through the living room.

The door to the nook under the stairs opens and Gage crawls out, knife in hand.

He grins at us, mouth wide and leering. "I've got a new game. It's called how many stabs."

The scream that tears out of me hits a seven on the horror movie scale. I windmill backward, away from Gage, keeping my eyes on the knife while calculating how fast I can reach the stair-case in these cursed boots.

"Run!" Archer shouts.

I shove the skillet into Archer's hands and bolt. Demario lobs the vase at Gage. It slams into his knee with a delicious crunch. Archer slides in with a full-extension swing of the skillet and catches Gage under the chin in one swift and fluid move. Gage goes down with a thump just as I reach the first step. Mariana screams as she whacks him with the canoe paddle.

"Go, go, go!" Demario shouts behind me.

I run up the stairs like an Olympic track star, my heart pounding in my ears. Every muscle and nerve ending syncs, propelling me forward and away from Gage. As I hit a curve in the staircase, Gage staggers to his feet. Archer swings the skillet again, but Gage grabs Archer's injured wrist and squeezes. Archer releases the skillet with a yell but somehow manages to land a kick in Gage's leg, throwing him off-balance before racing away. I take a couple of quick looks over my shoulder. By the time Gage starts clomping up the stairs, I'm hauling ass down the hallway, just in time to see Dylan sprinting out of my room, with my go bag swinging from his shoulder.

CHAPTER 11

"What if I told you that today you'll leave here different. I'm talking to you. Right here, you are going to witness an absolute spectacle."
—*Nope* (2022)

"Motherfucker," I hiss as Dylan disappears with the clown in hot pursuit.

Everyone scatters upstairs. Demario and Elise urge Taylor, Hailey, and Mariana to hide in a bedroom. Maddie, Charlie, and Vivek must've stayed on the first floor and I'm hoping Josh is with them. Splitting up is exactly what we're *not* supposed to do. Frustrated, I duck into my room, Archer right behind me, and slam the door. Gage is probably at the opposite end of the house by now.

"What a snake! Dylan heard me talking about my go bag and then he steals it?" I say, fuming.

"Yeah, I don't know what he's thinking," Archer says.

He takes in my room, the cheesecloth mummy throw pillows tossed on the messy bed, the upholstered velvet headboard and linen-blend curtains. Whereas the rest of the house is draped in traditional black, orange, and yellow for the party, I've gone for an elegant all-white Halloween theme in my bedroom. White-painted pumpkins draped with pearls sit on the dresser next to a display of silver and white cloches.

I pull out the drawers of the bedside table, but my iPad is gone. My schoolbag is also open, when I'm pretty sure it was closed before the party. A quick check confirms my suspicion: my laptop's missing too, along with my smartwatch.

Archer takes a seat on a 1930s Louis Vuitton steamer trunk, a thirteen-birthday gift from Mom. He stretches his long legs out in front of him, while I sit on the floor yanking off Mom's silver designer boots.

"I need that go bag back," I say.

"We'll find him, don't worry," Archer says. He slips into the bathroom, and I shove my feet into my worn combat boots because this is war. Not only with a homicidal clown but with Dylan too.

When I look over, Archer is sitting on the edge of the claw-foot tub and staring down at something. My heart skips a beat. The scent of vanilla bath salts lingers in the air. Low light spills out from the recessed ceiling lights and wall sconces. I didn't use vanilla bath salts today.

"What is it?" I ask. I clench and unclench my hands as I approach, nerves grating into shards.

"See for yourself," he says, standing.

I lean over the tub and suck in a sharp breath. It has been filled with water, and fish with razor-sharp buckteeth are swimming around. A collection of cell phones is at the bottom of the tub.

Our phones.

The water ripples as the fish zoom to the surface. *Snap. Snap. Snap.*

My laptop, iPad, smartwatch, and two more iPads that belong to my parents also rest at the bottom of the watery grave. Every muscle in my body locks, and no amount of Himalayan pink salt and frankincense will relax me ever again. I rub my arms, and the hairs on the back of my neck stand up. Now we know why my playlist stopped shortly after the flashbang.

Archer scrubs a hand down his face. We stare at each other for a moment, his eyes bright and perceptive. Something about the way he looks at me makes my stomach do a strange flip. I take a deep breath and lean against him. He pulls me to his side, fear and despair tugging at us both.

I point out an older-model phone. Its screen is cracked and its case is chunky and hideous. "Gage was taking selfies with that phone earlier," I say. "Why would the clown put his own phone in?" To make sure we didn't get our hands on it and call for help?

"Dude is unhinged." Archer touches his nose ring, a tiny gold hoop. It's something he does when he's concentrating. He reaches for the lever to drain the tub, but I stop him.

"Everything needs to stay exactly as we found it. For the police," I clarify. CSI. Castle Hill is now an active crime scene.

How much worse can this night get? I still can't wrap my

head around the fact that Kelsi is dead downstairs. She's supposed to be having fun with us, being catty and snarky, not lying lifeless in a pool of her own blood. I don't know if I'll ever be able to sleep in this house again.

We head back into the bedroom. My brain is a muddled mess. Archer is watching me, a question on his lips.

"Any idea who this guy is really?" he asks, like the thought has just occurred to him that I might know something.

I bite down on my lower lip. "No. I didn't share much information about who would be here when I hired him. I have no idea how he found out." My throat tightens.

"Maybe he got his hands on the guest list?" Archer says.

"But how? I didn't share it with anyone. Not even Demario," I say. "I used a delivery service to send out the invitations, and I sent the pin with my address only like an hour before the party. So either I got hacked or this guy has a connection to the couriers I hired."

Until tonight, everything had gone according to plan with Gage. Our entire correspondence was by email. His answers were always quick and to the point. We never spoke over the phone. I don't even know what his real voice sounds like. But from the moment I opened the door, there was no mistaking the cold depths in his eyes, even under layers of makeup. Eyes we now know belong to a killer.

The intercom buzzes again, and seconds later, merry-go-round music blasts from the recessed speakers. Josh's voice crackles through. My stomach begins to churn as another podcast episode begins.

Josh Sullivan: Welcome to *A Lot to Unpack with Josh Sullivan,* the culture podcast where no topic is off-limits. I'm Josh and today we're talking to Salford Prep's very own celebrity, Archer Mitchell, Mr. Billboard Hot 100 himself. He's got over ten million views on YouTube and a double platinum single, "Pursuit." What's going on, Archer?

Archer Mitchell: Not much, man. I'm having fun . . . enjoying the ride.

Josh Sullivan: And you wrapped up your first lawsuit. That makes you an official celebrity! [*laughs*]

Archer Mitchell: Yeah, happy to finally close that chapter.

Josh Sullivan: Right. So, let's talk about your journey up to this point. Piano lessons since you were five. You've done recitals, solo and ensemble performances. How did you go from being a classically trained pianist to singing pop and alternative rock? Critics say your style is over the top, loud and intense. What do you say to those people?

Archer Mitchell: It's all about perspective and how you connect with a particular piece of music. I don't know, maybe that's the point of music. To be whatever it wants for whoever's listening. If people are looking for wild and different, I'm just the artist.

Josh Sullivan: The artist with a new Porsche. Now, you know I'm all about the ride, so let's change gears for a minute. I heard you went down to Florida in February for the Daytona 500.

[*sound of revving engine*]

Archer leans against the dresser, arms crossed tightly across his chest. His jaw is clenched, all sharp edges and angles. I hate that my hunch was right about Gage knowing who would be at the party. He prepared this podcast episode for us too.

Archer Mitchell: [*laughs*] Yeah, Daytona's the real deal. Shit was wild . . . but I'm working on some new stuff for y'all.

Josh Sullivan: Okay, I just got curved about Daytona, but things were pretty messy for you back then. Anyway, folks, you heard it here first. Archer Mitchell's in the studio. . . .

The recording ends. Just like Kelsi's, the clip sounds totally random, but it's anything but.

"Shit!" Archer says. He pushes off from the dresser and paces between my bed and the entrance to the walk-in closet. "This is about the lawsuit."

Not long after his song "Pursuit" topped the charts, Archer was sued for copyright infringement by Bella Sara, an indie pop artist who claimed Archer had ripped off her song. He has always denied it.

"How do you know?" I ask.

"The song he forced me to play on the piano earlier is the one I was accused of copying," he explains, massaging the deep-purple bruise blooming on his wrist.

Goose bumps pop up all over my skin. "That's why he forced you to play Bella Sara's song. That's why he rigged the keyboard lid and played this clip. To punish you. This is about revenge. But what does that have to do with Daytona?"

Archer doesn't answer right away. His throat bobs. "That's where the lawsuit was filed."

I have more questions, but now isn't the time. Not when there's a killer clown after us. The recordings are clearly clues. "I invited the who's who of Salford Prep," I admit, cringing at how it makes me sound like a social climber. Everyone here tonight is popular. Influential. Privileged. What better reason for the clown to carry out a murderous agenda? Kelsi's got a modeling contract and half a million Instagram followers. Josh has even more followers than she does because of his podcast. Vivek's got over a hundred thousand following him for the latest news on his social networking site, Simmer. "I brought you all here to be slaughtered."

"You can't blame yourself, Noelle," Archer says. He tips my chin up, urging me to meet his gaze. "The clown is responsible for this."

"He has to be working with someone, though, but who? It has to be someone who knows us. Someone from school or maybe even a former student?" I might be grasping at straws, but we have to start somewhere. We spend the next few minutes pacing, tossing out names.

"What about Wolfie?" Archer asks.

"Doubt it," I say, shaking my head. Wolfie Marlow just laughed when he heard I was having a party. "He thinks my watch parties are lame. He wouldn't leave his own party to kill us. Our absence wouldn't upset him." Like, at all.

We toss out a few more names, like Lion Reef Wilson, a fellow senior who wears his girlfriend's blood in a vial around his neck; she wears his too as a proclamation of love. Lion is way too zen to do this.

"What about Jack Hudson?" I say, referring to a former classmate. "Dylan took Jack out of the game with an illegal hit. He was playing dirty but never meant for Jack to get *hurt* hurt, but he walked away with Jack's endorsement deal."

"Jack can barely walk," Archer says.

"But he has an older brother," I counter, remembering Levi, who was kicked out of school for threatening a teacher. "Levi's about the same height as the clown. Brown eyes. He knows us."

The more I think about it, the more plausible the theory feels. Could Levi Hudson really be Gage the Clown, out to avenge his younger sibling?

Archer's Adam's apple bobs. "But why go after all of us?"

A soft thud cuts me off. To the untrained ear, it's easy to miss, but I know all the quirks and noises of this house.

"What is it?" Archer asks.

I beeline for my walk-in closet again. "Someone's out there," I whisper, urging Archer away from the door.

I slide open the closet door and rush inside, past the white wardrobes and shelves of shoes and accessories, into the louvered closet at the far end where I store my winter coats.

"I didn't hear anything," Archer says, as I nudge him behind a thick metallic Ivy Park puffer jacket. The thing is big enough to hide us both. But is it insulated enough to stop a knife?

"Did you lock the door?" Archer whispers.

"Lock's broken," I say. Realization sets in. "I'm guessing that's not a coincidence."

"Probably not."

The bedroom door opens with a soft click, and I suck in a panicked breath. Maybe it's Demario, or Taylor, or Elise. Please let it be anyone but Gage.

Fear grips my throat like a vise and my heart drums an erratic beat. Archer shifts until he's standing in front of me, his back pressed to my front, ready to face off against anyone who comes in. The air between us evaporates.

A crash, like something's been thrown across the room, breaks the silence. I jump and grab fistfuls of Archer's shirt. Firm muscles stiffen beneath my touch, but he reaches back, catching my hands and bringing them around his waist.

There's a loud grunt, then the sound of furniture falling. Items shatter against the walls, followed by the unmistakable sound of fabric ripping. I rest my forehead on Archer's back and press my trembling lips together. He tightens his grip on my hands, and I breathe in his woodsy-citrusy scent.

"We're okay," Archer whispers.

We are most definitely *not* okay. We're about to come face to face with a killer clown. What is the clown doing? Has he left my room? I start counting slowly. My heart rate inches down toward normal. A moment later, someone busts into the walk-in closet.

I press against the wall, bringing Archer with me. A bolt of fear rockets through me. I see Gage through the narrow slit in the louvers as he flips on the closet light. A roll of toilet paper is tucked under his arm; in his other hand is the hunting knife. He slips the toilet paper between two handbags on a nearby shelf. His gaze roams around, settling on the square tufted ottoman in the middle of the closet. The clown raises the knife high above his head with both hands and plunges it into the footrest, then slowly rips the blade through the stool's tufted fabric.

Archer smooths his thumbs over my fingers, but the only thought running through my head is that if Gage opens the closet door, I'll have no choice but to push Archer into his waiting arms and run for my life. I hate that I'm even entertaining the thought, but truth is, Archer would want me to get help and find a way for everyone to get out of the house. Even though it means I'd be losing my most credible alibi.

Gage heads over to the cubby shelves stacked with shoes and handbags and unleashes more violence, swiping the contents of shelf after shelf onto the floor. I flinch with every thud. Archer keeps his grip on my hands, and we hold each other up. Gage reaches into the glass cosmetics display and sifts through my lipstick collection. He takes his time, removing one glove to apply swatches onto the back of his pale-white hand. When he settles on the right shade, he draws on a section of the mirrored wall, gliding the lip wand across it with smooth, angled strokes. I can't see what he's drawing, but when he's done, he steps back from the mirror to admire his work. He cleans the swatches from his hand with the toilet paper and tosses the roll onto the floor. Then he fixes his attention in our direction. He tilts his head all the way to one side, his ear dipping down toward his shoulder, deliberating his next move.

My breath comes in shallow pants because any minute now, Gage will find us.

There's a knock on the bedroom door. Gage turns and steps over a messy heap of shoes and bags, the knife in a firm grip. The door opens before he makes it out of the closet.

"Noelle?" Taylor calls, their voice barely above a whisper.

Run, Taylor! Get out of here! I'm screaming on the inside. I want to warn them, but the horrible truth is, if Gage attacks Taylor, I can run right past both of them and straight out the door. What kind of person does that make me? What kind of friend?

The one who survives.

Gage rushes out of the closet, knife raised. There's a slam of flipped furniture and the crack of what sounds like my Wiffle bat landing a blow. And screaming.

"My nose!" Gage yells, his voice muffled.

There's another flash of denim moving toward the door and then it shuts. I'm clutching Archer so tight I'm surprised he's still breathing.

"Is he gone?" I whisper. "What about Taylor?"

"They got away," Archer says, giving my hands a reassuring squeeze.

Gage storms back into the closet, one hand clamped over his nose. Blood trickles through his fingers. He snatches a gauzy cream cotton dress off a hanger and uses it to wipe his nose.

He tosses the bloodstained dress on the floor and kicks a handbag out of his way. Then he turns and picks it back up. It's my pink-and-white Birkin, a sweet sixteen gift from Dad. Gage opens the bag and positions it on the floor. He unzips his jumpsuit and shimmies his shoulder out to push the pant legs to his ankles.

He sinks into a squat.

What the fuck?

"Not the Birkin!" I mouth. *Please no, please no, please no.*

A blast of gas and shit explodes from Gage's ass. I bury my face in the puffer coat. The ass eruptions continue for what sounds like forever before Gage eventually lets out a sigh of relief. After he's undertaken meticulous efforts to clean himself, and scattered shitty toilet paper all over the room, he picks up the Birkin, dims the light, and leaves.

Minutes pass. I'm gagging. Archer eventually steps out cautiously. "Wait here for a moment, okay? I want to make sure he's gone."

"No way," I say, stepping out behind him. "I'm coming with you."

Whatever else I'm about to say dies on my tongue when I see the mirror. The message, artistically drawn in faux calligraphy with a blood trail design beneath each letter, glitters on the glass in the low light.

ONE BY ONE

"He's not leaving until we're all dead," I say. A lump rises in my throat.

"He's just one guy," Archer says, staring at the words written in showstopping red lipstick.

"There's got to be something in here we can use," I say, pulling out a fabric storage bin. Inside is an old forensics kit and prank items I got from Elise as a Christmas gag gift. I grab a flashlight and disposable scalpel from the kit. There's nothing to help me break out of the house, but at least now I've got a weapon. I slip the items into a small fanny pack and sling it on cross-body. I grab a bottle of itching powder and a potent fart spray as an afterthought.

Archer takes the spray from me and examines the label. "So, you plan to save us with a can of Liquid Ass?" he asks, grinning.

"If inhaling that stench buys us a few seconds to get away from Psycho Clown, it'll be worth it," I say, dropping the can into the fanny pack.

Archer picks up a broken photo frame from the floor. A deep crack snakes diagonally across the glass. It's a photo of me with Elise and Demario. We're laughing on the iron footbridge in Watkins Glen State Park. The painted words on the mirror taunt me.

I think back to the party's guest list. Rich and popular. The smug expression on the clown's face as he reached for my Birkin. "He isn't some rando on a killing spree, Archer. This is personal."

CHAPTER 12

"I just can't be running off in a panic because there's a room downstairs with a bed and a bucket."
—*Barbarian* (2022)

I look away from my butchered bed and try not to think about what Gage would have done if he'd found us in the closet. I take a deep breath. Dylan might have stolen my go bag with every tool that could help us escape but that doesn't leave me completely helpless. What would a Final Girl do? *Find a way.* I head to the bathroom.

Archer's brows furrow. "What are you doing?"

"Getting a few things together," I say. I stuff a washcloth inside a ziplock bag and slowly saturate it with bleach. Then I pour in a bottle of nail polish remover.

Archer crinkles his nose. "What's this?"

"Not-quite-chloroform, but I'm hoping it'll have the same effect," I say. I seal the bag and tuck it into the front pocket of my fanny pack. Archer's watching me with a mix of awe, doubt, and something else I don't have a name for.

"What's the safest room in the house?" he asks.

"The home theater," I say without missing a beat. It's windowless and soundproof. "The door's pretty thick."

My voice rises with a realization. "And there's a panic button on the control panel of the security system. We need to get there now."

"But the clown disabled the security system," Archer says.

"There's a backup panic button," I say, trying to remember the technician's explanation. "There's a SIM card inside the control panel that uses a cellular network to call the security company. We can call for help and hide until the cops get here."

I was home when the security consultant came by to upgrade the system. It's one of the most elaborate security systems on the market. A breach shouldn't even be possible, but here we are. Demario, Elise, and the others are still out there. No one is safe unless we get to that button.

"Demario can handle himself," Archer says, reading my thoughts. "He'll look out for the others, too."

"Right." I let out a soft sigh. "So, are we going to talk about how you took out Gage with a double backhand?"

Archer laughs. "I got him good, didn't I?"

"Damn straight," I say, adjusting the fanny pack.

Archer leans against the bedroom door, listening, and for a moment I expect Gage's knife to stab through the door and into his head, Ghostface-style, but nothing happens. Archer slowly turns the knob and peeks outside.

"Clear," he whispers.

When Archer reaches for my hand and my fingers close tightly around his, I can't help but smile. Even though the mere thought of going out into the hallway makes me want to run back to the shitty closet.

"Okay, let's do this," I say, exhaling roughly.

We've only made it a couple of steps out of the room when Maddie rounds the corner, arms flailing in her feathery black No-Face dress.

"It's coming!" she shrieks, eyes wide with terror. She stumbles, clipping the sleek metal grandfather clock that stands against the wall before she regains her balance. The clock wobbles and then rocks back into position.

"Who's coming? The clown?" I scan the area, but there's no sign of Gage.

"Omigod, omigod, omigod!" Maddie screams, the words rear-ending each other into a monosyllabic chant. She tugs on my arm, urging me to run with her, then runs past the guest bedroom and disappears into Mom's office. Then I hear it: an erratic clip-clop, the distinct sound of hooves. A small horse prances into the hallway.

"You've got to be kidding me," I say. *There is a horse inside my house.* A white miniature horse to be exact, with a long silky mane falling on both sides of its neck. It skids at the corner of the hallway, unable to navigate the floor. The horse slows, throwing its head back with a frustrated neigh.

Dangling from the horse's neck is a wooden square on a rope, which it's trying to shake off without luck.

I'm no horse whisperer, but I make a clicking sound with my tongue, the same one that I use to get Old Girl's attention. The horse slowly approaches and I reach out tentatively, stroking my hand down the length of its neck. Warm breath from its nostrils brushes my hand as I quickly loop the sign over its head. The horse trots away the moment the burden is lifted, and I follow Maddie into the office, my heart pounding. Archer makes a quick scan of the hallway and follows.

Mom's office is a dream of soft pinks and nudes. Maddie sits in a far corner, hyperventilating and hugging her knees. She's staring at at a deep-red stain on the carpet. If I didn't know it was from Mom's wine accident, I'd be freaked out too. She lifts her head slightly, just long enough to tuck strands of damp, limp hair behind her ears.

"It's gone, Maddie," I say, closing the door.

"Why is your horse running around in the house?" she asks, wiping away a stream of tears with the back of her hand.

"It's not mine. The clown must have brought it," I say.

Maddie gasps. "How does he know I'm afraid of horses?"

This is news to me. "I think he knew who would be here tonight. He hijacked my party to terrorize us."

"This letter board belongs to my mom," I say, tilting the board in Archer's direction. A message is pinned to the felt board with plastic changeable letters.

Archer reads it out loud:

HIT AND RUN
TWICE THE FUN

Maddie raises her head and something in her expression shifts. Her gaping mouth flattens into a line, and she stands slowly, smoothing the front of her dress.

"Does this mean anything to you, Maddie?" I ask.

Her eyes flick around the room.

"Do you know what the sign means?" I ask again. We don't have time for secrets. If Gage sent the horse after her, he might be nearby to get her reaction.

Maddie finally looks at me. "No. I don't."

She's lying.

I decide to try a different tactic. "Archer, what about you?"

He catches on right away. "I haven't heard anyone at school talking about a hit-and-run, but maybe this is about something else entirely."

I don't miss the way Maddie's entire face shutters, shifting into resolute stoicism.

"I don't even drive," she says after a long pause.

Now, that *is* true. Maddie takes an Uber to school most days until recently, when she started riding with Charlie.

"I need to find Charlie," Maddie says, her voice stitched with urgency. She gathers up her dress like a debutante princess and heads for the door.

"Come with us to the home theater," I urge, but Maddie slips out before either Archer or I can stop her.

"You know she's lying, right? She kept crossing and uncrossing her arms," Archer says, holding the door open for me to exit first.

"I noticed. And I think she knows exactly what this message means."

We slip downstairs, pausing on the landing to scan for any sign of Gage. The orange light on the security panel beams like a laser across the entryway. My fingers come away dusty when I touch the access control pad.

"He's already been here," I say, frustrated, showing Archer the loose screws. I push the small red button near the bottom of the pad anyway, but as I expected, nothing happens.

Archer digs into his pockets, then one hand reemerges with a small multi-tool. "I never leave home without it." He quickly pries the control pad cover off and examines the inside panel.

"I've been looking everywhere for you," a male voice says from behind us.

I jump clean out of my skin. Josh eases out of the dim dining room and comes to stand a few feet from us, a hiking pole from the mudroom in his grip.

"Demario and Elise aren't with you?" I ask, panic rising.

Josh glances upstairs, a frown deepening on his forehead. "We came face to face with the clown in an upstairs bathroom and everyone just ran. What are you two doing?"

"Trying to activate the panic button," I explain.

Archer holds up two severed wires. The slot that housed the SIM card is empty. Our mission was doomed before it even began. I glance over at the biometric padlock fixed to the front door, thinking of the scalpel in my fanny pack. I'll cut one of the clown's fingers off if that's what it takes to get out of here.

"Let's check the other doors again," I say.

The temperature inside the house dips as we creep around, as if a draft is blowing in from an open door or window. My heart pounds as we move through the dining room toward the yoga studio. Light filters under the door leading out to the covered patio. I almost cry with relief when I see that the door is ajar.

I nudge it open with the toe of my boot and wait a few seconds just in case it's a trap. I glance over at the pool house, which is connected to the main house. It's Mom's newest renovation project, and all the furniture's been cleared out. It's a large rectangular space with a pool in the middle and literally nowhere to hide. Across the lawn, the strobe lights in the fun house switch from purple to red. A harrowing scream comes from inside the fun house. The fear monster in my chest grows claws and teeth. Josh doesn't hesitate. He rushes toward the noise with his damn pole like a Viking, but I don't take a single step. I throw one arm out to stop Archer from following.

"Hold up," I say, patting him on the chest. We can't afford to be reckless.

"Charlie needs help!" Maddie shouts from the fun house, her voice faint and muffled.

"Okay, can we go in now?" Archer asks.

Converting the guesthouse into a fun house for tonight was one of my best ideas, but at this very moment I'm terrified to go inside.

"Guys!" Maddie sounds even farther away this time. "No, no, no, no!" she shrieks.

I enter the fun house and into a maze of mirrors. My nerves are sparking. *We need to get out now.*

"Maddie?" Josh calls out. His voice reverberates across the room.

A burning scent wafts into my nostrils. Smells like that nasty-ass candle Josh pranked me with earlier. I take tentative steps forward behind Josh. Archer moves with me. Tension rolls off him, thick and formidable.

"Maddie!" There's a sharp edge to Josh's tone this time that sends chills through me.

She answers with a scream.

A chain saw rumbles, then roars throughout the fun house. I can't tell which direction it's coming from. A bright light switches on inside the maze, disorienting me for a few seconds. We turn a corner and stumble across Maddie. She's on the floor, crab-walking backward while Gage approaches with a hedge trimmer. He lurches forward, sweeping the garden tool from side to side, the long blade narrowly missing Maddie's feet.

"Charlie needs help!" Maddie's voice echoes, but Maddie's not the one speaking. The clown's painted red lips contort as he repeats the impression, and it prompts Maddie to spring into motion. She flips over onto her knees and pushes up, and Josh hauls her the rest of the way.

"Come on!" Archer says, pulling me along. We are almost back at the entrance to the maze—me and Archer now ahead of Josh and Maddie—when we hear fast-moving clunky footsteps. The clown is chasing us, his bulbous shoes clomping into a steady stride as he makes woodchopper slashes in the air with the hedge trimmer. Josh grips Maddie by the hand, urging her along, but her heeled boots are slowing her down.

Gage leaps forward. Everything happens so fast and it's so wild that Archer and I halt. The clown stumbles on landing and the blade of the hedge trimmer makes a wild, haphazard arc and comes smashing down, grinding through the flesh and tendons of Maddie's shoulder. "Whoops!" Gage shouts. Then he chuckles. Maddie's knees buckle as a mist of blood sprays into the air, splattering the wall and Josh. She tumbles, her shoulder blade separated from her clavicle, and collapses into a heap, wailing. Josh stares down at her mutilated body sprawled out like a horror show reenactment. Gage plants one foot on Maddie's lower back and jerks the hedge trimmer out of her flesh. The hedge trimmer makes a loud buzzing sound as if jammed, before it comes away with a roar.

Josh takes off. Archer and I scamper out of the fun house. I'm screaming my head off. Josh's ragged breathing isn't far behind us. We cut across the lawn, heading for the front gate, but running on wet, slippery grass is not the move when you're trying to dodge a killer.

Gage appears from the other side of the guesthouse and cuts us off. Now would be a damn good time for a flock of birds—only New York's finest—to descend on Gage, like in Hitchcock's *The Birds*. He raises the hedge trimmer and revs it, forcing us to double back to the house.

A moment later, Gage's *Hunger Games* clown horn blasts.

Maddie Xu is dead.

CHAPTER 13

**"But, uh, how were we supposed to know
that you were, um, really good at killing
people? Which is actually sort of weird,
by the way."**
—You're Next (2011)

We rush back inside the house and lock the door. I peek through the curtains, searching for Gage, but he's faded into the night. Shadows leak out from all corners and phantom sounds have me twisting my neck around every six seconds. Archer's never more than a few inches away from me. One of Mom's favorite sayings comes to me: *Stay ready so you don't have to get ready.* We're moving in sync, fluid and flexible, expecting the unexpected.

That is, until we arrive at the foot of the staircase and realize Kelsi's body is gone. I lose my footing. A white chalk outline has replaced Kelsi, but it isn't an outline of Kelsi's actual body. It's more like a drawing of a person walking by and waving hello. All traces of blood are gone, and the scent of lemon floor polish and disinfectant lingers in the air. Small yellow crime scene markers numbered from one to four are positioned around the chalk outline.

Archer and I step around the outline as if it might be a trap. Explosive paint or some kind of superglue. I squat next to one of the tented cards and examine it closely without touching it, just in case Gage dusted it with something poisonous.

"There's writing inside," I say.

Josh walks away, checking for any activity. He hasn't uttered a word since Maddie was murdered right in front of him.

I grab a pair of plastic tongs from a nearby salad bowl and use it to flip open the first card. Like everything else tonight, it makes absolutely no sense.

THEY FUCK YOU UP

"Let's see what's on the other cards," Archer says. There's an urgency in his voice. We're out in the open in my vast living room, visible and vulnerable to an attack. I grab the remaining cards. Josh reappears and we check out the rest in order.

YOUR MUM AND DAD
THEY MAY NOT MEAN TO

"'But they do,'" Archer says, quoting the final card before I even open it.

"What is this?" I ask, confused. "How did you know it?"

"It's a verse from a Philip Larkin poem," Archer says. My blank expression prompts him to explain further. "English poet."

"You're into poetry?" The question bursts out of me before I think to stop it. Archer's lips curve into a smile, and if not for the dim light and the murder, I'd call him out for blushing.

"I read a lot when I'm not writing," he says, downplaying it.

I file that tidbit away for later. I read the verse again and again, trying to make a connection between the words and Chalk Outline Kelsi.

"Is he saying that Kelsi's the way she is because of her parents?" I ask, unable to refer to Kelsi in the past tense. I slip the cards into my fanny pack. When this is over, I'm handing all of this evidence over to the police. I'm determined to be around when this night is over.

"Is this some Jason Voorhees revenge plan over something our parents did?" I ask. "Or," I say, with a dramatic pause, "what if an actual parent is behind this, like how Jason's mom was the original killer in *Friday the 13th*?"

Archer rubs the back of his neck. "I don't think so. The poem's about how parents mess up their kids. It's about a cycle of burden, pretty much." He recites the entire poem as we head to the server room. His voice is low and even though it's the most unromantic poem I've ever heard, my entire body tingles.

"So basically the poem's saying that future generations are screwed?" I ask.

"Yes, and the only way to break the cycle is to not have kids," Archer says.

"That's bullshit," Josh says, breaking his silence.

"I don't think anyone at this party is thinking about having kids," I grumble. I'm struggling to wrap my head around the poem as it might relate to a deranged clown's thinking.

We need to regroup. Find a spot to get our thoughts together. The panic button was disabled, and the fun house maze turned into a death trap. The clown did a freakishly believable impression of a teenage girl's voice. Nothing is what it seems.

"Maybe we can escape through the garage," I say. "My dad keeps a bunch of spare keys in the server room. The key that can get us into the garage is in there. I'm sure of it."

Archer nods. "Okay, let's do it."

Josh stares down at his bloodstained hands. "Whatever gets me the fuck out of here."

The server room is long and rectangular and painted dark industrial gray bordered by white crown molding. Equipment hums on metal racks along one wall. Archer closes the door behind us, and I wait, listening, hoping that we're alone. Goose bumps rise all over my arms. The air conditioner is running, with a quiet hum. On the opposite wall, the four monitors linked to the security cameras outside are dark. Disconnected. Shouldn't that have triggered a call from the security monitoring company? *Did the clown sabotage this too?*

My eyes adjust to the darkness and a shadow shifts in the far corner, stretching into discernable arms and legs. A scream gathers in my throat.

Demario appears from behind tall stacks of cooling racks. "Aye, it's me."

Elise and Charlie pop out from behind him. My lungs legit seize and I double over, forcing myself to take deep breaths. "I'm so glad to see y'all."

Archer and Demario share a weird half-hug, pat-on-the-back thing. I've never been so happy and relieved to see anyone in my whole entire life. Elise crushes me to her, sobbing into my hair. I blink away the tears pooling in my eyes and pull away because what we're not gonna do is get wrapped up in big emotions while Gage slips in and hacks us all to death.

As thunder rumbles outside, low and hungry, Josh watches us, shifting anxiously from one foot to the other. I can't blame him for being antsy.

"Shit, what happened to you?" Charlie asks, noticing Josh's blood-splattered face and clothing.

I take a deep breath and push my back against the tall filing cabinet. "It's Maddie. The clown got her." For a moment, Charlie is speechless. He opens his mouth and closes it, scanning the faces in the room, silently daring anyone to dispute what I said.

"What the fuck happened?" His voice shakes and he stumbles back a few steps.

Archer relays a shortened version of the story, leaving out the gory bits. Charlie's hands fly up and clutch the sides of his head. "No, no, *no!*" he screams.

He pushes off the wall and storms toward me. Archer and Demario immediately block his path, but he slams up against them. He leans around Archer and points a shaky finger at me.

"I am not going to die in your goddamn house, Noelle. You hear me?" he cries. He takes a ragged gasp as Archer places a hand on his chest to stop him from coming any closer. "I need to make it out of here alive. My little sister has a soccer game this week and I need to be there. I've never missed a game." He stops midsniffle and pats his pockets frantically. "I'm out of Xanax. Fuck!"

I turn to Demario while Elise tries to calm down Charlie. "Did you find Dylan?"

"I lost him. Dude's fast," he says.

"What about everyone else?" I ask.

Demario throws his hands up. "They all disappeared."

"The podcast episodes are clues. They might be pointing to Gage's motivation," I say, sharing what I discovered with Archer earlier. "Most of us have been on *A Lot to Unpack with Josh Sullivan* at some point."

"I've never been on Josh's show," Elise says.

Demario shrugs. "Me either."

"Jump Scares," I say suddenly. "Everyone here's a member."

"That's true," Elise says. "But who hates on a horror movie club *this* much?" Her voice trembles. I'm saddled with so much guilt I can barely look her in the eye. If I can't handle a moment like this with one of my closest friends, then how am I going to face everyone at school on Monday?

"Do you remember anything unusual about booking the clown?" Archer asks. "Any weird vibes?"

I shake my head. My nose burns from a surge of tears threatening to fall. "Our emails were always short. Professional. Nothing to make me suspect that I was hiring a freaking murderer!" A hard lump of emotion rises in my throat.

"Don't do this," Archer says, gripping my hands. "This isn't your fault."

An uncomfortable silence settles over the room like a thick cloud. He's trying to make me feel better, but we all know his words don't ring true. We wouldn't be here if I wasn't trying to schmooze with the most popular kids at school to boost my follower count and have them hype me up ahead of my podcast.

While briefing the others on my plan to escape through the garage, I search the filing cabinet for anything we can use but find only cables, manuals, and loose papers. The lockboxes have all been emptied out. Josh hasn't said much. He stares blankly at a spot on the wall, absentmindedly picking at the dried flecks of Maddie's blood on his arm. In the bottom drawer, I find a zipped leather binder with design plans for the kitchen remodel. Tucked into the back pocket are a few spare keys, including the one I'm looking for. My shoulders sag as I let out a sigh of relief. "And what happens if we can't get out through the garage?" Charlie asks. He drags a hand through his hair and starts pacing.

I tuck the key into my fanny pack. "Then we go to plan B. If we can't get out, then we'll hunker down inside. We'll go to the home theater."

When I tell them about the message on the letter board and the poetry verse, Charlie straightens.

"You know Maddie moved here from London, right?" he says. "She's afraid of horses because she had an accident back in England."

"Any idea what 'hit and run, twice the fun' means?" I ask.

Charlie's brown eyes shift from mine to Archer's. "What did Maddie say?"

"Not much. Is there something else you want to tell us?" When Maddie first arrived at Salford, Charlie managed to convince her that he needed extra tutoring in Mandarin for job prospects. Since then he's become her closest friend—and based on what I saw tonight, maybe a bit more.

Charlie's shoulders slope downward. "I don't know if I should say anything. It's not really my story to tell."

Maddie's no longer here to tell it. The thin thread holding me together snaps. In an instant, I'm in Charlie's face. "You want to die?"

His head snaps up. "What?"

"Shit is as real as it's ever gonna get. If you know something that can help us get out of this horrendous mess, you better start talking," I say.

Charlie sighs. "When Maddie lived in London, she and a friend stole a horse and carriage on a dare. The horse got spooked and ran into a parked car."

I don't hide my surprise. I don't know what I was expecting to hear, but this isn't it.

"Why would she steal a horse when she's afraid of them?" I ask, confused.

"She wasn't afraid before the accident," Charlie explains. He pushes his hair away from his face. "The dare was Maddie's idea. But her friend hurt his back pretty bad."

"So that's why she left London?" I ask.

Charlie nods. "Maddie felt guilty. She would visit him at the hospital but couldn't stand to see him in so much pain. She could barely look the guy in the face after he told her the doctors didn't know if he would ever walk again. Her parents let their lawyers deal with everything and Maddie moved back to New York after that."

"Her folks made it all go away," I say.

I mull over the message on the letter board. "Hit and run, twice the fun," I murmur.

"It wasn't her first accident," Charlie says. His voice catches.

He sighs. "She had one the week she arrived in London, too. You know how they drive on the opposite side of the road? Well, Maddie hit another car and her dad used his expatriate status to get her out of the traffic charges."

Archer and I exchange concerned looks. "But how does the clown know this?"

"No clue. Maddie never talks about this stuff," Charlie says.

"Has the clown been stalking us? Digging into our lives to uncover secrets?" I wonder aloud.

"We've all got stuff we don't talk about," I add. I'm thinking about one thing I've done in particular, but there's no way Gage could know about it. I haven't even shared it with Demario.

"We're not dealing with a rational person here," Demario says. "If he killed Kelsi over fruit stickers in a cake, who knows what else he'll do."

We sneak out of the server room, heading to the garage, and I take a peek outside. Heavy mist swirls across the surface of Cedar Swamp Creek. The water shimmers in the moonlight, rippling in the light wind and rain. Dad's rowboat peeks out at the end of the jetty and an idea teases my thoughts. And just like that, I know exactly how we're going to escape from Castle Hill.

CHAPTER 14

"Nothing is ever going to be okay again."
—*The Purge* (2013)

"The rowboat seats four, but we'll make it work," I explain, going over the new plan. "The boat's at the end of the jetty. We jump in and go."

"You mean row," Archer says, grinning.

"I'm getting another alibi. One who doesn't make dad jokes in a crisis," I say.

"Noted," he says with a smirk.

Archer peppers me with questions about the boat, whether the seats slide or not, about the oars and how the oarlocks are mounted. I answer the best I can, but rowing is mainly Mom and Dad's thing. I've always been happy to stay dockside, jotting down notes for my next film review for the Jump Scares website or getting lost in a good horror book.

We head down to the den and as soon as we enter, I notice Quilly's cage is open and that she's no longer inside.

"Quilly's missing," I announce.

"Your porcupine is not who we should be worried about," Demario says, pointing down.

I gasp at the bloody footprints before I spot the latest message. It's writen on the wall, painted with fresh blood.

HELP ME

"Holy shit," Elise says.

"So much blood," I whisper. *Whose blood, though?* "I don't think an injured person wrote this."

"How do you know?" Archer asks.

I gesture at the floor. "No blood trail, no droplets. The footprints are actually leading away from the wall. I think the blood dripped onto the floor while Gage was writing it." Did Gage bring blood to the party? Or is it from someone in the house? The thought gives me chills.

The French doors leading from the den to outside are closed, but the room glows orange and blue from the firepit.

A chilly blast whips around the room from a broken window next to the doors. I examine the mess of glass on the floor and the patio. Unease creeps up my spine. Something isn't right.

Beneath the window is a long, smooth black piece of iron. I snatch it up right away. "My Obliterator!"

"Your what?" Archer examines the tool in my hands.

"My demolition hammer. It was in my go bag," I blurt out.

"Do you think Dylan got away?" Elise asks, nibbling on her nails.

I don't know why she's so concerned about him after he stole my bag. "I'm surprised Dylan didn't take the boat, too," I say. Elise has always had a soft spot for Dylan, but she's also always denied being attracted to him.

"He wouldn't do that," Elise says. "If he escaped, I'm sure he'll send help."

Josh scoffs. "Dylan looks out for Dylan. Thought you'd figured that out by now."

Elise turns away and goes over to where Archer is examining the French doors. The lock has been jimmied. Glancing at me, Archer turns the knob.

The fog is even thicker than it appeared from inside, covering the water's surface and rolling halfway up the pier. A flash of lightning lights up the sky, illuminating the end of the pier. Cold wind swirls around my shoulders and the light rain pelts me, but I'm too wired about the imminent danger to be bothered.

"Hang on a minute," I say, crouching down to examine the glass fragments.

Elise rolls her eyes. "Listen, girl, we don't have time for this *CSI* shit."

I ignore the barb and make my point anyway. "Most of the broken glass is inside the house. That means the window was broken from the outside. But the doorknob was broken from the inside."

"Dylan didn't take the boat, so maybe he forgot something," Demario says.

"C'mon, we don't have time for this. The clown could be anywhere," Archer says, offering his hand to pull me up.

"Let's get out of here," Charlie says, rubbing his arms.

Elise takes off running down the pier, her feet thumping against the wooden slats. Mist swirls around our legs and the ripe smell of algae and wet earth hangs heavy in the air.

Wispy tendrils of fog rise off the water and curl into clouds around the rowboat. Elise has a solid lead, but she doesn't slow down when she reaches the edge of the pier. She vaults herself into the rowboat, just as a shape sits up ominously behind her, like Michael Myers in all three hundred *Halloween* movies.

I'm almost at the end of the pier just as the clown reaches for Elise, knife in one hand, and I scream. It's a solid warning cry. Elise swings around and stumbles backward as Gage lunges forward, a menacing look etched into his features. He tosses the line of rope onto the pier and the boat lurches away.

"Elise!" I yell.

Adrenaline pushes me faster, even though the boat is now too far away from the dock for me to help. Thick clouds drift over the moon and the fog acts as a sheer curtain, transforming Gage and Elise into two actors performing on a smoke-filled stage.

Demario sprints and then leaps, arms outstretched, fingers clawing the air. His body slices into the water with none of his usual grace or precision, creating a mammoth splash.

"No!" My voice dissolves into the night. Archer's arm hooks around my waist, tugging me away from the edge of the pier.

Gage thrusts the knife forward, burying the cold steel blade into Elise's stomach. He jerks the knife up, as if gutting a fish. Elise doubles over, her screams piercing the night. The rowboat twists and turns with each violent movement. Demario swims faster, his arms shredding the water. Clutching her stomach, Elise tumbles forward, ramming one shoulder into Gage and sending them both careening sideways as the rowboat flips and drifts away in the wide, churning creek. Josh and Charlie rush to the end of the pier, calling out for Elise and Demario.

Demario dives under the capsized boat, emerging seconds later, frantically searching for Elise. Archer and I scan the water, squinting through the dense layers for any sign of activity. Demario takes a deep breath and goes under again, just as Elise breaks the surface, gasping, several feet away.

"Over there!" I yell, pointing at Elise. Her wig is gone, leaving her lush curls tucked under a nylon stocking cap. She flips on her back, doing her best to float.

"Where's Demario?" My chest aches. Charlie swears and kicks off his shoes.

The water ripples as Demario rises to the surface again. This time he spots Elise and breaks into a freestyle sprint. A thick band of clouds eclipses the moon completely, plunging the river into murky shadows. A red wig breaks through the water behind Demario and my heart nearly ruptures in my chest. Gage swims with his eyes just above the water like a hungry alligator. I holler and holler, but Demario is so hyperfocused on Elise that he doesn't sense Gage behind him. Elise's head tips back in the water as if she's losing consciousness. Demario is now only a few feet from her, but just as he reaches her, Gage erupts from the water like a geyser and drags Demario under.

Shit. I start to tug my boots off. "Demario!"

There's a huge splash as Charlie dives in after them. He slices through the water, powered by grief and rage over losing Maddie. The rowboat spins sideways with the tide and drifts into the mist. Gage pops up. Demario doesn't. I call for Demario again, the chilly wind ripping his name from my lips.

Gage throws one arm out in Charlie's direction and a tiny object sails through the air, whacking him in the face. Charlie howls a string of curses.

The boat disappears completely into the mist. Tears race down my face. This can't be happening. The clown disappears once more and Charlie spins in circles, treading water, but Gage is gone. Charlie comes back to the pier, and Archer and I haul him out. Blood streams down his face from a fishing hook embedded in his cheek.

I hold Charlie's head in my lap while Archer uses his utility tool to ease out the barb.

"Where's that sick fuck?" Charlie snarls, clutching his cheek.

I stare out at the water, looking for the clown, but see nothing. There's no sign of Demario or Elise either. Thunder rumbles and the sky opens, beating us with hard, punishing rain.

"Noelle, we need to go back inside," Archer says, his voice pained.

"We can't," I say. Walking away feels like giving up on Demario and Elise. "I have to wait . . . just in case."

My feet move of their own accord, edging me closer to the end of the pier. Just as I'm about to turn around, cold, wet fingers curl around one ankle, tugging me toward the inky-black waters. I try jerking away, but Gage's grip is iron tight, his fingers digging into my skin. Josh and Archer scramble back to help me.

"Let me go!" I shriek. I raise the Obliterator and bring the hammer down hard on Gage's hand. Bone crunches. His fingers release, and I race up the pier, blood and fear humming in my ears. Archer opens the door and I glance over my shoulder, only to see Gage using his elbows to clamber out of the water. He stands there, motionless, water pooling at his feet.

Heavy fog blankets the creek. My best friends are out there, lost in the cold, fractured night. A new wave of guilt squirms inside me, but I rush indoors, ignoring the crunch of broken glass and fissured hope around me.

I have a meltdown as soon as we reach the laundry room. Elise is badly hurt or worse, and Demario . . . My heart cracks completely open. He's missing, possibly stabbed underwater and drowned. Josh stands at the door, his eyes peeled for any threats in the hallway. Charlie flips through a stack of folded laundry and emerges with a towel for his face.

"Demario's one of the best swimmers on the school team. And he's a lifeguard, remember?" Archer says. He hooks one finger under my chin, tilting my face up to meet his fierce gaze. "If anyone can survive out in the water, it's him."

Rationally, I know Archer is right, but I can't shake the memory of Gage dragging Demario underwater or of the knife sinking into Elise's stomach. I rest my forehead against Archer's chest for a moment and he hugs me close, his embrace warm and reassuring.

"Oh god. I should have . . ."

Archer shakes his head. "There's no way you could have known any of this would happen."

"Archer's right," Josh says.

Charlie doesn't say anything. He just adjusts the pressure of the towel on his face.

But I should have known. A true Final Girl would have known.

I exhale loudly, breath whistling between my teeth. I manage a tiny smile. "Thanks for helping me back there," I say to Archer.

He takes the demolition tool from me. "Think I'll name my next album after this . . . Obliterator." He chuckles and sets it down on top of the dryer.

"Ugh, please don't," I say. My throat burns from unshed tears. I should have stuck to the original plan and gone to the garage. I should have stopped Elise. I should have done more than just stand there.

Josh tugs out a sweatshirt from a pile of clean laundry and hands it to Charlie, who's shivering.

"I don't know what to do," I admit.

Archer reaches for both my hands and squeezes them tightly. "We're going to find a way out. I need you to believe that."

He actually sounds convincing, and I want to believe that he's right, but Gage has been one step ahead, and so far all my brilliant ideas have only put people in danger. The panic button was a major miss and the rowboat getaway ended in tragedy. I want to go back to the pier to look for Demario and Elise, but maybe that's what Gage wants, for us to return to the scene of the crime so that he can add more bodies to the count.

I become aware of how close Archer and I are. He's leaning against the washer and I'm standing between his legs, pressed up against him, my fingers still linked with his. He's staring down at my lips almost as if he wants to— I banish the thought immediately. Kissing Archer would be a stress response.

Demario is Archer's friend too, and I know that he's worried. And even though he's too decent to ever admit it, Archer blames me for what's happened here. He has to—everyone must. As if aware of the rising heat between us, Archer straightens, and I step back.

I close my eyes, listening to the silence. A door clicks some-where upstairs. I pick up the demolition hammer, bolstered by the weight of it in my hand.

"I'm going back to the pier," I announce suddenly. If Gage is still lurking, I've got the Obliterator ready. "I have to check for Demario and Elise. Just in case they need help."

Archer doesn't argue. Charlie tosses the bloody towel into a basket and he and Josh follow us out of the laundry room. We sneak around the dark corners of the house. The door leading from the yoga studio has been locked and secured with a bio-metric padlock similar to the one on the front door. My feet slip on something wet. A set of footprints leads away from the door and into the hall.

Josh leans in. "Are these from the clown?"

"No, too small," I say. I still don't know how Gage managed to swim with those massive boat-sized shoes on his feet. I point at the shape of the print and the toe impressions left on the floor. "These were made by bare feet."

We follow the watery trail to one of the guest bedrooms. While Josh and Charlie debate whether we should go in, Archer eases open the door. I guess we're entering.

Nothing is out of place. The bed is made, the window blinds closed. Outside the wind howls.

Archer checks out the bathroom. "No one in there."

"Look in the closet," I say.

I stand with the Obliterator raised while Archer pulls the closet door handles in a swift move. The closet should be empty, but six identical gray clown suits hang from evenly spaced hangers. For a moment, I don't take a single breath. I'm tempted to toss the suits into the bathtub, but instead I dust them with the itching powder I grabbed from my room, giving extra attention to the crotch. Josh reaches into a rattan basket in the corner and lifts out a soaked clown suit.

"He was here," he says.

And now he's on the move again.

CHAPTER 15

"This ain't no funeral home! It ain't the Terror Dome neither! Welcome to Hell, motherfuckers!"
—*Tales from the Hood* (1995)

"Are you sure going to the theater is the best idea?" Josh asks.

After what just happened to Elise, I don't want to take any more chances. The garage might be another trap.

"It's the closest thing to a safe room," I say. "We need to think tactically. We can't spend the rest of the night running around the house when there's a murderer on the loose."

"So that's your plan?" Charlie says with a hard edge to his voice. "Spend the night holed up there until this guy comes to finish us off in one go?"

I wrap my arms around myself. "He's armed and dangerous. We have to be smart about this, Charlie. Our best chance at staying alive is to stick together. I don't want to lose anyone else."

My body is numb. From finding Kelsi dead to seeing Gage plunge a knife into Elise and then try to drown Demario to the hedge trimmer attack on Maddie, I don't know how I've remained standing. I want to tell Charlie that he's lucky he didn't witness Maddie's murder, that he doesn't have it imprinted on his brain forever. Josh keeps swiping at his face with his sleeve, trying to wipe away blood that's no longer there.

When we arrive at the home theater, I open the door and take a step inside. Flickering light from the movie screen fills the room. The seats are empty and in various stages of recline. The pillows on the long sofa are rumpled from recent use. Less than two hours ago, Archer and I sat on this very sofa enjoying a movie. I was sure that he was going to ask me out. And now it's possible that tonight is where everything ends.

"Hello? Anyone in here? It's Noelle," I whisper tentatively into the semidarkness. I take only two steps into the room in case the clown is hiding here.

"Aye," Demario calls. He pops out from behind the wet bar, relief washing over his face.

My legs start moving as my brain processes the shock. Demario is alive. He looks exhausted and is shivering slightly, but he's mostly dry. He's wearing a gray sweatsuit I recognize from my dad's closet.

Archer, Josh, and Charlie spill into the room behind me. Archer locks the door. My pulse quickens as Taylor, Mariana, and Vivek crawl out of their hiding places between the seats.

Demario crushes me to him in a giant hug, and just for a moment the prickling fear in my chest eases up.

"I'm so glad you're all here," I say, wiping away tears. I take a step back, taking Demario in while simultaneously scanning him for injuries. "Are you okay?"

Demario nods. "Yeah, considering that the clown tried to take me out."

"And Elise?" I ask, hopeful.

Demario's shoulders curve inward and he pushes up the sweatshirt's too-long sleeves. His forearms are covered with scratches. "I got her back in the rowboat, but she was unconscious." He takes a shuddering breath. "She didn't have a pulse, Noelle, and she'd lost so much blood. The boat got tangled up in some reeds. I tried to get it out, but I couldn't, and I couldn't carry Elise back on my own. Maybe I should have stayed out there with her."

We both know that there's no way he would have survived if he did.

After witnessing an almost drowning at a birthday pool party when we were younger, Demario got into swimming and volunteering as a lifeguard at the local pool. Not being able to save someone is his biggest nightmare.

"Did you do CPR?" Josh asks.

Demario's jaw clenches. "Of course I did. What kind of question is that?"

Josh huffs out a hard breath and pushes back his damp hair. "Right. Sorry, man."

I catch the others up on everything that's gone down since we separated. Taylor clings to me when they learn about Maddie.

"This can't be real," they say, sobbing.

I want to sink down to the floor and bawl my eyes out with them, but I can't. My energy needs to be focused on one thing: staying alive.

"What about Dylan? And Hailey?" I ask.

Mariana's eyes are red. She tugs on the hem of her ripped dress. "We saw Dylan upstairs and went after him. But then the clown jumped out of one of the bedrooms and we got separated."

"Dylan was upstairs?" I say. What was he doing up there? "I thought he would use something from my go bag to find a way to save us."

Mariana wipes away a tear with the heel of her hand. "He didn't have anything in his hands when we saw him."

Hmm. Did he stash the bag somewhere? Why hasn't he tried to break us out of here? There's a bolt cutter in the bag for precisely this kind of situation. *Unless he's not on our side.* I chase away the tendrils of doubt in my mind. His girlfriend was murdered. Even if he and Kelsi had a lovers' quarrel, Dylan wouldn't plot against us all, would he?

Archer double-checks the locked door. It's solid, and the room is soundproof, so unless Gage has a battering ram and superhero hearing, we should be okay for a minute. Yet I can't help but wonder where the clown is, or if he's busy laying another trap.

"Hold up," Charlie says, turning his full attention to Demario. Half of his face is swollen from the fishhook injury. "How'd you get back inside the house?"

"The French doors were open," Demario says. "I guess the clown didn't bother to lock it since the boat's gone."

"Well, what the fuck are we waiting for?" Charlie says. He makes a beeline for the door. "Let's go."

"Bad idea," Archer says, blocking his path. "The rain's just getting started and you saw that lightning earlier. It's safer indoors."

"It's true," Josh says.

Charlie sinks into a seat. "I'll take my chances with the lightning," he mumbles.

"Hear me out. I think the clown was in a hurry to change into a dry suit, and that's why he left the door open," I say. I fill them in on the spare costumes in the closet. "I want out of this hell just as badly as you do, but even if we get outside, where are we going? The only thing back there is the creek, which is swollen, and rising fast and furious."

Vivek sits off to the side of the movie screen on the wide console. He stares down at the floor as if the carpet pattern is the most captivating thing in the entire world. I know he's running the scenarios and calculating all options and risks. Taylor paces the back of the theater, in front of the velvet wall. For once, I wish the room had windows. It's beginning to feel claustrophobic. I suppose, regardless, we'd be eyeing the spiny shrubs strategically planted around the house. Josh grabs a can of Dad's hard seltzer from the wet bar and starts to chug.

"Whoa, take it easy on the hydration," I say, half joking.

Josh shrugs. "I had bladder Botox just before school started. I'm good for a few hours."

My mouth falls open. Elise had told me all about "the Hamptons bladder," the awful traffic and the lengths people went to just to avoid a bathroom break on the drive there. Demario is the first to speak.

"You had what *where*?" Demario says. He lowers the water bottle he grabbed from the minifridge from his lips and scoffs. "Bro, you wildin'."

For the first time since Gage darkened my doorstep, we

laugh. My camera sits on a table between the seats. I should've thought of this sooner, but it can't hurt to take a few pics and film a bit. Any video recorded tonight could be considered evidence. I'll have valuable footage for investigators to re-create what happened at Castle Hill. Video may be the only way tonight's story gets told accurately if none of us are around to testify. A chill washes over me. I can't think about dying, so I focus on living. Although I still have Archer as an alibi, I'll need proof if I make it out and he doesn't, so the cops don't try to tie me to the murders. The image of Gage driving the knife into Elise clouds my vision and I press one palm into my right eye as if I could push the memory back, deep into my hippocampus.

I can't fall apart now. Final Girls don't fall apart, right? They keep going, against all odds.

The movie screen flickers on and everyone gasps. Hailey appears. She's sitting on a stool in the family room against a backdrop of floral wall hangings. She faces the camera, tears streaming down her face. The family room is at the opposite end of the house. Gage must have nabbed Hailey after she got separated from Mariana and the others.

"Oh my God," I say, staring. I reach for Archer and he laces his fingers through mine. My hands are clammy and I feel a tremor in his fingers, too.

"Is he live streaming?" Demario asks.

"Doubt it. He blew up the router, remember?" I say, although it's possible Gage has another phone. "But how did he know we'd be in this room, at this instant?"

No one answers and the mood in the room descends into

something far more depressing. Did Gage see us come in here or is he watching us on hidden cameras? "I thought you liked a good sign," Gage says, from behind the camera. Even though his voice is altered with a device, it radiates coldness.

"Please," Hailey begs. Gage chuckles.

Hailey's most viral videos aren't the ones where she's demonstrating the best organic makeup products, but the ones where she holds up handwritten signs bringing attention to important social issues like inhumane working conditions and mental health awareness.

"Let's move this along. I'm kinda busy, Hails," the clown says, using Mariana's nickname for her.

Hailey stiffens and glances down at her lap. She holds up a white index card scrawled with black marker.

I AM A MEMBER OF 12 SOCIAL JUSTICE ORGANIZATIONS

Hailey shudders as she reaches for another card. A bitter taste floods my mouth. Around me, no one moves. Our eyes are glued to the screen. I'm afraid to watch, but I'm even more afraid of how the recording will end.

I STAND AGAINST ALL FORMS OF INJUSTICE
I SHARE TWEETS AND PROMOTE HASHTAGS
BUT!
I NEVER VOLUNTEER
I NEVER ATTEND MEETINGS
I PROTEST FOR <u>CONTENT</u>, NOT A CAUSE

Hailey hesitates with the last index card. She stares at it, fury flashing across her face. Then she holds up the card, her arm taut with defiance, before throwing it down at the clown's feet.

WHAT WOULD YOU DO FOR CLOUT?

"What the hell is going on?" I ask, eyes fixed on the screen.

"This is such bullshit," Taylor says. "Everybody tweets and uses hashtags."

We hear Gage clapping off-screen. "Such a natural."

"It takes courage to be an activist," Hailey says, an unmistakable challenge in her voice. "Having a voice makes me feel present, and I'll never stop speaking out against oppressive systems."

"Yes, because all you do is talk," the clown says.

Hailey's eyes are wide, like a deer caught in the headlights. She keeps glancing at the door, as if debating whether she should make a run for it or stay there in the hopes that someone will come in and distract the clown so she can save herself.

There's shuffling in the background and Hailey jerks upright. "What are you doing?" she asks, panicked.

Dread uncurls in my belly, snaking its way around my ribs and into my throat, where it settles. More shuffling, and then the crackle of Velcro ripping. My heart is beating its way out of my chest. He's about to kill Hailey on camera and there's nothing any of us can do about it. He recorded this video and is playing it for us, a glaring piece of evidence for the cops. What if Gage has no intention of surviving the night? If he has nothing to lose, it makes him even more dangerous.

"I'm unsubscribing from your channel," Gage says. "'Why isn't anyone talking about this,'" he says, mimicking Hailey's catchphrase. "I'm so tired of you self-righteous activists, expecting people to rise up at every single global event and injustice. War in Ukraine, Uighur genocide in China, military dictatorship in Myanmar, racial justice, cancer awareness, climate change," he rattles off, then lets out an exasperated groan. "You have an infographic for everything, don't you?"

"You're a heartless, intolerant pig!" Hailey shouts.

"I watched all two hundred seventy-eight of your videos. Now, *that* is the epitome of tolerance." The image wobbles, like the clown is dancing around Hailey. "But you know which was my favorite? The vulnerable one where you told the world about your mental health woes and your greatest fear, of being silenced as a woman."

The video stabilizes, and Gage zooms in on Hailey's face, catching each of her hyperventilating breaths.

"What are you going to do to me?" she shrieks.

"Plenty." Gage laughs and starts circling her again. "I see right through you, Hailey. You shame people into activism while you avoid doing the actual work."

"You don't know what you're talking about," she says, defiant.

The clown snorts. "I know attention isn't action. I know only a small slice of the money you earn hiding behind your computer is going to helping people."

Hailey dips her chin and leans forward on the stool, arms crossed over her chest. In the background is a clinking noise, like Scrabble tiles hitting against each other. Gage adjusts the camera angle, capturing the moment he empties a bag of keyboard keys onto a hand-painted chinoiserie tray.

He positions the camera on a tripod and one hand pops into the frame. He dons a multicolored silk glove with red pompoms, then shuffles over next to Hailey and pours water into a highball glass.

"Eat them," he says, gesturing at the keys.

I gasp. Archer and Vivek swear. Demario shrinks, turning his head away.

"No fucking way," Hailey says.

Gage laughs a whiny, high-pitched laugh. "Hang on, I have just the thing for this moment."

There's an unzipping noise, followed by the sound of rummaging before Gage slips back into the frame again. He marches right up to Hailey, knife extended.

"Any funny business, and I'll cut your face from ear to ear," he says, cackling.

Hailey lets out a strangled cry as Gage jams a pink knitted pussyhat onto her head so far down it almost covers her eyes. It's like the ones we all wore to the End to Inequality march last spring.

"How's that for solidarity?" Gage says. He examines the hat, his head slightly cocked, before stepping forward again to tug on the hat's pointed ends.

Hailey's face is flushed.

"Okay, Hails. Showtime," the clown says. He nudges the tray of tiles at her.

Hailey reaches for a key and places it far back on her tongue.

She tilts her head back and gulps from the glass as if she's taking a pill. She makes a gagging sound and clutches her throat.

"I can't watch this," Taylor says, turning away.

Mariana collapses into a seat. Demario sits next to her, and she turns and sobs hard into his shoulder.

I don't look away from the screen even though I can't stand seeing Hailey like this. I've watched tons of gory horror films. I can stomach gross things. Maddie's face flashes through my mind. I've seen worse.

I wish I could go back in time and uninvite everyone from this party. When my parents announced they were going to the Adirondacks, that should have been my cue to binge a bunch of movies over the weekend alone and work on finishing my Premiere Critic application. Kelsi, Maddie, and Elise would still be alive.

"Oh, wait," Gage says. He rushes from behind the camera, back to the tray, and picks up the long space bar. "Can't have you choking on this. That would make me a monster."

"This is unhinged," I say.

Charlie looks like he's about to faint. Archer fixates on the cuts on his wrists. Hailey gags and coughs. She's about to throw up.

Minutes tick by. Eventually, Hailey's eyes are only partially open and rolled back, with just the whites showing. Hardened superglue seals her lips shut, and her nostrils are filled with the same adhesive. Blood mixes with the glue in the cracks in her lips, from trying to tear her lips apart.

The video ends.

I stare at the frozen image of Hailey's tear-streaked face. "Do you think she . . ." I can't bring myself to say it.

Archer inches closer to me. Even in the dim light, he looks pale. "So he's doing this because he hates performative activism?" He shakes his head and stares up at the ceiling. None of this makes sense to him either.

"Hailey's last video was about getting off the internet and working to make a real life change," Vivek says, his voice barely audible.

"Uh, no. Actually, it was a compilation of our best TikTok dance challenge videos," Mariana says with a loud sniffle.

I start pacing, pulling a few threads together. "Look at Kelsi. Her apology cake for seniors was a major fail. Maddie steals a carriage, her friend gets hurt, and just like that she's on a private jet out of London. Gage is accusing Hailey of not walking the walk when it comes to her activism."

"But Hailey does the work. This asshat doesn't know what he's talking about," Mariana says.

"I'm a good person," Vivek says to himself. Mostly. He's sitting hunched over and rocking, and I don't think I've ever seen anyone so broken as he looks right now. Another spear of guilt tears through me. I'm the reason he's here.

"And Hailey *wasn't*?" Mariana leaps out of her seat and charges over to Vivek. "What the fuck you trying to say?"

"Whoa," Demario says, putting himself between Mariana and Vivek. "I don't think—"

"I didn't mean it like that," Vivek says, looking even more miserable. "Hailey and I used to talk a lot about how Simmer was a good channel to amplify voices."

Mariana's lips tremble and she flops back down into her seat. "I know. She was excited about all the connections she made there."

With the bomb defused, we get back to the discussion about the clown's possible motive. But now I'm worried about staying in the home theater. After all, the clown knows we're in here. What if he's on the way?

Taylor paces. "Okay, but what did Kelsi get away with? Or Elise, for that matter?"

I think back to the podcast episode and the Larkin poem next to the chalk outline of Kelsi's body. Is it that, according to Gage, Kelsi was following in her parents' self-serving footsteps? After all, in a PR stunt, she sent cake with nonfood to the elderly after her mini cancellation over the parking lot situation. Kelsi's parents are all about themselves and what makes them look good. And Kelsi is basically a mini-me version of her mom.

Gage had watched Hailey's videos. Did he read the messages in the Jump Scares group chat too? We get pretty honest in there. My social media content is carefully curated. Until this moment, I've never stopped to really consider how our professional content can be used against us personally and how being so open online gives loons like Gage unfettered access.

But if my hunch is right and Gage is coming after us over stuff he thinks we got away with, then I've got my own problems. There's a niggling whisper in my head that things done in the dark eventually drift into the light. And that's enough to put me on edge and hold me there.

CHAPTER 16

**"Congratulations. You are still alive.
Most people are so ungrateful to be alive.
But not you. Not anymore."**
—Saw (2004)

Josh Sullivan: Welcome to *A Lot to Unpack with Josh Sullivan,* the culture podcast where no topic is off-limits. Today I'm here with Vivek Bhatia, founder of Simmer, the new social networking site that everybody's talking about. Vivek, tell us about your baby.

Josh's voice comes through the powerful speakers of the theater with stunning clarity. Vivek groans. He leans forward and holds his head in his hands. Another recording has begun to play. I need to talk to Josh about his podcast, because if you really think about it, *A Lot to Unpack* is an extension of Josh. He's been interviewing celebrities on Spotify, and though nothing's been confirmed, Josh is on track to being one of the youngest nationally syndicated podcast hosts. Josh and his podcast are everything Gage hates. Could he be saving Josh for the end?

Vivek Bhatia: [*laughs nervously*] It's a social network run on a decentralized platform. I just wanted a safe space for students to hang out online, and it sort of took off from there.

Josh Sullivan: Let's be real, you're giving off some serious Zuckerberg vibes here. How does it feel to be a tech overlord?

Vivek Bhatia: Nah, I'm not there yet.

Josh Sullivan: Modest, I see. Simmer is hot right now. It's where everyone wants to be digitally. It's run on a software platform that you built yourself, right?

Vivek Bhatia: Uh, yes, built on an open-source protocol.

Josh Sullivan: Speak English! [*laughs*]

Vivek Bhatia: Simmer works like a microblogging site with a social networking service where users can create sites, join groups, and initiate private chats. Anyone can set up their own server on Simmer and carve out their own online community space.

Josh Sullivan: Genius, man. I've connected with some cool people on Simmer.

Vivek's eyes are squeezed shut. He sits still, the subtle twitch in his jaw the only movement. The rest of us are wearing matching confused expressions.

"What's happening with Simmer?" I ask outright.

Vivek stands. "It's complicated." He runs his hands through his hair. "We've got legal trouble."

"What kind of trouble?" I ask.

"Some far-right figures started their own communities on the platform and now all these hate sites are popping up," he says with a deflated breath.

"What?" My voice hits a high note. "How long has this been going on?"

Vivek glances around the room as if looking for an escape hatch.

"A few months . . . So far I've kept them contained to their own community spaces, but I didn't create Simmer for people to spread hate." Vivek pinches his brows together, something he does when we're squabbling in chemistry.

"Can't you kick them out?" I ask, glancing at the door. Gage knows we're in here, so I can't stop wondering how much longer we'll be safe.

Vivek sighs. "Technically, there's no functional way to shut them down because they're just implementing Simmer's open-source code. They hijacked my infrastructure, Noelle. I isolated some of the sites and blocked a few domains and that's when the legal trouble started. I'm being sued for violating their First Amendment rights," he says gloomily.

"You gotta be kidding me. So, hate speech gets to masquerade as free speech and you're the one getting sued?" Demario questions.

"Can't you shut down the whole thing?" Taylor wonders.

Vivek shakes his head. "It's not as simple as that. I came up with the coding, but some influential people bankrolled the whole thing. I can't just pull the plug."

"So they're not fazed by what's happening with Simmer?" I ask. I feel bad for Vivek. He created Simmer with the best intentions, but now he will be branded as an enabler.

Vivek huffs. "As long as the money rolls in, they don't care. I had to reinstate the banned accounts until the lawsuit is over. The whole thing's a mess."

"Maybe Gage was radicalized by one of these groups?" I ask, cautiously.

Vivek shrugs. "He forced Hailey to wear a pussyhat and swallow computer keys. I wouldn't rule anything out."

"Some people are just gullible, easily manipulated. They fall for anything," Charlie says. He holds an ice pack made from paper towels and a cold Coke can he grabbed from the theater minibar up to his cheek.

"Like how they fell for your Koro coin bullshit?" Josh says, poking Charlie in the chest. "I convinced friends and family to buy into your bogus crypto scheme and then the whole thing collapsed."

"Hey," Charlie snaps. "Crypto is volatile. You run the risk. You know the security got compromised and Koro took a big hit. Sometimes you win, sometimes you lose."

"I never lose," Josh grumbles.

"Now isn't the time for this," I say, trying to defuse another situation. "We're all stressed right now."

Demario and Archer are already nudging Charlie and Josh away from each other, but Charlie shrugs free.

"Whatever, man. I'm out," he says, sidestepping me and heading for the door.

"No, Charlie, wait." I take off after him. "Stay together, remember?"

Charlie yanks the door open. "Going to find Dylan. I'll take my chances with the clown."

"At least carry this." Taylor offers Charlie a flashlight they grabbed from a side table drawer.

Charlie hefts the heavy flashlight in his hands and mumbles thanks before slipping out of the theater.

A frustrated breath whistles out of me as I meet the nervous faces staring back at me. "You know he's not coming back, right?"

The movie screen flickers on again. This time with a message.

Five minutes

"Five minutes to what?" I ask, panicked. *Should we stay or should we run?* Having us run out of the theater in a panic might be just what he wants. Or Gage could be lining the doorframe with explosive putty to blast his way in. "Get away from the door," I whisper-yell, urging everyone deeper into the room. A countdown clock appears on-screen. We need to come up with some ideas real quick. The time we spent bickering could have been better spent coming up with a plan of attack.

We raid the theater for anything we can find. Archer grabs the marquee off the wall and Mariana snatches up the fancy velour ropes while Demario grabs a post. We line up everything else on the counter of the minibar for easy access: glasses, metal ice buckets, a bottle opener, and a countertop popcorn maker. I take the scalpel out of my fanny pack, finding comfort in holding the metal handle.

Thirty seconds.

Fifteen. We fan out around the theater, ready to launch everything at the door the second it opens.

Ten.

I heft a heavy whiskey glass, adrenaline surging. "If that clown comes in here, I'm aiming for his head."

Five.

"Crack it wide open," Archer says on my right.

"Down to the white meat," Demario adds from my left.

The clock hits zero. We wait. And nothing happens.

"Fuck!" Demario screams.

I pinch the bridge of my nose to quell the burning sensation building there. Taylor rubs their eyes. I hope they don't cry, because if they do, I won't be able to hold back the lump of tears expanding in my throat.

I can't let Gage psych me out. I remind myself that I've prepped for this scenario. I've done half-marathon training to get my energy levels and endurance up, just in case, you know, I have to outrun a killer. I've studied the Compendium of Physical Activities, so I know the MET—the metric for measuring energy expenditure—I'll use if I have to drag Archer or Demario out of the house to save us.

Archer coughs and makes a raspy sound, clearing his throat. Vivek sneezes. The burning sensation in my nose intensifies, scorching its way down my throat. "What's happening?" I croak.

Archer shields his eyes with his hands, but I can still see they are red and irritated. He jabs a finger at the ceiling. "It's coming through the vents . . . feels like pepper spray."

"More like bear repellent," Vivek says, coughing into his

sleeve. "Whatever it is, Gage must have released it into the air vents."

The clown is flushing us out like rats.

I gasp for air as I rush to the door. My skin burns and the pain in my throat is unbearable. I don't think about whether Gage is waiting on the other side of the door. I yank the knob, but it tears away from the door with a snap.

I stare at the knob in my hand in disbelief. "That motherfu—" I wail.

"The door's jammed," Archer says.

Taylor screams. Their eyes are shut and they hold on to Vivek for help, but Vivek trips on a step in the center aisle and they both go down in a tangle of limbs. Josh and Mariana try to help them up, but the spray's also got them messed up.

"Get back," Archer says to me. He does a running kick, slamming one foot into the door. It rattles on its hinges. Archer lands another two kicks before the door swings open. We all tumble outside, crying and gasping for clean air.

"Kitchen," I whisper, gagging. My chest is tight and my throat feels like it's coated with liquid fire. I can barely manage a full breath. "Water."

We rush to the kitchen, stumbling from the burning pain. Broken glass crunches beneath our feet. The kitchen is a mess, the floor littered with food, paper plates, and broken glasses. I practically dive into the sink, holding the sweep spray faucet up to my eyes. Vivek reaches into the fridge for a gallon of milk and we take turns splashing it over our faces and skin.

We're covered in the liquid irritant. It's soaked into our

clothing, hair, everything. I'd love nothing more than to strip off my clothes and jump into the shower, but given the shower murder scene in *Psycho*, that's probably a really, *really* bad idea.

"We can neutralize the pepper spray," I say, remembering the research I did before going out on social justice protests with Hailey. I dump out a bowl of tortilla chips and fill it with a mixture of dishwashing liquid and water. Archer grabs a jumbo roll of paper towels from the stand and we use the soaked towels to apply the mixture to our skin and clothes.

"Feeling better?" Archer asks, handing me another paper towel.

"Yeah, a bit." The stinging in my eyes is subsiding, but my skin still tingles and my throat is raw and itchy. *Where's Charlie?* I'm getting more worried. If that's even possible.

Archer's cheeks are red and blotchy. He's lucky that his *Squid Game* costume has long sleeves—he's been spared the worst of it. Taylor fills a spray bottle they took from the cleaning supply cabinet with the dishwashing mix and spritzes their hair and clothes before passing it to me.

"So, are we going to talk about how you karate-kicked the door back there?" I ask.

Archer chuckles. He takes the bottle from me and spritzes his jumpsuit. "I did what I had to do."

Our eyes connect and I can tell, jokes aside, we're both wishing we were anywhere else. "We would still be stuck in there if not for you. Thank you."

Vivek ventures into the living room and returns a moment later. He found Gage's sharp-tipped rainbow umbrella near the door, but it's just a regular umbrella now, the blade removed. Still no sign of Charlie.

Outside, a clap of thunder rumbles and the rush of a fresh downpour lashes at the windows. The overhead lights flicker as lightning splinters the night sky. I search the room for unusual shapes, the curve of a clown's shoe, the hand of a killer. *Where is he?*

Archer reaches up and traces a finger across my cheek. I lean into his touch. My skin tingles all over, but this time it has nothing to do with pepper spray. "We're going to make it out of here," he says.

"How do you know that?" I ask, desperate to believe him.

"Because we have a lot to look forward to," he says, inching closer. He brushes his thumb across my cheek once more before dropping his hand. "We have college next fall. I also have my tour . . . and I'd really like to get to know you better in the meantime."

Me too, I want to say, but instead I spin away from him. "Did you hear that?"

"What?"

Click.

A sudden bolt of lightning sends light flooding through the oversized windows, from the kitchen all the way to the living room, scattering the shadows that had leaked out of the dark corners. I rub my eyes with the heels of my hands, quelling the irritation still there.

Gage bursts into the illuminated space, with a struggling Charlie at knifepoint. The light reflects off his wig, creating a demonic red glow around him. A metal dental retractor protrudes from Charlie's mouth, stretching his lips and cheeks. Drool dribbles down his chin when he tries to speak, his words garbled and wheezy. Charlie grinds his wrists against the too-tight handcuffs, which have already broken his skin, leaving raw, fleshy indentations.

"What did you do to him?" I yell at the clown.

Charlie's sweater is ripped and stained with blood. The wound on his cheek is bleeding again.

"How badly do you want Finance Bro back?" Gage asks.

"Just let him go," I say.

"And where's the fun in that?" Gage says, rolling his eyes. "How about we play a game?"

"We were supposed to be playing hide-and-seek until you murdered Kelsi, you psycho!" I shout.

The items we grabbed to defend ourselves in the home theater are scattered on the kitchen floor. Demario snatches up the short metal pole and storms toward Gage, but the clown pulls out a syringe and holds it inches from Charlie's arm.

"There's enough ketamine in here to put down a horse," the clown warns.

Demario drops the pole.

The clown hauls Charlie into the living room, prompting us to follow. A rope ladder hangs down from the second floor.

"The key for the cuffs is at the top of the ladder. Climb the rope, grab the key, and you can free him yourself. But the gag stays—this one loves the sound of his own voice."

The rope ladder doesn't look stable at all. The rungs are frayed and worn, as if they've been deteriorating outdoors for years. It's a death trap.

"I'll get the key," Archer says, stepping forward.

"Uh, no," I say, tugging him back. No way am I letting him anywhere near that flimsy rope. "Y-your hands . . . ," I stammer, pointing at his puffy wrists.

The clown clears his throat. "Actually, I want *her* to get the key." He fixes his glare on Mariana.

Mariana yelps and backs away. "Me? No. I can't. I can't."

Archer and I exchange concerned looks. Mariana's afraid of heights, like deathly, panic-attack-inducing afraid. How does Gage know this?

Charlie groans, but it comes out as a strangled gurgle.

"Gage, please," I plead. "Let me do it. Mariana can't, she's—"

"I'm faster," Demario offers.

The clown rolls his eyes. "Either she climbs that ladder or Finance Bro joins his girlfriend in the fun house," he says, all authoritative.

"C'mon, man—" Archer starts.

"This," the clown says, waving the syringe frantically in the air, "is not a democracy." He turns to Mariana. "Hop to it."

Mariana sniffles loudly as she walks over to the rope ladder. Gage shifts closer to the front door. Mariana tests the first rung with one foot, then backs away. She wipes her palms on her dress. Her shoulders rise and fall with each hyperventilating breath.

"You can do it, Mariana," I say.

Everyone else chimes in and Mariana steps onto the first rung. The ladder stretches and creaks. We encourage her all the way up, getting louder and cheering when she hits the halfway mark and pushes higher. She stops several times, frozen, and I'm afraid that she won't make it.

"I see the key!" she shouts as she nears the top. She wobbles in excitement and the rope ladder begins to sway. Mariana squeals.

"Easy," I warn.

"Toss it down to us," Archer says.

I hold my breath as Mariana tentatively stretches her arm to grab the handcuff key from the second floor. With a slight flick of her wrist, she drops the key. The clown steps away from Charlie and picks up his umbrella sitting by the front door.

I rush for the key, but Archer beats me to it. He tosses it to Demario, who unlocks the handcuffs. Charlie immediately claws at his mouth, desperate to remove the dental retractor.

The rest of us are so focused on Mariana that the gust of cold air catches us by surprise.

The front door is open.

"Get the door!" I yell, racing around the furniture. We won't get a chance like this again. Josh takes off for the door without a backward glance, knocking over a side table on his way. A lamp crashes to the floor. I'm torn between leaving Mariana and escaping, but I move closer to the door anyway. The clown is standing outside in the rain under his umbrella. Mariana climbs down the ladder, her movements jerky and frantic. The ladder wobbles precariously with each step down. Charlie cuts across Demario's path on the way to the front door, causing him to trip. Total dick move. Mariana screams and I glance up just in time to see the rope snap.

Mariana plummets in a blur of peach and black lace. She hits the floor before I can take a single step. There's a distinctive crack as her head slams against the tile. Taylor rushes to her side, but I already know there's nothing they can do. Nothing any of us can do. I examine the ends of the rope. It's been partially severed near the knot. There's no way anyone would have seen it. Not even Mariana. Outside, the rain turns the landscape white and blurry.

Why is Gage just standing there in the rain?

Charlie bolts past Josh, knocking him into a family of mannequins, scattering them in all directions. He blows through the door clocking a top speed and charges right into a thin garrote wire stretched between the portico's columns at neck height. The wire slices through his neck, severing muscles and blood vessels. His head flops to one side, but his legs are still running like a headless chicken's, until he pitches forward into the fountain.

"Oh my God," I whisper, staring at Charlie's unmoving body.

The heavy rain dilutes the blood trail leading from the steps to the fountain, creating tiny red rivers between the cobblestone pavers of the driveway.

"Damn, that could've been me," Demario says, stroking his neck.

Gage reaches into his pocket for the horn and pumps off two quick blasts. Another streak of lightning flickers across the sky, catching the knife blade sticking out from the waistband of his pants.

The body count is now up to six, assuming that Hailey is dead. What were we thinking? That Gage would just open the door so we could stretch our legs in the front yard?

The clown approaches, ducking under the wire, and we hurry to close the door but he's too fast. He bulldozes through it and I scream, and this time, it's a solid ten out of ten on the horror movie scream rating. I bolt for the kitchen, toward the garage, fumbling inside my fanny pack for the key to the mudroom door. There's got to be some tool in the garage we can use to unseal the windows or jimmy open a door, or something. *Anything.*

We race through the kitchen, toward the mudroom, slipping and sliding on the floor, which is still wet with water and milk from the pepper spray–neutralizing event. Anxious tremors dance along my nerves.

"Where is he?" I ask as we all but crash into the mudroom. I rush to the locked door leading to the garage. My hands shake as I slide the key into the lock, willing it to open.

"I don't know. Just open the door," Archer urges.

I unlock the door, but it only opens a few inches, obstructed from the other side. "Something's blocking the door," I say. Demario joins me and we take turns ramming against it.

"Get back," Archer says, gearing up to kick.

"Don't go Cobra Kai on another door," I warn. "We're gonna need that leg."

Taylor grabs me by the arm. "He's coming."

Slow, heavy footsteps grow closer. We're trapped. I've never been religious, but all of a sudden, I'm chanting the Holy Spirit's name over and over like an old church auntie.

I search the mudroom for anything I can use as a weapon, but there isn't much I can do with scarves and coats. I grab a pair of Dad's size 12 Timberland boots from under a bench. Mud slicks down my forearm when I grip the boots over my head, one in each hand, ready to pounce.

Gage steps into the kitchen holding a metal bucket that sloshes with every step. He narrows the space between us with creepy dance footwork, a forward and back shimmy that sums up our entire night as predator and prey.

The sloshing in the bucket grows louder as Gage closes in. My adrenaline spikes, and my heart pounds against my ribs. Behind me, Archer, Demario, Josh, and Vivek are ramming the door. It yields a few more inches but still not enough for a person to get through.

"Open the fucking door!" I scream.

Gage appears in the doorway. He stalks toward us, each predatory step more ominous than the last. "So, who wants to go next?"

My heart jackknifes. Gage raises the bucket and the liquid inside splashes up against the sides. I'm haunted by a nightmarish vision of acid rain scalding me from the head down, melting away hair and skin like in *Amityville Uprising*.

Behind me, there's mad clamoring at the door. Gage comes to a stop a few feet away. His lips peel back into a wide, sinister smile. He's enjoying himself, reveling in our screams and curses, our primal fear. I adjust my grip on the boots.

The clown lunges forward. I hurl the first boot at his head. It whizzes by, missing him. The next one clips his shoulder but doesn't break his stride. I stagger backward as the door finally yields. Archer hooks an arm around my waist and hauls me inside, but not before Gage's arm arcs up and he tosses the contents of the bucket straight into my face.

CHAPTER 17

"Brothers don't last long in situations like this."
—*Scream 2* (1997)

Confetti explodes before my eyes and swirls around me in a blizzard of color. Large pieces of tissue paper and shimmering metallic foil float down and cling to my face and damp clothing. I slap at my arms and dress, frantic and confused. Vivek rushes to slam the door, and it barely clicks shut before the weight of the clown's body slams against it. Archer picks up the metal chair that was used to block the door and jams it back into position, while Gage's screechy laughter surrounds us.

A wave of dizziness overtakes me, trapping my breath in my airway. I gasp for air and rescue from this living nightmare.

"A confetti bucket," I say between raspy breaths. A corny magic trick where the water is sealed in a separate compartment of the bucket and the audience is showered with confetti instead.

"What are we going to do?" Taylor says. They are running their fingers through their hair, tugging at the roots.

No one answers.

I brush away the confetti stuck to my shoulders. The recessed lights flicker as I make a quick assessment of the garage.

The rack of garden supplies has been cleared out—the shovel, rake, and shears all missing. The toolbox with the zip ties is gone. The garage smells of cold cement, dirt, and car tires. The tires on Mom's Range Rover have been slashed; a pink box cutter with a gold blade sticks out from the back tires. The ones on Dad's BMW are busted too. My windshield is covered with small cracks as if it was struck multiple times. I circle the SUV, relieved to find its tires remain intact.

"At least he didn't slash your tires," Demario says. "Probably was too busy out front flattening everyone else's."

"Or maybe he's planning to use my Tiguan as his personal getaway vehicle when the night is over," I say. My car key is still missing and I can't remote start without my phone.

I hit the switch on the wall that opens the garage door. The motor makes a loud grinding noise, but the door doesn't budge. "A malfunction? Seriously?"

"It's jammed," Archer says.

"Most garage doors have a backup battery, but it looks like it's damaged," Vivek says.

"Can we fix it?" I ask.

"Doubt it," Vivek says, "but there should be an emergency release somewhere."

The spark of hope I felt a moment ago evaporates faster than fog in daylight. We keep turning corners only to run headfirst into a wall.

"Can't we make a bomb with this?" Josh asks, kicking at a giant bag of fertilizer slumped on the floor. "I watched a documentary one time about the Oklahoma City bomber."

"No. The chemical compounds in household fertilizer aren't explosive," I explain.

A faint sound comes from the trunk of Mom's car. I hesitate, wary of what might be inside. If the clown found a way to bring a miniature horse indoors, there could be another, not so friendly four-legged animal trapped in there. Two hard thumps sound from the trunk.

"Someone's inside," Taylor says.

Archer pulls open the rear door. "Help me push down the back seat."

Low, muffled cries come from the trunk and it takes us a few minutes to find the lever and pull away the paneling, where we discover Dylan bound and gagged. One of the vintage Tiffany spoons I sent with the party invitations sticks out of his mouth, secured with a mass of duct tape.

"Get him out of there," I say, frantic.

A clump of hair sticks to a bloody gash on Dylan's temple. He rips the tape from his mouth and spits out the spoon the moment his hands are freed. There's a note scrawled on a napkin in bright crayon and stuck to his chest like a runner's bib.

"The clown knocked me out and I woke up in the trunk," Dylan says, fuming. "I thought that asshole was going to kill me." And now I'm wondering why he didn't.

Archer reads the note with a grim expression. He hands it to me and gets back to freeing Dylan's feet.

THE PEOPLE COME TO UNDERSTAND THAT HEALTH IS NOT
THE FRUIT OF LABOR BUT THE RESULT OF ORGANIZED,
PROTECTED ROBBERY.

Dylan rubs at his wrists. The skin is bright red with angry welts.

"Frantz Fanon," Archer says.

"Great! We're on the run from a poetry-quoting, philosophizing murderer," Taylor says, rolling their eyes. "Can this night get any worse?"

Yes, I want to say. The worst outcome is that the electrician shows up in the morning and discovers our dead, mutilated bodies.

"You were in the trunk this whole time? Where's my go bag?" I demand.

Dylan's expression turns sheepish. "I lost the bag. He ran after me and I dropped it. I came here to check for functioning cars, but he was already waiting."

Gage is preying on our fears, weaponizing terror. Kelsi was pretty fearless, but maybe Gage knew how much she hated not being the center of attention. He killed her first, quickly, as if she was nothing. He manipulated Maddie's fear of horses, Hailey's fear of being silenced, and Mariana's fear of heights. Demario is afraid of not being able to save himself or someone else from drowning.

What am I most afraid of?

Being exposed as a fraud. As someone who bribed a contact at Premiere Critic to push my application to the top. Sending in a video would just be a formality. In exchange, I gave them the

Nets season pass with courtside seats that I got from Dad. But what choice did I have? Working twice as hard when the playing field isn't level is a scam. Hard work only pays off for people with money or a legacy. And that's a fact. So I did what I needed to for my future.

Dylan takes stock of us.

"Where's Elise?" he asks.

I tilt my chin up and take a breath. I will never get used to what I'm about to say. "The clown killed her."

"Fuck!" Dylan turns away and buries his face in his hands.

I tell him about the others. He leans against the car, his eyes squeezed shut.

"Is there any chance that she could still be alive?" he asks.

"So, now you care about Elise?" Josh asks. His voice booms like the never-ending thunder outside.

"Watch your mouth!" Dylan says, squaring up. Archer positions himself next to Dylan, in case the two go at each other.

My eyes flick from Josh to Dylan. "What's going on?"

Josh folds his arms. "This dirtbag's been stringing Elise along for months."

My mouth falls open. I knew Elise was hung up on someone. All she would say is that the guy wasn't available. "Dylan's the guy?"

"*He's* the guy?" Demario repeats. He looks ready to kick Dylan's ass. How many times did we have to cheer up Elise after her mystery guy bailed on her? According to her, he promised they would be together once he broke things off with his girlfriend. Elise kept saying the situation was messy.

"I loved her," Dylan says, glaring at Josh.

"Of course you did. That's why you lied to her and rubbed your relationship with Kelsi in her face every chance you got," Josh says.

"It wasn't like that," Dylan spits. "It's complicated. I was going to break it off with Kelsi after graduation."

"Dick move," Archer murmurs.

"How are you involved in this?" I ask Josh. Elise hiding her situationship with Dylan from me is one thing, but to confide in Josh?

"I found out by accident," Josh says. "I told her to stop giving this loser the time of day."

The constant bickering between Elise and Josh now makes sense. It stings that she didn't come to me, but Elise knew I would have put Dylan on blast. And when a relationship is toxic, you only come clean when you're ready to end things. She must not have been.

"Can we please get back to the part where we don't die tonight?" Demario asks.

Vivek flicks the switch again and the garage door makes another awful screeching noise.

"If I had my car keys, I would just blow right out of here," I say.

"Let's do it," Dylan says. He turns to Demario, who's still giving him serious side-eye. "You're the fastest one here and you know the house."

Demario snorts. "Horrifying shit is going down and you're asking the only Black dude to go out there for some car keys? You trippin'." D, like me, is trying to make it to the end.

"Yeah, we need another way," I say. I pause for a moment, thinking.

"Okay, the question is, how did the clown get out of the garage after he put Dylan in the trunk? We had to break in here, remember?" I say.

Gage is toying with us, playing the ultimate predator game of catch and release. He trapped Dylan in the trunk instead of killing him, just like he pulled the confetti bucket stunt. A sinking feeling in my gut tells me that the next time we come face to face, we won't be so lucky.

"Did Gage say anything to you before he knocked you out?" I ask Dylan.

"Nothing much," he says. The muscles in his jaw clench, and he looks at Vivek, who keeps flicking the door opener back and forth, causing grating frustration.

Through the wide windows in the garage, we can see the slow-moving fog descend around the house. I can barely make out the tall shrubs behind the cloudy curtain. Dylan shifts from one foot to the next, his gaze moving from his raw wrists to the door.

"What did he say, Dylan?" I ask, losing patience. We won't be able to stay in the garage much longer, and after the pepper spray incident, I prefer to leave on my own terms.

"He said we brought this on ourselves," Dylan says. A shudder rolls through him and his breath catches. "That's all."

"Right. He hates rich people. Think we've already established that," I say.

I don't miss Josh's eye roll. I know he hates being called rich;

he prefers the term "person of wealth," as if it makes a real difference to a mass murderer.

"It's because of your dumb podcast," Dylan snaps.

"Some people don't like what I have to say or what my guests say, but I'm not about censoring content. I've never been," Josh says.

A new flash of lightning lights up the garage and Gage's face appears at a window, staring at us. I squeal and recoil, terror winding its way around my body. I jab a finger at the window, but by the time everyone else looks, he's gone. Was it even real, or is my brain playing tricks on me?

"He's out there," I gasp.

Our group moves toward the windows, but only the drizzly haze remains. The windows in the garage aren't functional and don't actually open. They're just for aesthetics and natural light, bolstered with shatterproof technology.

Demario adjusts his grip on the metal post from the theater and I uncap the scalpel, ready to inflict as much damage as possible. Taylor grabs a can of rust inhibitor and a small garden spade tucked inside a tower of plant pots.

I catch sight of a dark object on the top shelf and rise up on my toes. "There's something up there," I say to Archer.

He plucks the item off the shelf. It's an old handheld two-way radio.

"Well, hello friend," Archer murmurs to the radio. He hands it to Vivek, who opens the back cover of the radio and is already running mental diagnostics.

"That's from my dad's boat," I say, recognizing it. If Vivek can fix it, we can call for help. "Does it work?"

Vivek examines the radio. "I'll have to test it, but if we can find the battery pack, we can charge it up and try to find an open channel. If we're lucky, we'll pick up a nearby boat or maybe even the Coast Guard."

Archer rifles through the rest of the items on the shelf and pockets a small spool of nylon string for the hedge trimmer. I'm not sure it's strong enough to restrain the clown but it's better than nothing.

It doesn't take long to find a battery pack and connect it to the charging station plugged into the wall, but even after we do, the charge light doesn't come on. My optimism deflates. Again.

We're running out of time. For all we know, Gage could be sitting right outside, sucking on a lollipop, waiting to take us out *one by one*, just like he's been doing.

I venture over to the window and Archer comes to join me. The rain is picking up again. We just stand there, silently staring out at my backyard, watching raindrops chase each other.

"We're going to get out of here," I say, forcing a bit of confidence back into my voice. I'm running on adrenaline; it's the only thing that's holding me together like a thin thread. "I won't let him win."

Archer links his fingers through mine and squeezes. "Here," he says, gently picking a piece of confetti from my cheek, "you got a little something."

"Goddamn confetti bucket," I mutter. I laugh and cry at the same time because tonight may be the most ridiculous and terrifying thing we'll ever live through.

A pair of headlights breaks through the fog as a vehicle coasts up the driveway.

"Someone's coming!" I say. Everyone rushes to the window. My first instinct is that the clown has called in backup to finish us off, until the car gets close enough and I realize who it is.

"It's Lauren from down the street," I say, hopeful. "Mom must have asked her to come check on us because of the weather."

Lauren drives around the fountain and parks by the front door. The intercom clicks on.

"Ding-dong," the clown sings. "Someone's coming to join our party."

"No!" I shout, even though Gage can't hear me. Or maybe he can. Maybe the entire house is bugged.

The driver's door opens and Lauren steps out of the car. Charlie's body is still floating inside the fountain, but Lauren doesn't notice it. She's too busy fighting to open her umbrella against the rain.

"Help!" I scream. We're banging our fists against the window and hollering, but she can't see or hear us.

"We have to get to her," I say, moving toward the mudroom door. "If Lauren comes in here, she's as good as dead."

"Noelle, wait," Archer says. He lowers his voice. "Gage could be standing on the other side of the door because he wants us to come out."

I return to the window with a sigh. "You're right. But we need to warn her."

Lauren marches up to the front door and rings the doorbell.

The intercom clicks on again. "Noelle, can you be a doll and get the door?" the clown asks.

I freeze. Archer's right. The clown wants to lure us out of the garage. Vivek flicks the garage door switch yet again, restarting the loud, grinding noise. It catches Lauren's attention and she takes a few steps back from the front door, turning her head in our direction. *Yes.* I motion for Vivek to keep going.

Lauren rings the doorbell again and takes out her cell phone. She's probably dialing me and wondering why it's going straight to voice mail. *Please call the cops. Call my mom. Help us.*

"Noelllle," the clown drawls. "It's really rude to keep a guest waiting." His altered voice is tinged with anger. "If you don't invite her in, what happens next is on you."

My stomach flips. Lauren swipes at her phone and redials. She tucks the phone into the crook of her neck and rings the doorbell again, this time with urgency. A loud explosion blasts her high into the air, sending her skating down the steps. She lands in a crumpled, unmoving heap near her car. Both her legs are badly mutilated and she's missing a foot.

"Lauren," I croak.

I want to throw up.

"He must've put an explosive device under the welcome mat," Vivek says. His hand is frozen on the garage door switch.

"Activated by the doorbell," Archer adds. He scrubs his hands down his face.

"This is my fault," I babble. Another death is on my hands. "Gage said if I didn't get the door what happened next would be on me."

Archer tilts my chin up. "And he would have gotten us too. Did you think we would let you go alone?"

Demario nods. "We got your back."

A bang sets us on high alert. The door to the mudroom vibrates as if being hit with a sledgehammer. The clown is back, and he's taking the door off its hinges.

An icy chill snakes through me. As useless as it feels, we rush to barricade the door. Gage throws his weight against it, sending a shower of paint and wood chips splintering down on us.

The door groans and shudders in its frame with each swing of the hammer. There's a moment of silence. If we yield an inch, the door will come crashing in, leaving us to face off against Gage.

The vibrations send a bolt of pain up my arms and down my spine. By the fourth swing, it's clear that Gage isn't giving up and we can't hold the line forever. The crack in the center of the door lengthens. One more hit and there won't be anything left to hold up. We're out of time.

"Go," Archer says to us. He says something else to me, but his words are garbled by thunder. We scatter to the dark corners of the garage, just as the door cleaves open. The electricity cuts off and for the second time tonight, Castle Hill goes dark.

CHAPTER 18

"You've gotta be fucking kidding."
—*The Thing* (1982)

Some nightmares are real. My recurring nightmare about being chased is nothing compared to this. My vision goes black. Every light is out. The garage is blacker than midnight. The intercom crackles on.

Josh Sullivan: Welcome to *A Lot to Unpack with Josh Sullivan,* the culture podcast where no topic is off-limits. Today, I'm with Mariana Martinez, lead actor in Salford's original musical production *Amor en Spanglish.* You're not going to break out into a *Hamilton* song, are you, Mariana?

Mariana Martinez: We'll see. [*laughs*]

Josh Sullivan: So you're an actor, a singer, and now a playwright! How did *Amor* come about?

Mariana Martinez: I went down to Puerto Rico to volunteer with a community project, and I came back excited to celebrate everything about my culture, my language, my people. *Amor* is a love letter to my home. Just being there was, like, restorative, you know? The idea for *Amor* just sprang at me, out of nowhere.

Josh Sullivan: It looked to me like inspiration came to you while you were sunbathing on a yacht in Fajardo? I saw your photo dump on Insta. [*laughs*] What kind of community work was it you were doing, again?

Mariana Martinez: [*clears throat*] Wellll . . . at a small theater, but it didn't exactly pan out. I had some creative differences with the organizers.

Josh Sullivan: Creative differences, yes. I saw something on Reddit about you complaining about the heat.

Mariana Martinez: [*laughs*] We were rehearsing outdoors and it was like a hundred and two degrees, bro.

Josh Sullivan: You also came back as a supporter of statehood for Puerto Rico. I understand this is a major theme in the play?

Mariana Martinez: Yes. If we want to talk about equal representation, freedom, and self-determination, we have to talk about statehood for Puerto Rico. Throwing us a few paper towels after a Category 5 hurricane doesn't cut it, you know? It's time to abolish the colony.

Josh Sullivan: I hear you. So, tell me more about *Amor*. Can we expect some original songs?

Mariana Martinez: [*laughs*] *Amor* is about my love for my family and friends. For my culture. And how I'll go all out to protect the people I care about. I'm pledging a portion of the profits from the play to funding community theater projects on the island. As for original songs, you'll have to come to the show to find out. As we say in the show . . . pa' la cultura!

The snippet ends. This episode is from a few weeks ago, just before opening night of Mariana's play. My stomach muscles twist and loop into knots. I can feel Archer's body next to mine; his breathing is quiet and steady. I think of Hailey's YouTube channel and Gage's hostility about her activism. Did Gage target Mariana because she's a statehood activist? Something about that angle doesn't quite sit right with me because we've all marched or spoken up for one cause or another. *Amor* was successful, with rave reviews and a media blitz. Elise and I had a blast at the show. It was a high school musical but with a ridiculous budget and an over-the-top production.

Or is it because Mariana bailed on the community work? Could the clown really be deranged enough to care that she gave up on her project in Puerto Rico?

From what I've seen tonight, absolutely.

Slow, shuffling footsteps sound along the cement floor as the clown moves through the three-car garage. I can't see my hand in front of my face, but I can smell him. The sickly-sweet scent of bubble gum fills the space. I'm tucked against the side of my car. I rub my finger along the flat edge of the box cutter, feeling vulnerable. It's the one we found sticking out of Mom's tire. There aren't many places in the garage to hide, but the darkness works in our favor. We're tucked between the cars or hiding at the back of the garage near the tiered plant stands and storage cabinets.

The legs of a metal chair scrape against the floor, followed by something else heavy. My heart bottoms out and lands somewhere inside my stomach as the realization sinks in. *He's barricading the doorway.* What should have been a straight shot to the open door is now an obstacle course.

Where is he?

The silence between Gage's footsteps scares me more than the darkness. Each one sounds closer yet farther away at the same time. I feel the walls and the ceiling closing in.

Something clicks to my right, but I don't get a chance to react. Lighting splinters the sky once more, flooding the garage with bright-white light that catches the shimmery fabric of the clown's outfit. My heart stops as Gage pounces on the first person he sees. Vivek scrambles to get away, but he's not fast enough. I can tell by his pleading. A power drill rumbles to life now, and the air vibrates the moment the drill bit sinks into flesh. Vivek howls.

Pressure builds in my ears, muting the yelling around me. My feet start moving before I tell them to and I bolt from behind the car, arms outstretched, blindly racing toward the yawning pit of the doorway. The drill cuts out and heavy footsteps sound behind me. The air thickens with the noxious, fruity bubble-gum smell.

A hard shove from behind pitches me forward. I stumble, and just as I right myself, my feet connect with something and I totally biff it into the cement floor. The box cutter flies out of my hand, clattering away out of reach. My cries die in my throat because the night is also on my side. I slink away, careful not to make a sound. Something metal falls to the floor and I hold my breath as footsteps pound past me. Someone is making an escape out of the garage. A moment later, the clown honks his death horn from somewhere inside the house.

"Noelle?" Archer calls out, but I'm too stunned to answer.

I back away from the entrance to the mudroom in case the clown decides to double back.

Archer calls out for me again and this time I manage a hoarse reply.

Warm arms wrap around me. "Are you hurt?" Archer asks.

I'm trembling like a deer in headlights on a sheet of ice, and I shake my head before realizing that Archer can't see it.

"Vivek?" Archer's silence and Taylor's sobs tell me all I need to know. I fish the small flashlight out of my fanny pack and switch it on. The beam bounces across the wire shelves and plant pots until it lands on Vivek.

Vivek is slumped against a wall, a drill-bit-sized hole in the middle of his forehead like a third eye. Blood trickles down the sides of his nose like bloody tears, each drop adding to the blooming stain on his shirt. The air stinks with iron-rich blood and urine.

"Vivek?" I say, knowing he'll never answer me again. The flashlight wobbles in my hand.

"He's gone," Archer says softly. He tries to tug me away, but I don't move and I can't look away. Seeing Vivek like this fills me with guilt that's permanent and persistent.

The intercom clicks on again, and there's heavy breathing. "I've got a huge mess at the front door to deal with," Gage says, irritated. "If you're thinking of ways to escape, just know there are two more things that go kaboom hidden in the house."

Josh buries his head between his knees. His shoulders shake with silent sobs. Taylor sits next to Vivek, eyes closed as if willing some of their life force into him. Demario paces back and forth, his gaze fixed on the door. I scan the garage. Dylan is gone. My eyes drift back to Josh and I realize something's missing.

"Where's the radio?" I ask.

Archer kicks away the mess scattered around us, but the radio isn't here. Not even pieces of it. Even if we had it, Gage killed the only person techy enough to fix it.

"How is it even possible that he had time to grab the radio when he was trying to murder us?" Taylor asks.

From the window I see the clown dragging what's left of Lauren into the back seat of her car. He's probably stolen her phone, too.

A heavy moment of silence passes. I don't know how long it will take before any of us can really begin to process the trauma being birthed at Castle Hill.

"There's no way the clown is doing all of this alone," I say. I recap all the weird stuff that's happened tonight, from broken locks and drafted notes to letter boards and animals roaming the house.

"I'm pretty sure Dylan pushed me," I say, recalling the moment inside the garage. I just don't know whether Dylan was running from the clown or running with him.

"What are you saying?" Josh asks.

I chew on the inside of my cheek. "One of us is helping him."

In the yellowish glow of the flashlight, Josh's eyes grow wide like two full moons. He glances over at Vivek and his jaw tightens.

"It just doesn't make sense," Archer says.

"Doesn't it?" Ropes of guilt tighten around me, keeping me in place. Like Kelsi and the others, Vivek's death is on my hands.

Archer picks up an item from the floor.

"That's my portable phone charger," I say, grabbing it from him. "It was in my go bag."

"This thing looks like it packs some serious juice," he says.

"How else am I gonna watch TikToks during the apocalypse?" I say.

Archer snorts. "What are you trying to say?"

"I'm wondering if Dylan actually lost the bag *or* if he gave it to the clown," I tell him.

A tense look passes between us, but Archer's already shaking his head.

"Dylan?" Demario laces his hands behind his head. "Nah, there's gotta be another explanation. We found him tied up in the trunk. You really think he staged that?"

"Fine. Let's consider it. The other possibility is that someone else, some rando, is in my house." It's one thing to be looking out for the clown, but an unknown accomplice is a thousand times worse, like confronting two Ghostface killers in the *Scream* movies. The thought is even more disturbing.

Outside, the fog is lifting. Taylor rubs their arms, making a point not to glance at Vivek's body. "I hope Gage doesn't come back. Hasn't he killed enough of us?"

"Hope isn't a strategy, Taylor," I say, sharper than I intended. Gage has parked Lauren's car behind Josh's Tesla. He's sitting in the driver's seat, bathed in the bluish glow of a cell phone and it looks like he's texting. My stomach sinks. He's probably texting Mom from Lauren's phone, telling her that everything at the house is fine. That's what I'd do if I was a sociopath.

"We need a plan. I have to get the spare key to my car," I say. I don't say where the key is just in case the garage is bugged or I'm right about one of my "guests."

Archer rubs his hands together. "Ready when you are."

A dark thought flashes across my mind. Before Lauren showed up, I thought the clown planned to steal my Tiguan, but what if his real game is that he's planted an explosive in it? I swing the flashlight until the light lands on a plastic owl on a shelf, something Mom bought to keep the birds out of the garden. The ornament never really worked, but it gives me a new idea.

"This has a motion detector. It might come in handy," I say, taking the owl down.

Josh shakes his head. We're all on edge, but Josh is extra finicky. He's trying to give himself Reiki and do breathing exercises. Hearing that Dylan might be involved in the murder plot has clearly freaked him out.

"Guess we can't stay here forever," he finally says, deflated. More than half the original group is dead, and Josh seems resigned to join them.

I chew on my lower lip. "Okay, but we stick together."

Josh extends one hand with a silent ask for the flashlight. I press it into his palm, and we file out of the garage, one by one, led by a narrow cone of light.

By the time we reach the living room, the clown is no longer in the car and the biometric padlock is in position on the front door. We debate using the demolition hammer to knock it off but then think better of it. Making noise will only draw Gage to us and then what? We need to be smart. Instead of being on the run, it's time for a more tactical approach. Problem is, when we see him again, then what?

"We need to set a trap," I whisper. The room is alight from the orange glow of the fireplace. Taylor crouches in the warmth, arms wrapped around themself. They're staring into the fire, lost in thought and grief. Hailey and Mariana were their closest friends and they're both dead.

I know I should probably say something, comfort them, but how can I? Saying sorry doesn't even come close to expressing how awful I feel.

I don't know how we're going to get the upper hand with the clown, but I know we can't keep running around mindlessly. Eventually we're going to have another confrontation.

"Did you bring the string for the trimmer that we found in the garage?" I ask Archer.

He reaches into his pocket and hands me the spool.

"What are you up to?" Demario asks.

I quickly loop the string around the bony feet of the giant skeleton and stretch it taut a few inches above the ground, before tying the opposite end to a chair leg.

"Let's see how he likes being messed with," I say. The sooner I get my car keys, the sooner I can ram the garage door and get out of here. We head for the stairs.

"Hear me out," Josh says. "I think we should go to the basement."

"No." Every instinct tells me not to go down there. "C'mon, you know the rules. No basements, no attics."

"You don't even have an attic," Josh says, rolling his eyes.

"How do you know? You've never been to my house before," I say.

He crosses his arms. "You said so in the Jump Scares group chat. Listen, if you're right about Dylan working with the clown, we need to hunker down somewhere. Stick together, remember?"

"Fuck that. I'm not going down there," I say.

Dappled moonlight seeps through the large windows, illuminating the room just enough for us to see each other's faces. I take down a musical snow globe from the fireplace mantel. It was a gift from Dad to Mom on their second or third date. If you wind it up, it plays "Somewhere," the love song from *West Side Story*. Inside the globe is a couple wrapped in each other's arms, snowflakes drifting around them. Mom loves sappy old movies. She was really excited about my movie club until she realized it was all horror. She's never asked about it since.

Archer watches me gazing into the snow globe. Our eyes connect for a moment, filled with unspoken words. I look away first and set the snow globe down on a nearby side table. Now isn't the time to think about our dance earlier, or what spending time together will look like after tonight. Both feel eons away.

Josh gets all fidgety again. "It's late. What do you think that clown is doing? I can't fucking die tonight, Noelle. My dad needs me."

I pause. "How's he doing?"

Josh's jaw twitches. "Still having seizures. The doctors are running tests." He glances at the dark hallway, where a monster could very well be hiding.

"So, are we going to the basement?" Taylor asks. I can tell they're antsy, too.

Josh looks to me for a final decision. I don't want a repeat of the pepper spray incident and the clown has already showed us how creative he can get.

"I'm not going to the basement," I say. This isn't negotiable. "Let's check the windows and doors again. Maybe try to get a window unstuck. And actually, I've got an idea for the perfect trap."

And then I tell them exactly what we're going to do.

CHAPTER 19

"They will say that I have shed innocent blood. What's blood for, if not for shedding?"
—*Candyman* (1992)

I double-check the piano and its bench for any strange wires and jam the piano lid open just in case. Archer takes a breath and starts to play. It's the Bella Sara song from earlier. The rest of us are hidden behind the heavy curtains, shielded by darkness.

"I don't know about this plan," Demario murmurs. He hides the metal post behind the curtain.

As predicted, the music lures Gage out. He slinks into the room, knife in hand. Archer falters but doesn't stop playing. A smug smile spreads across the clown's face.

I hold my breath as Gage inches closer to Archer. I'm about to leap out from behind the curtain as a distraction when someone zips into the living room.

It's Dylan. Shit!

"Hey!" Dylan shouts. "Get away from him!"

I want to scream. Dylan's about to ruin everything. But his

recklessness does make me wonder—would he rush in to save the day if he was really working with Gage? Thankfully, no one breaks their cover. We stay put. Maybe this can still work. Or maybe it's going to be a murder buffet.

Gage turns in a slow circle and shakes his head. "You guys are dumber than I thought."

I squeeze Demario's fingers. It's time.

"You sure?" he mouths.

I nod.

I slip out from behind the curtain. Dylan does a double-take at my appearance but moves closer to me. "You killed my friends and my neighbor. Innocent people," I say to the clown. I suck in a breath, immersing myself in Final Girl energy.

"And I'm going to kill you too," he says, leering. Then he charges at me, knife raised.

I sprint away, screaming at the top of my lungs. I skip over the string, leading him right into the trap. My heart is beating so fast it's about to burst.

The moment the clown's foot connects with the nylon string the room erupts. Gage lurches forward, desperately trying to break his fall, but the twelve-foot skeleton is already crumbling down on top of him.

"Fuck!" the clown screams. He tries to claw his way out from under the pile of ribs, femurs, and vertebrae, but Demario's already on him, choking him from behind with a curtain tie while Josh and Dylan try to wrangle his legs together with the rest of the nylon string.

Gage clutches at his neck and screams like a wounded

animal, and I leap forward and blast him full in the face with Liquid Ass. He gags as the smell and taste hit him hard in the back of the throat. He struggles to get up, but Archer flattens him with a serious whack to the back with the post.

I reach into my fanny pack for the ziplock bag of not-quite-chloroform and smash the washcloth over Gage's nose and mouth.

He bites my hand, and I'm screaming my head off but not easing up. After almost five minutes the not-quite-chloroform kicks in and the fight drains from his body. Demario, Archer, and Dylan drag him to the front door.

"I'm in the same chemistry class as Noelle and I can't cook up this kind of stuff," Demario mutters.

We didn't anticipate how hard it would be to lift Gage's upper body to get his hand on the biometric padlock. Or having to figure out which finger deactivates the lock. And then the biggest worry: not knowing when the not-quite-chloroform will wear off.

"Try the thumb on his other hand!" I say, frantic.

We struggle to switch sides and after we've tried both thumbs and index fingers, we try the rest of his fingers on one hand before moving to the other. We're down to two fingers on his left hand when the clown suddenly makes a fist.

Shit. My measurements for the chloroform must have been wrong.

Archer clobbers him in the head with the post, but Gage is so enraged that he barely flinches from the blow and jumps to his feet. He lurches at Dylan, who takes a swipe at him with the clown's own knife, which he picked up when the clown passed out. Dylan slashes the front of the clown costume, revealing a black armor vest underneath.

Archer lobs the post at the clown's head and we take off running.

"When I get my hands on the rest of you," the clown yells, "I'm going to take my time! And I'm going to make it hurt."

Not a threat but a promise.

"Gotta catch us first!" I shout, racing away on pure adrenaline.

When we get to the French doors leading into the den, I'm hit with a realization. "This is where he made the video of Hailey."

Josh sweeps the room with the flashlight, and it lands on Hailey's slumped body. Bile floods my throat. Watching Hailey swallow keyboard keys was horrific, but what we see of her afterward is far worse. Hailey's features are distorted, twisted into a final grimace.

Archer rubs his hand gently up and down my back and I lean into him.

"Reconsidering that basement yet?" Josh asks.

"Nope," I say.

"He needs to pay for what he's done to us," Taylor says. They sniffle and wipe their nose with the back of their hand.

We do a quick check of the windows of the den and nearby rooms. Archer tries to get a window unstuck using his multitool, but the window sealant is way too thick.

We eventually kill the flashlight and use a wall as a guide.

I insist on checking the side door, just in case. A biometric padlock matching the one on the front door dangles from the doorknob. It's a reminder of our botched attempt to escape.

Tonight should have been so different. We were having fun before the clown showed up. I should be booed up with Archer now, making enough memories with him to fill a double-page spread in my journal. Instead, Archer just might be a witness to my villain origin story, because if I have to separate this clown's hand from his body to get his fingerprint to disable these locks, then that's just what I'll have to do.

CHAPTER 20

"Uh, yeah no, Black people don't need to be summoning shit."
—*Candyman* (2021)

A shadow peels away from the wall just as we're about to head upstairs. I don't wait to find out who, or what, it is. I pirouette and take off in the opposite direction, down the hallway toward the guest rooms. Footsteps pound the floor as the others follow me, screaming.

Wispy cobwebs brush against my cheeks. They thicken as we go deeper, crisscrossing from the ceiling to the floor, until we find ourselves in what feels like a spiderweb. Silvery spirals dangle from the ceiling and then come to an abrupt stop. I didn't put up any ceiling decorations in this part of the house. We've run right into a trap.

"Back up," I say, already retreating. "This isn't supposed to be here."

I brush one hand against my cheek, surprised to find dust there, and glance up. There's a net filled with black balloons stretched across the ceiling. Before I can warn everyone not to move, Taylor flicks away one of the dangling foil spirals. There's a slight ripping sound and the giant net completely covers us.

Bones and dust shower us. The mass of black balloons drifts to the floor, obscuring my vision. I immediately claw at and rip through the net. Dried bones crunch beneath my feet. I've got bone fragments in my hair, dust in my nose and mouth. The air stinks of decomposing flesh. Demario untangles himself and quickly helps free Taylor. Archer and Josh use their feet to sweep the net aside, clearing a path in the hallway.

"Animal bones," I say, picking up a small femur before tossing it back on the floor. A balloon pops and we all scream. The owl lawn ornament feels heavier than it did a moment ago. Taylor starts to hyperventilate. They step on what's left of a decaying rib cage, and I swear they're about to faint. Understandable but something we absolutely don't have time for.

Gage does a high-knee sprint past the arched doorway at the end of the hall. He turns and shouts, "Guess the cat's out of the bag!"

Oh. Okay. Gage the Clown has some morbid jokes. The floor is littered with hundreds of animal bones while the fishing net lies in tatters. Gage stretches his arms out and tucks his head down into a classic dab dance move, then transitions into a jerky, awkward dance routine before flashing a knife.

"What's with the animal bones?" I ask loudly. Every move Gage makes is tied to one of us.

"Silas works at a pet cemetery," Taylor whispers, referring to their ex.

And . . . I have my answer. But I don't have time to process the latest information. We're out of there, our footsteps echoing against the tiles as we push deeper into the house. Instead of chasing directly after us, though, Gage races around to cut us off at every turn, forcing us to divert.

"Damn it," I swear. I set the owl ornament down on the floor. We're breathless, except Demario, who looks like he just took a short jog around the block.

I stand with my back against the wall outside the laundry room, my breath coming in uneven puffs. Our options are limited. We can either move toward the family room near the back of the house or toward the living room. Between the two and right in front of us is the staircase to the basement. I have no idea where the clown is, but it feels like he has us exactly where he wants us. He's been herding us like cattle the entire time.

Archer stares at the staircase, as if he's thinking the same thing I am.

"Are you going down?" I ask Archer.

"Not if you aren't."

He shifts and his arm brushes mine. He leans down, voice low in my ear. "I have no intention of letting you out of my sight."

He grins, but it doesn't reach his eyes, and I have to stop myself from flinching. In horror movies the traitor is always the one you least suspect. I'm still suspicious of Dylan, but what if I'm wrong? I've been confiding in Archer since Gage hijacked the party. What if it's been Archer the whole time? My tongue is suddenly tied up in knots. "I—I'm glad you're here," I say convincingly enough.

His fingers find mine in the dark. "Me too. I would have lost my shit if I had to deal with this mess on my own."

His voice cracks, heavy with emotion.

I nudge him with my elbow. My apprehension fades almost as quickly as it came. He's genuine—I know he is. "After tonight Castle Hill will be known as Castle Horror."

He chuckles. "You'll be famous."

"More like infamous." Which is certainly not what I wanted ahead of the party. Tonight was supposed to be about gaining more followers and getting everyone hyped for my new podcast. Not any of this.

I switch on my flashlight. The beam lands on the framed family photos hanging on the walls: Mom and me in Italy making epic Leaning Tower of Pisa poses, wearing matching shayla headscarves while visiting the Grand Mosque in Abu Dhabi, and swimming in the Blue Lagoon in Iceland.

It's wishful thinking, but I keep visualizing not only walking out of this house but also going on another vacation one day, when the trauma of the night wears off. I think of Paris, because I can't afford to allow negative thoughts to take root. Final Girls never give in to the fear. I let my breath out slowly, air whistling between my lips. My flashlight dips in my hand, its light bouncing off an object propped against the wall a few feet away.

"There's something there," I say, forcing my feet forward. "A sign."

It's one of my protest posters from summer. A new name, drawn in blood, sits below what I'd written.

SAY HER NAME
ATATIANA JEFFERSON
CHELSEA GOODING

"Who's Chelsea Gooding?" Demario asks.

Taylor gasps. They pick up the sign and the tiniest of sobs escapes them. In an instant, months of progress in therapy unravel. I'd met Chelsea only once or twice at the golf country club with her parents. She had a real down-to-earth vibe about her, and I could see why she and Taylor were friends.

"Taylor?" I say gently.

They wipe their cheeks and set the sign facedown on the floor. "I'm good."

"Chelsea was a friend of mine," they say to Demario. "She was a volunteer at an animal shelter and told me about some abuse she saw there. My boyfriend at the time, Silas, used to hang with some guys from an animal rights group. They were pretty militant. Anyway, it was his idea to raid the shelter and free the animals. Chelsea agreed to help, but a bunch of us got arrested and Chelsea got a raw deal."

"Damn," Demario says. "That's messed up."

"Silas said Chelsea would be fine, you know. Her family's got a lot of connections. We weren't worried," Taylor says.

Taylor told me everything afterward. The raid went sideways. Someone—Silas—set a fire after they got the animals out and Chelsea was fingered as the mastermind because she left a door unlocked for him and his crew to get inside. So while Taylor and most of their friends were released from the police station after only a few hours, Chelsea got hit with all kinds of charges, including arson and criminal damage, and ended up at a juvenile facility. I heard Chelsea was assaulted while she was there and attempted suicide months after her release. Taylor's been racked with guilt and spiraling ever since. And yet, this wasn't even the reason they and Silas are over, despite arson being a major red flag.

"Gage is messing with us, Taylor," I say. I can't afford for them to fall apart now. We all need to stay focused on getting out of here. "You did everything you could for Chelsea. You visited her every week, convinced your dad to get her the best legal team, and you bitched out Silas for his dumb idea to raid the shelter in the first place."

Taylor shakes their head, flicking away my words. "Did I, though?"

I wish I knew the perfect thing to say, but even if I did it's up to Taylor to give them power. So I reach out instead, linking my arm through theirs, and right at that moment, the motion detector inside the plastic owl is activated, and its wide eyes start flashing red.

CHAPTER 21

**"If I didn't know any better, I'd say
I'm the bait."**
—Beast (2022)

There's a rolling duffel bag parked in the hallway, its handle fully
extended. The suitcase makes a whirring sound and begins to
oscillate on its wheels. We all back up. The suitcase rolls toward
us like a robot.

"What the hell?" I say, realization setting in. "That's my dad's
tennis ball launcher." It's sleek and portable and looks like a piece
of luggage.

There's a loud pop, followed by another, and then yellow
tennis balls come hurtling at us. We take off running toward the
family room. A ball whizzes past my head and my stomach folds
in on itself. The tennis balls are spiked with long nails.

A ball catches Taylor, nails sinking deep into their shoulder.
They cry out and clutch at the wound, but continue running.
Archer runs in a crouched position, but the balls are flying high
and low, fast and furious. I scream as a ball lodges in my hair,
which saves me from a nail stab to the head. The balls are relent-
less, the force and speed set to inflict maximum damage.

One catches Demario in the back of the leg, and he goes down with a groan. Archer and I double back to help him up. Blood is already soaking through his sweatpants, tiny pinpricks blooming into a dark-red circle at the back of his knee. We move as fast as we can, helping Demario along. The cut on my arm burns like an open wound brushed with pepper, but I remain focused. We're nearly to the family room when the clown steps in front of us with a small remote in his hand. We skid to a stop and immediately start backing up. Getting ripped up by a bunch of spiked tennis balls can't be how it ends for us.

Behind us, the suitcase rolls to a stop, whirring and clicking as more balls slot into the loading chamber.

I don't waste a second. As soon as the ball launcher has halted, I turn, leaving Archer to support Demario and racing toward the machine to topple it. "Quick! Before it reloads!" I scream to the others.

The clown laughs. "Okay, let's see you outrun eighty-miles-per-hour balls."

I'm less than two feet from the launcher, ready to flip it on its side, when the machine whirs and spins. We're out of time.

Archer screams my name as the ball launcher trundles toward us again. We're trapped between a high-speed death contraption and a maniacal clown. Gage shrieks and squeals.

Out of options, Josh throws open the basement door and drags Taylor inside with him. The rest of us follow behind them, slamming the door in our wake and locking it. The emergency glow-in-the-dark lights illuminate the steps. The basement—turned–wine cellar is quiet, the air heavy with the smell of old cork and wood, but I'm relieved that we're the only ones down here.

Archer pulls me close. "Are you hurt?" His gaze rolls over me, and his face blanches at the blood trickling out from the small gash near my elbow.

I finally untangle the ball from my hair and hold it out to Archer. His eyes widen and he swears. I came so close to being bludgeoned in the back of the head. He opens his arms and I step into them. He lowers his forehead to mine, and we stay like that for a moment, oblivious to the others' curious stares. The door thumps, repeatedly pummeled with rapid-fire balls. And then there's silence. I wonder where Dylan is hiding. If I'm wrong about him working with the clown, I hope he's somewhere quietly trying to get a window open.

Taylor takes a few steps and collapses. How many times were they hit?

"Taylor, c'mon, get up," I say, kneeling next to them. Their pulse is fast, their skin pale and clammy. They blink but don't speak. Their breathing is fast and shallow, and their eyes unfocused, trapped in a Castle Hill nightmare.

"I think Taylor's in shock," I say.

Their only visible injury is the ball that's still jammed into their shoulder. I glance over at Demario, who's sitting with his back to the wall. "How're you doing over there, D?"

"Been better," he says, grimacing as he straightens his leg. He hisses as he pries out the spiked ball, and for a moment it seems as if he's about to pass out. Blood leaks through his fingers and spills onto the stone tiles.

"There's a first-aid kit down here somewhere," I say, heading past rows of redwood diamond shelves, a bottle of pink champagne tucked inside each one.

"We need to do something about your arm," Archer says.

I shrug him off. The wound hurts like hell, but Demario and Taylor need urgent attention. I can't think about myself right now. Josh sits on the floor, propping Taylor up.

In the middle of the basement is a small marble-topped island with decanters and wineglasses arranged on it. I slide open the drawer at the bottom and rummage through the collection of wine openers and stoppers, relieved to find the first-aid kit. I hold my breath as I flip it open, almost expecting to find it empty, but thank God, it's fully stocked.

I rush back to Demario and Taylor with antiseptics and bandages. Josh sucks in a breath, looking peaky. "Really sorry about this, Taylor," he says. He helps Taylor onto their side, and in one swift move, yanks the ball out. Taylor lets out a low groan and their eyes flicker shut. Josh clamps a wad of gauze to Taylor's shoulder to stem the bleeding.

Nearby, Demario's bleeding all over the floor, the bandages doing nothing to stop the flow streaming from the puncture wounds. I suspect that a nail might have nicked a vein. I hope I'm wrong. Please, let me be wrong. Even if Demario somehow stems the bleeding, he's going to need a lot of help moving around, and the next time we come under another surprise attack, his reaction time might be his downfall. I can't let anything else happen to him.

Blood trickles down my arm and drips onto my pink dress.

The bright red contrasts with the dark-cranberry stains of the fake blood spatter from earlier.

"Let me take care of this," Archer says softly. He gently swabs my arm with hydrogen peroxide. I flinch and hiss, and he sweeps his thumb along my wrist, murmuring apologies. I'm sure he can feel my pulse hammering through my skin. His hand trembles slightly, and I can't help but wonder if he's as affected as I am, or if the piano cover messed up his hands more than any of us realized. He wraps the bandage around my arm. The stabbing pain dulls to a steady throb. Archer has a few scrapes of his own, but he hands the first-aid kit to Demario and douses his cuts with my dad's top-shelf whiskey. Then he sinks down to the floor next to me and puts his arm around my shoulders.

Demario takes the whiskey and pours himself a shot. He offers to pour one for Archer too, but Archer refuses. Josh doesn't. He throws one back and wipes his mouth with the back of his hand. "We're so fucked," he says.

Taylor slowly comes to. They sit up, staring around the wine cellar and I explain that we're in the basement, but Taylor only nods. Josh offers them some water and they take slow, measured sips, eyes focused on the bloody pieces of gauze on the floor.

Demario finds his way to a standing position, supporting himself with the wall. "Okay, y'all ready?"

"Ready for what?" Josh asks. He pours himself another shot and sets the bottle down next to him.

"We can't stay in my basement forever," I say, standing too. I don't want to think about what other kind of trap might be waiting for us upstairs.

Josh's brows shoot up. "You're leaving?" He glances at Demario and shakes his head. "And how far do you think you'll get on that leg?"

"I'll get where I need to get," Demario says.

"Gage forced us into this room," I say, feeling another wave of uneasiness roll through me. "There was nowhere else to run. We dodged several bullets, just barely. But we ain't safe here."

Josh abandons the glass, choosing to swig from the bottle instead. He lowers the bottle from his lips and starts rapping an old G-Eazy song.

"It ain't safe, it ain't safe,
it ain't safe, it ain't safe."

He raises the bottle again, but Archer takes it away. "You're not getting sloshed now," he says. "Even if you have twenty thousand reasons to get wasted besides escaping a killer clown."

All eyes flick to Archer and Josh.

"What are you talking about?" I ask.

A weird look passes between Archer and Josh. No words are uttered, though. If one of them doesn't talk soon, some even crazier shit is about to go down in this basement.

"I invested twenty grand in Koro coin because of Charlie, and it tanked," Josh hisses. "Dad restricted my credit cards and he's been a total asshole about it ever since."

My mouth legit falls open. "You invested *twenty grand* in cryptocurrency? Are you nuts? Where'd you even get that kind of money?" I know we're all well-to-do, but I didn't think Josh would have access to his trust fund until he turned twenty-one. Earlier tonight he said crypto was bullshit. And Charlie's talk about never losing was just a front, because he lost stacks of cash. But why would Josh lie? And how far would he go to get back at Charlie?

"I sold an old Rolex I got as a gift from my dad," Josh says with a shrug. "Besides, Charlie made a ton of money trading crypto. And how was I supposed to know that the dumb watch was passed down from a dead great-great-uncle?" He kicks at an unopened case of brut rosé.

"One bad decision after another," Taylor scoffs.

"You're not the only one who lost money," Archer says to Josh.

I turn to Archer in disbelief. "You tossed money down the crypto black hole too?"

Archer's face flushes. "Yeah . . . just a few thousand."

"Miscalculations were made," Demario says. He's adjusted the tourniquet on his leg a few times and tested out putting weight on it, but his prognosis doesn't seem good.

"Whatever," Josh snarks. "Let's see how far you get dragging that leg behind you." There's a hard edge to his voice that wasn't there before.

"Man, fuck you," Demario says. He grabs a broom from the corner and tries to fashion it into a makeshift crutch. "Noelle, you ready to dip? I'm not about to die squatting in a basement."

"Wait, what's that over there?" Taylor asks suddenly.

Tucked beneath a row of shelves is a brown trunk—a real one this time. It's the one the clown was carrying when I first opened the door, unknowingly unleashing hell on myself and my houseguests. Archer slides it out and we stand around, silently debating what to do next.

"I say we open it and use this clown's bag of tricks against him," Josh says.

Tempting as that prospect is, I shake my head. "Not so fast. I mean, he forced us down here. I'm sure he wanted us to find this."

"But what if there's something inside we can use to get out?" Josh asks.

"Like a phone?" Taylor says. For a moment, none of us speaks.

Josh doesn't wait another second. He lands a solid kick near the handle and the trunk latches fly open.

Hundreds of white mice start scurrying around, clambering over the case's plaid lining. That's probably why we didn't hear them squeaking. The mice swarm the cellar, transforming the floor into a living white carpet. Their tiny feet hit the floor like rain on a pavement. My chest seizes.

Pandemonium breaks out in the wine cellar. We're screaming and running, scrambling to stand on top of crates. Mice scamper over my boots and I die a million deaths. Josh jumps backward and trips over the case of brut rosé. He struggles to stand, but a few of the vermin have already disappeared up his pant legs. I make a break for the stairs, ignoring the crunching sound of tiny bones beneath my boots.

I grab the largest bottle from a nearby shelf, a ginormous Nebuchadnezzar, and smash it to the floor, creating a river of red wine and glass through the swarm. The air fills with the rich scent of black currant and plum. Josh kicks away a cluster of red-stained mice, his face etched with disgust. Demario hobbles up the steps behind me, beating back the mice with the broom. They dive into the diamond shelves, bouncing against the bottles. I let Demario do the honors and he yanks the basement door open. We rush outside. With the coast clear, I sprint down the hallway ahead of everyone else. Archer yells after me, but I need air. I can still feel the mice squirming against my legs, their warm, furry bodies trying to burrow inside my boots and their *eek-eek-eek* noises as they scampered around.

I stop to gag, tasting bile. The house is quiet, but my mind is an angry soundtrack, a dark, humming orchestra building up to a whirlwind of chaotic strings and zero fucks to give. I hear the footsteps of the others as they run to catch up, but I'm too worked up to acknowledge them. The room is warm and toasty. The fireplace casts a warm orange glow, with enough light to illuminate the terror on our faces.

"Timer?" Archer asks, pointing at the fireplace.

I shake my head, feeling a fresh wave of fear. Did Dylan do this or was it Gage? I push an ugly image of one of us being pushed headfirst into the fire out of my mind.

"Noelle, listen. We're out. We're fine," Demario says, being rational when I'm feeling anything but. We're currently standing just feet from the chalk outline of Kelsi's body.

"None of this is fine, D!" I say. My voice is way louder than it should be, like a beacon summoning Gage out of the darkness. Rage pulses inside me like a second heartbeat. I'm not going to let him win. He can't have any more of us. He can't have me.

I kind of want him to come out, to have a showdown, to get this night over with, once and for all.

"Just take a breath," Archer says, his voice low and reassuring. "We'll do whatever you want."

I hate feeling like a cornered cat. Final Girls are supposed to be levelheaded. They know exactly what to do and when to do it. The fantasies I've entertained about what I'd do in this situation seem silly and half-baked now. Fact is, I don't know what to do, just that I can't give up.

"I think those mice got me in the balls," Josh says. After giving Demario shit, now Josh is limping too.

"So, what now?" Taylor asks.

"I have an idea," I say. I hate the idea of splitting up, but Gage has predicted our every move and forced us to go exactly where he wanted us. Maybe Dylan had the right idea about going solo.

"Y'all should head back to the garage. Look for some hiking poles. It's the closest thing we have to crutches," I whisper.

"I'll stay with you," Josh says. He glances in the direction of the garage. Vivek is in there. Dead.

"No." My voice is firm and steady. The opposite of how I'm feeling. "Stay with Taylor and Demario. I've got something else to do. I'll be right back."

Josh tilts his chin up. I can tell he wants to argue, but he doesn't.

Demario scrunches his nose. "You know people who say that never come back, right? Isn't that what you said earlier?"

"Yeah. Good thing I'm not any old people," I say. My throat feels tight, heavy with emotion.

I take a deep breath, scattering the tension twisting up my insides. "Can you go upstairs with me?" I ask Archer.

"You don't even have to ask," he says. He holds my gaze and I know he's got me.

I tell myself that I'm keeping him close because he's my alibi, that he'll back me up when I tell the cops this crazy story about how the clown I hired turned on us. I tell myself that Archer's just an unfortunate emergency shield, but that's only half true. He's so much more than that. Tonight has bound us together in unexpected ways. I know I'm prepared to be a Final Girl. But how would I survive all the tomorrows without Archer and my friends in them?

CHAPTER 22

"No screaming while the bus is in motion."
—*Freddy's Dead: The Final Nightmare* (1991)

"Where to?" Archer asks. He matches my pace easily with long strides while I storm upstairs.

"My dad's office," I say. I slow down when we reach my bedroom. There's a sign hanging on the door. It's a giant novelty check, the kind that lottery winners pose with for a photo op, excitement plastered on their faces.

Archer stares at the check, at the dollar amount on it, and then at me. My face heats up with embarrassment. The clown knows my secret. I need to come clean. I want to be honest about everything because I need to start this whatever-this-is with Archer right. He deserves the truth—I'm the reason why we're in this mess—even if it changes the impression he has of me.

Dad's office is in the east wing of the house, away from the bedrooms. It's a large room with high vaulted ceilings, hardwood floor, and an executive desk that overlooks the gardens. I set the flashlight down on Dad's desk. The office smells like him, a mix of pine and leather. I peek through the window, searching for movement. There's no sign of Gage. I pull the blinds shut, just in case he passes by.

"So what are we looking for again?" Archer asks.

"My spare car key. Dad took the SUV for a service check last week and he never puts the key back where it's supposed to be," I say.

We stand in awkward silence for a moment and then we both start talking at the same time. "There's something I need to tell you," he starts just as I say, "Archer, I need to explain. . . ."

I drift off, both of us breaking into short, tense laughter. "Okay, you first," he says.

Guilt closes around my throat, but I push the words out and admit the thing I've never admitted to anyone, except my therapist, Dr. Dillard.

"I bribed someone to get priority consideration on my internship application," I blurt out. I can feel Archer's eyes on me, but I can't bring myself to meet his gaze. "My parents know how badly I want to be a movie critic. I was working with a college advisor, but even with all the help, I couldn't compete with the Hollywood nepotism babies. Landing this internship is the experience I need to get ahead."

I finally peer up at Archer, my need for self-preservation battling with embarrassment. His expression is one of empathy and something ferocious. "Noelle, you don't owe me or anyone else an explanation."

"People have this idea that I'm so brave and business savvy, so put together like my parents. I mean, if not for the horror movie club, I'd be nothing." I start babbling.

"Trust me, that's not possible," Archer says, giving me a heated look.

"So, I bought my way in. Some people do so much worse. Why shouldn't I go after what I want?" I ask. Bitterness coats my tongue. By paying my way in, I'm edging someone else out. Someone who's probably busting their ass just like me to get in.

I start to pace. A mess of conflicted feelings float to the surface. Archer must think I'm such a fraud.

"Noelle." Archer steps forward, a tender expression on his face. "This one act doesn't make you a bad person."

Ever since I hit send on Cash App, I can't shed this guilty feeling that I got something I didn't deserve, even though I haven't officially gotten the internship yet.

"You worked hard to get where you are. You're talented and really smart, Noelle. I'm sure you can get into a good film school without an internship. Look at all the work you've done to build Jump Scares. Trust yourself. You got this," Archer says. He runs a hand through his hair. "I get it. My parents aren't thrilled about my music. They want me to focus on a serious career in business like they are with the store chain. They don't even know that I applied to Juilliard."

"You're so talented, Archer. Juilliard would be foolish not to take you," I say.

I appreciate Archer. He's been solid from the jump. I walk over to him and rest my head against his chest for a moment. His breath is warm against my ear. I exhale and tilt my head up.

He brushes his thumb against my cheek and anticipation surges through me like a wildfire.

He bites down on his lip and takes a step back. "Listen, I really need to tell you something."

"Or you could tell me later?" I feel confused. Shouldn't we be kissing? Shouldn't we give each other a moment of reprieve from all this chaos?

"There's more to the story about that copyright lawsuit," he says. "I did sample a vocal loop from Bella Sara's song, but I thought my team had cleared it. They were supposed to sort out the legal stuff. By the time I found out they didn't, the song had hit the charts and . . ." He trails off and shoves his hands deep into his pockets. "They were supposed to work out a deal with her, but then she filed a lawsuit and things got nasty."

"That's not on you," I say.

Archer shakes his head. "Yeah, it kind of is. I said we did everything by the book without double-checking. My fans went after Bella Sara hard. They doxed and harassed her until she shut down her socials. No one's heard from her in the longest time. I wanted to come forward publicly with the truth, but my team said to just let it blow over."

"Okay, but I saw your video message asking your fans to leave Bella Sara alone. And you can still take control of the situation and tell the truth. It was a legal oversight; someone dropped the ball. Don't beat yourself up over this," I say.

"She didn't deserve that. Cancel culture can be the worst. I don't want anyone to ruin someone for me," Archer says. "If we make it out of here—"

He grins. "*When* we make it out of here," he corrects, "I'll make things right."

"I'm going to withdraw my internship application. I'll figure something out," I say. I take a settling breath and step away from him, ready to search for the spare car key, the reason why I raced up here against my better judgment. There are no easy ways out on the second floor.

Archer reaches for my hand. "One other thing."

My heart is beating double time. His eyes lock with mine. "When I wrote 'Pursuit,' I was thinking about you." He takes a deep breath, never breaking his gaze. "I wrote it for you. I know we're going to make it, but I just . . . needed to tell you that."

"What?" I replay the song in my head, and appreciate how the vulnerability of a boy with a major crush blends with its relatable soul-shredding lyrics.

My brain struggles to catch up to what he's really saying as I calculate the album's production timeline and release date and realize that he wrote those lyrics over a year ago. Am I hyperventilating? Totally.

"Why didn't you say something earlier?" I whisper.

Archer shrugs. "Scared, I guess. I thought maybe you wouldn't feel the same."

A part of me melts. "What if you thought wrong this entire time?"

"Can I remedy that then?" he asks. I nod before he lowers his mouth to mine. The moment our lips touch I'm lost, engulfed with emotions. I deepen the kiss. It's just us. In our own universe. Nothing else, none of this shitty stuff, exists.

"So," I say breathless when we finally pull apart, "if you wrote 'Pursuit' for me, does that mean I get royalties?"

Archer laughs, his breath mingling with mine. I step away and cool air floods the space between us, reminding me how we got to this point.

"Let's keep looking for the key," I say, clearing my throat. I head over to the bookshelf and search for the cedarwood cigar box where Dad stashes the spare keys. Inside is a graveyard of fobs, and it doesn't take long before I find the key to my SUV. I grab the spare gate remote just in case and shove them deep into my fanny pack. Archer's putting the box back when he almost knocks over a stack of documents and I spot the manual for Dad's countertop coffee machine. It's time for a new one, but Dad likes to think he's handy. He likes the idea of fixing things, but he's really just a tool enthusiast.

"Noelle?" Archer says.

"The manual," I say. An idea kindles into a full flame. "Dad keeps manuals for everything." I rush over to the tall filing cabinet. It's a long shot, but I can't dismiss the slightest possibility of escaping this nightmare.

"What manual?"

I pull out a giant stack of manuals from the bottom drawer and start flipping through them. My fingers tingle with excitement. "When Vivek was trying to open the garage door, he said the backup battery was damaged, but there should be some kind of emergency release," I say.

"Like a backup to the backup?" Archer says.

"Exactly. But he didn't find anything and then the clown

showed up and . . ." My voice trails off and the grief lump in my throat returns full force.

I comb through the mess of manuals until I find the one for the garage door. Archer and I flip through pages of illustrations until we reach the troubleshooting section.

"This!" I say, tapping the page. " 'How to Disengage Your Garage Door.' Says there's an emergency cord that releases the door from the opener."

This is it. This is how we escape.

CHAPTER 23

**"Reporting live for Black TV. White folks
are dead and we gettin' the fuck
outta here."**
—*Scary Movie* (2000)

When we head downstairs, Demario is alone in the kitchen tending to his leg with a wad of kitchen towels. Outside the rain has eased up, but lightning continues to streak across the sky.

"I thought you were waiting in the garage," I whisper. "Any sign of Dylan? Where's Josh and Taylor?"

"We heard this weird tapping sound, and they went to check it out," he says.

"What? And you *let* them?"

Demario gestures at his leg. "It's not like I could run after them. Taylor got it into their head that it was Dylan trying to get our attention."

"Do you think Dylan found a way out?" I ask, feeling a spring of hope.

Demario shrugs. He's in pain and trying to downplay it. I know that he hates not being able to do more.

I tell Demario about the garage door, still peeved that Taylor and Josh took off. Archer wants to go look for them, but I stop him. I don't need him wandering around the house in the dark too.

"Taylor doesn't believe Dylan's working with the clown," Demario says. He grimaces as he flexes his leg. "I think they're having some kind of breakdown, for real. They keep talking about Silas."

"But the cat bones must mean something, and Silas worked at the pet cemetery, right?" I say to Demario. "What if Silas is the killer?"

Demario leans in. "I think Taylor would still recognize their ex, even in a clown suit."

"True, but he could have orchestrated this whole thing," I say, pensive.

I'm mulling over this new possibility when Archer makes a sudden flagging signal with one hand. Demario and I immediately go on the alert. We slip into the dark corners of the kitchen, away from the glow of the full moon shining through the fog, listening and waiting.

I hear the soft click of approaching shoes. Two sets, so not Gage. Or at least not only Gage. I don't move until I hear voices.

"I'm getting an emotional support dog when this night is over," Taylor says. "A Cavalier King Charles spaniel."

We slip out of the shadows and into the living room, ready to usher Taylor and Josh back to the garage now that I have the solution to our problem. I spot a flash of red upstairs. Gage is watching us from the second floor. Our eyes meet. Gage climbs onto the top rail.

"Fuck this guy," Taylor says.

Gage stands on the railing, arms outstretched horizontally.

Then he jumps.

Time slows as he plummets. His ankles are secured with a bungee cord. He shrieks all the way down with a laugh like the Joker straight out of a *Batman* movie. Josh scrambles backward, dragging Taylor with him, out of the clown's reach.

The bungee cord recoils and Gage rebounds. Taylor rushes forward and starts screaming obscenities at the clown. I'm begging them to run with us, but Taylor does the unthinkable. They grab an empty silver platter from a nearby coffee table and run headlong at Gage as he descends.

Gage releases the body harness and launches himself at Taylor, knocking them to the floor with his weight. His hands go to their neck. Taylor kicks and screams. We rush forward just as Gage clasps a black leather band around Taylor's neck and it locks with an audible click. Archer lands a kick in the clown's shoulder, knocking him off Taylor, and Josh and Demario drag Taylor away by the armpits. Taylor claws at the band around their neck. The metal clasp digs into their skin.

"Get it off," they gasp.

The clown scuttles backward on his ass and springs to his feet. "Stay back or I'll fry them!" he snarls. He lifts a pom-pom button on his costume to reveal a receiver. "Thought you would appreciate the dog collar," he says to Taylor. "This one's supercharged to fifty thousand volts. Hey. Did you know vegan leather isn't real leather?"

"Don't do this," I plead, even though it's useless. The clown is enjoying this way too much.

Taylor's eyes are wide and their mouth is open, but only a strangled cry comes out. Gage starts to back away.

"Didn't you want to play a game, Noelle?" he says. "Welp, tag, you're all it!" He cackles.

My heart seizes. I take slow, measured steps away from Taylor, quickly sidestepping the fireplace, never taking my eyes off Gage.

Heat licks the air around me from the roaring fire, but my body is a solid block of ice. I back farther away, my hands raised in a defensive position. Mom and I enrolled in a self-defense class two summers ago and I wish I'd paid more attention to the moves instead of fretting about sweating out my hair.

"This has gone far enough, Gage," I say. The moment the words leave my mouth, I feel like an idiot. Empty words that hold no meaning.

Uneasiness dances beneath my skin like raw nerves, and I shift around until I'm positioned behind the sofa. My porcupine, Quilly, darts out from under a side table in the living room and scurries along the length of the baseboard, making me jump. Relief surges through me to see my prickly pet still alive and around just when I need her. I glance up at the wall clock and realize something. I resist the urge to smile.

"Noelle, let's get out of here!" Archer shouts.

Not yet.

Gage licks his lips with anticipation. My brain toggles between the urge to run and waiting out the clock. My leg hits the side table, causing it to scrape jarringly along the floor. It's eleven o'clock. I suck in a breath, just as the Roomba vacuum bursts to life on schedule with a whirring noise and trundles its way across the living room floor.

I use Gage's surprise to my advantage and shove the accent chair into his legs, throwing him off-balance. I grab the snow globe from the side table and dart away. Gage is fumbling to untangle himself from the chair when the vacuum swerves around his feet. He stumbles and lands on all fours, putting him eye to eye with Quilly.

Dylan, appearing seemingly out of nowhere, rushes down the stairs, his shirt stained with blood. I'm trapped between Gage and Dylan, equally afraid of both and unsure from which direction the next attack will come.

Quilly and the Roomba already have a complicated relationship, but with all the extra noise, my porcupine is now officially triggered.

Quilly's teeth chatter, and she makes a hissing sound. Gage tries to scramble away, but not before the porcupine flips around and bares her ass in the clown's face, quills raised. She blasts Gage in the face and scampers away into the cover of darkness. Gage's voice bellows like the thunder.

We don't waste any time. I nod toward Demario, who hobbles into the garage to search for the emergency cord I described from the manual in Dad's office. Josh drags an incoherent Taylor away.

The clown stands, pulling himself up to his full height. Quills stick out of his face in all directions like Pinhead in *Hellraiser*. And he's pissed.

I clutch the snow globe to my chest. I can sense the gears

turning in Gage's head. He steps away from the accent chair, moving slowly until he stands in front of the fireplace. An orange aura blooms around him. Archer and Dylan are whispering, apparently hatching some kind of plan, instead of fighting. Where the hell has Dylan been? And if he's not the one helping the clown, then who is? Demario, Josh, and Taylor are out of sight. I'm hoping the boys can figure out how to get that thing off Taylor's neck.

Gage's attention flicks from me to the guys, where he believes the bigger threat lies. He fingers the receiver under the pom-pom, reminding us that he still has the power. I hate the idea of Taylor getting hurt, but fifty thousand volts is the output of a Taser. It won't kill them. Hopefully Gage won't get a chance to press the damn button.

I lower the snow globe, the love song from it humming in my head. As the killer clown sets his sights on Archer, I think about what he said about "Pursuit." If I was to close my eyes, I know I would still feel Archer's lips moving against mine, the sensation of glitter drifting down around us like the couple intertwined inside the globe. I've imagined my first kiss with Archer a million times, but now, no matter how many more kisses might be in our future, the first one will always be tied to a memory of this night. To Gage. And to all the death that's taken place.

Rage erupts into vengeance. I swing my arm back. Gage folds his arms in a silent dare to Archer and Dylan. They hold their positions, waiting to see who will make the first move. No one expects it to be me. That's Gage's mistake.

"Come at me," the clown taunts Archer and Dylan. He extends one hand to them, beckoning with four fingers. "Come face your truth."

His arrogance is astounding.

I release the snow globe and it spins toward Gage, catching him by surprise. He jumps out of the way at the last minute, and the globe crashes right into the fireplace.

Gage starts to laugh, but the pain from the quills buried in his cheeks cuts it off. The cocky bastard thinks I missed.

I motion to Archer and my voice is laced with a warning. "Get down."

His eyes grow wide as understanding dawns, and he tugs Dylan to the floor with him. We hit it as the glycerin and mystery chemicals from the snow globe ignite and a ball of fire explodes out of the fireplace. I push up on my knees and peep over the back of the sofa. Gage is rolling all over the floor, extinguishing himself. The entire right side of his reddish wig has melted away, leaving a few strands of sandy hair and patches of an angry scalp. The pom-poms on his costume are smoldering and the receiver is nothing more than a clump of melted wires. The clown's knife with the wooden handle clatters to the floor a few feet away.

"Noelle, you good?" Archer calls out. He takes a few cautious steps toward Gage, who's sprawled on the ground, groaning. Dylan snatches up the knife.

"Yeah," I answer from behind the sofa.

"Whew, you're smoking hot when you do chemistry," Archer says.

A giggle escapes as I slowly rise, and I let this joke slide. I point at Gage's smoldering body. "What about him?"

Gage glares in our direction, his expression murderous. "What about me?"

The voice changer attached to his neck is gone. His natural voice is cold and filled with sharp edges. The hairs on the back of my neck stand up. I've heard this voice before, but I don't remember where. Dylan storms forward with the knife raised.

"This is for Kelsi," he says, moving in. But Gage reaches under himself, pulls the ring from a small black canister, and tosses it at us.

CHAPTER 24

**"Get that bitch, Leatherface.
Get that bitch!"**
—*The Texas Chainsaw Massacre 2* (1986)

Thick red smoke billows out of the smoke grenade, swirling like spilled ink, cloaking everything. It's not a flash-bang like before, but we're barely able to see a few feet ahead of us. Gage could be anywhere. Aware that we don't have much time, I lace my fingers through Archer's and lead him back to the garage, the rest of our group straggling behind us.

I sit the flashlight on a shelf and pounce on Dylan the moment I'm sure we're in the clear.

"Where the hell have you been?" I ask, suspicious. "You keep running off. No one's seen you since we tried to unlock the door with Gage's fingers. We almost died!"

Dylan staggers back a few steps as if pushed. "Me? You're the ones who keep disappearing. I slipped into the laundry room and when I came out you were gone. Then I heard screams, but I only found a bunch of dusty-ass bones scattered along the hallway. I even went into the basement. That's where I just came from. It's a fucking mess down there. Mice everywhere." He scans our faces, and he really does seem hurt.

A dull pain throbs in the side of my head, probably an adrenaline comedown or another stress response. I realize that Dylan was probably minutes behind us. I want to believe he's telling the truth, but it doesn't change the fact that someone in my house isn't who they're pretending to be.

Demario limps over to the garage door. "I found the emergency cord," he says, tugging on a red cable that he's pulled from a box on the wall. The garage door groans, but nothing happens. My heart falls. I start toward Demario to examine the box myself, only to have my attention pulled away when Archer speaks.

"What's up with you?" he asks, giving Dylan a weird look.

Dylan's hand is under his shirt and he's scratching himself again as if he's having some kind of allergic reaction. I'm wondering what on the menu could have triggered an allergy when it hits me. The thought is so sinister that I go hot and cold at the same time.

"Oh my God, it is you, isn't it? I knew it!" I say, moving away from Dylan.

Dylan scratches a spot at the back of his neck. "What are you talking about?"

"I'm talking about you wearing one of those clown suits in the guest bedroom," I say, remembering the itching powder. "I always thought Gage was too fast, the timing of his attacks too synchronized, that it was odd you kept breaking from the group, and it's because there were two clowns all along."

"What?" Dylan has the audacity to appear confused.

Archer lurches forward, grabbing Dylan by his shirt collar. "What the hell are you up to?"

Dylan shoves Archer hard. "I wasn't wearing a clown suit. That's crazy! I hid in Noelle's closet when the clown went into another room and then I got the hell out as soon as I could. Why the hell would I wear a creepy clown suit?"

I turn away frustrated. Then I take a deep breath and process. How well do I really know anyone here tonight? How many people have serial murderers as friends and have no idea that they're kicking it with cold-blooded killers?

Demario pulls the cord in a different direction and the garage door releases and opens a few inches. I gasp as moonlight spills under the door. It's suddenly all hands on deck.

"Grab the bottom of the door. We need to open it manually," I say, shifting my focus from Dylan to the door.

Maybe I was wrong about Dylan. He did try to help us back there—unless going after the clown with a knife was part of the performance—but that doesn't mean there isn't a rat in the house. I examine my remaining guests from my peripheral vision. Josh has been a bit distant since his dad got sick, but why would he get involved in a murder spree? His family has more money than all of ours put together, and his podcast is mad successful. Did Charlie make some kind of wager that went wrong, or what about the bad people who took over Vivek's platform, Simmer? Did they band together to teach a bunch of influencers a lesson? We've spent the entire night on the run trapped inside this house, and I'm tired. No more running. As soon as this door opens, we'll be playing a different kind of game. The one where I'm gone.

The garage door clangs and squeals louder than I've ever heard it, vibrating hard enough for everyone in the house to hear it. When the door opens wide enough, Josh rolls under first, then pulls Taylor through. Demario goes next. He taps the spot over his heart, then points to the sky before slipping outside.

Cold air floods the garage and my teeth chatter from the sudden blast. Moonlight cuts through the low-lying clouds, ushering in an eeriness over Castle Hill.

I fumble around in my fanny pack for the spare car key I grabbed from Dad's office. The zipper to the compartment where I stuck the key is open.

"Shit, shit, shit." I keep digging around, even though my brain has registered that it's gone. My mouth goes dry and for the first time tonight, I think I might actually pass out.

"You lost it?" Archer asks.

Cue the panic.

"It must have fallen out when we were in the living room," I say, the words coming out in a wheeze. "We have to go back."

I take two steps before Archer cuts me off. "No. It's too dangerous. Gage could be waiting for one of us to slip up. Let's just go."

"I'm not going from running around inside the house to running around outside the house. We need to get to the cops," I say.

"I'll find the key," Dylan offers.

"Um, no," I say. I'm not trusting anyone else to do this.

Without further discussion, I sprint through the mudroom and the kitchen, weaving around furniture and into the living room, still under a lingering red haze from Gage's smoke bomb. I retrace my steps, hoping to find the car key and grateful for the glow of the fire, which burns even brighter now.

Gage, who has quickly regrouped, emerges from a dark hallway with a baggie filled with ice pressed to his scorched scalp. I spot the key fob on the floor behind the sofa. Fear unfurls its wings inside my chest, beating hard. The smell of burned hair and bubble gum sucks the oxygen out of the room. Gage's face is bruised and dimpled with quills, his red eyes burning hot with hatred. He spots the key fob the same time as I do, and his eyes widen with vengeful ambition.

Archer and Dylan are behind me. Archer swears under his breath. When I sprint and dive for the key the clown darts forward. I grab the key and dash into the kitchen. Gage races around the opposite side of the kitchen island, trying to cut me off, but he slips in a puddle of spilled milk from the pepper spray incident and ends up mopping the kitchen floor with his ass.

"Fucking shoes!" he yells, scrambling to his feet.

But by then we're almost at the garage, trailed by Gage's raspy breathing, which sounds feral, ravenous. I run and don't turn back. I don't slip and fall like some corny wannabe Final Girl either. I'm pressing the hell out of the remote and I cry out with relief when I hear a familiar beep and the lights flash in the garage.

"Go, go, *gooo!*" Dylan yells behind me. I can hear him tossing whatever he can get his hands on as he sprints, dumping obstacles in the clown's way.

"Can't run from the Jester forever!" the clown yells. He's wearing a new voice changer and sounds even raspier than before. His laughter sends a bolt of panic through me.

"Jester?" I say to Archer. I almost slip as I reach for the door of the SUV. "It's the troll I've been blocking all day." I think back to earlier tonight, to the comment from @DisturbingJester calling me a sucky loser. Repeatedly.

"For real?" Archer says.

I swing myself into the driver's seat and Archer jumps in on the passenger side. An awful stench coats the inside of my nose and mouth. We are not alone. Archer swears before I see them. Kelsi and Vivek are strapped into the back seat, with my poop-filled Birkin positioned between them. Son of a bitch.

Dylan tips over a giant metal shelf. It goes down with a groan and crashes, its contents spilling like entrails onto the concrete floor. I shift into high gear just as Dylan sprints past us, heading for Lauren's car, where Josh, Demario, and Taylor are already piling inside. The clown dumped Lauren in the car, and unless he took the fob with him, the car will start. Gage rushes the vehicle and I hit the gas. He makes a grab for the back door, but I'm already peeling out, with the lyrics of Beyoncé's "Haunted" blasting from the speakers.

CHAPTER 25

"I'm scared to close my eyes; I'm scared to open them. . . . We're gonna die out here."
—*The Blair Witch Project* (1999)

There are dead bodies in the car. That's all I can think of as I gun it down the long driveway, narrowly avoiding crashing into one of the parked cars.

Streaks of moonlight slice through the haze, just enough to see the rainwater cascading down the sloped driveway like a mini waterfall. The SUV slices through the water, creating high arcs like a cresting wave, and I grip the steering wheel, praying I don't hydroplane.

What's worse than a dead body in a car?

Two dead bodies in a car *while* hydroplaning.

"Shit, he's behind us," Archer says, checking his side mirror.

In the rearview mirror I see Gage chasing us on an electric scooter I've never seen before. He glides through the water with jumps and twists like a wakeboarder. I click the unlock button on the gate and the light on top of the station starts to flash. It takes a few seconds for me to process that the gate isn't sliding open.

"It's not opening!" I scream. Lightning illuminates the interior of the SUV with bright-white light and I flinch.

"The sliding track might be blocked with debris," Archer says.

"Or the clown jammed it, too," I say. Behind us, Gage is still coming and Josh is only now moving off in Lauren's car. Is he having car trouble? We don't have time to get out and try to clear the track, so I punch the gas and the SUV surges forward. I can't stop now, not when we're so close to escaping.

"Noelle," Archer says, realizing that I'm accelerating. "What are you doing?"

"Crashing through the gate. Hold on," I say.

"*What?*"

Time slows. I focus on the flashing dome mounted on the gatepost. I curl my fingers tightly around the wheel and brace for impact. I holler as the SUV closes in on the gate. Archer does too. There's a million ways this can go wrong. But I am visualizing and manifesting that this SUV is plowing right through the gate, blowing it off its hinges.

Instead, my dashboard lights up like a Christmas tree, and an alarm blares as the car's emergency braking system activates. We screech to an unceremonious halt mere inches from the gate. The Birkin flies from the back seat and slams into the already shattered windshield before tumbling down into the driver's-side footwell. Kelsi and Vivek flop over like two crash test dummies.

"What the fuck?" I pound my fists against the wheel.

"This can't be happening" is all Archer says, gasping. He's rubbing his chest where the seat belt locked him into his seat.

I think I might be going into shock, because I'm just sitting there staring at the locked gate. Water begins to leak inside the car through the windows Gage broke. Archer's talking to me. His lips are moving, but I'm having a hard time understanding. The only thing I can think about is that I'm about to die, trapped behind a hand-forged fleur-de-lis iron gate accented with gold leaf.

I've seen this scene play out before, where the side character you're rooting for gets slaughtered within the last fifteen minutes of the movie, paving the way for the Final Girl to take her last stand. Gage is closing in. I can hear him laughing. My life is so tragic right now I could cry. But I don't. I start giggling, a hysterical and paradoxical kind of laughter that leaves me gasping for air. This can't be how it ends.

"Noelle?" Archer says, panicked.

"Do you know why my dad chose this car for me?" I feel the hysteria bubbling up more. "The Tiguan was named a top national safety pick! Three years in a row!" A fresh set of giggles erupts. One day this will make a hilariously macabre joke, but ain't nothing funny about this shit today.

Archer chews on his lower lip. He's worried, and he should be, because some random troll that filled my comments with vomit emojis has showed up at my party to kill me. To kill all of us. I feel like I'm no longer existing inside my own body.

In the rearview mirror, Gage bobs and weaves through the water on the scooter. It must be one of the waterproof ones. Josh is slowing down. My heart is trying to beat its way out of my chest.

"What are you doing?" Archer asks. He's watching me track Gage, watching him get closer and closer.

If my parents taught me anything, it was strategy. They built their businesses from the ground up, knocking on doors designed to keep them out, so they made their own doors instead. They failed hard along the way, but each time they went down, they got back up swinging. This isn't the last fifteen minutes of a movie and I'm not a side character. *I am Noelle Layne, Final Girl, the rightful Queen of Castle Hill, Escapologist, Main Character energy, and the great serial killer Survivor of Nassau County.*

I chuck the car into reverse.

"Noelle." This time, my name comes out of Archer's mouth as a warning.

And I press the gas.

It catches Gage by surprise. He swerves and goes down. The SUV jerks as it rolls over something.

"Omigod, omigod, omigod," I say.

Archer and I exchange horrified expressions. The only sound comes from the water gushing through the ornate bars of the gate.

Lauren's car is smoking after the millionth lightning strike, with sparks erupting in all directions. I'm hollering and ugly crying. I reach to unfasten my seat belt, but my hands are shaking so bad that Archer does it for me. I hop out of the SUV to the sound of panicked screams. The air is thick with the smell of burned fuses and melted rubber.

Gurgling water lashes my ankles and seeps into my boots. I back away from the SUV until I can get a good look underneath. The scooter is a mangled mess, but the clown is gone.

Archer and I rush to Lauren's car. Smoke streams from the melted tires and under the hood. The vehicle is completely fried. I can see shell-shocked faces inside the car. Dylan is first to open the door. He takes a moment before he steps out, as if contemplating whether he's about to be electrocuted. Realizing that it's safe, Josh, Taylor, and Demario hop out after him.

"Is everyone okay?" I ask.

"Definitely not," Archer says, running his hand through his hair.

"Understatement of the century." I want to hug him, but there's absolutely no way that we'll be out here in the open canoodling when there's a disappearing lunatic running around.

We're waiting for Gage, but there's no sign of him anywhere. He used the smoke as a cover to escape. Archer brushes a few loose hairs away from my face. "We can hide outside, just lie low."

"Where? Until when?" I ask, feeling the futility of the situation. Cold air is already biting my bare shoulders, nipping at my bones. My *Carrie* costume was meant for indoors with the fireplace burning. Thanks to the rain, my hair has reverted to its natural curly state, and I pull it into a low ponytail. I slosh through the muddy water and take a quick look around. Most of the trees are already bare, except for the evergreens close to the house. With the fog lifting, we'll be too exposed. The doors to the stables are open and I'm suddenly afraid for the horses, but guess who won't be going over there to check it out?

Cold, dirty water laps at our legs. The road beyond the gate is flooded and there isn't a vehicle in sight. Gage will have a harder time hunting us down out in the open. But that doesn't mean I'm staying put. I stomp through the waterlogged grass toward the perimeter wall. Demario, Josh, Dylan, and Taylor head down to the gate to see if they can dislodge whatever is jamming it.

Dad thought the razor spikes welded to the top of the fence would deter a burglar, but they might rip me to shreds. If the clown catches us he'll do much worse.

"Noelle," Archer says, cautioning me.

I brace my hands on the wall and glance over my shoulder. "You gonna boost me up or what?"

Archer sighs but links his fingers, creating a step with his hands. I step onto his palms and he hoists me up as high as he can. My fingers grapple for a hold on the wall and I rub the toe of my boot against it for friction, but I don't even make it halfway up. Gravity takes over, tugging me right back down to the mud. Abysmal. The others abandon the gate, which appears deliberately sabotaged, and come over to watch my latest desperate attempt to scale the wall.

"Again," I say, determined.

Archer rubs his palms against the bricks, shaking his head. "Feels like anti-climb paint. It's designed to ensure no one can scale the wall."

I sigh. Can a girl catch a break? There's a downed power line dangling in the floodwater outside the gate, so it's probably not a wise idea to scale the gate either. Another bolt of lightning zigzags down from the sky and there's a loud boom from somewhere in the neighborhood. How did the weatherman get this so wrong? We were caught in the eye of the storm.

"It's really jammed up," Dylan says, wiping his hands on his pants. "If I can get into my car, I've got a tool I can use to pry it open."

Dylan leads the group back up the long driveway with Archer and me trailing after.

"It's dangerous out here," I say to Archer. I look up at Castle Hill, shrouded in rain-misted darkness. The thought of going back inside sends my stomach plummeting. "Everything's going to be okay," Archer says. "We'll figure it out."

He links his fingers with mine, giving my hand a reassuring squeeze.

Then he stops and turns. "You hear that?"

There's a whirring noise coming from over by the pool house, which is attached to the main house. I glance down at the key fob in my hand. "It's the skylight over the pool. I must have opened it when I was trying to open the gate."

Dylan's Mustang is parked between Elise's cute Mini Cooper and Josh's Tesla. Taylor's pickup is parked behind the Mustang. Taylor grabs a piece of brick from the debris scattered across the driveway and hands it to Dylan.

"It's your car," they say with a shrug.

Dylan sighs and takes the brick. He steps back and with perfect aim busts the driver's-side window. He reaches in to unlock the door just as the clown rolls out from under the car, knife in hand. His face is twisted with contempt and anger. Gage slashes at Taylor with the knife and it rips through their jean jacket as they move out of the way. They scream and sprint toward the stables. Dylan races around the back of his car and follows them.

Demario isn't so lucky. He tries to run too, but his leg gives out. Gage has the knife pressed up to his neck in seconds.

I'm frozen next to Dylan's car. Beside me, Archer takes a small step forward but freezes when Gage jerks the knife against Demario's neck. Gage takes a step back, hauling Demario with him. From the corner of my eye, I can see that Taylor and Dylan have stopped running and are watching us from a grassy spot by the shrubs.

"This was fun. Blast of fresh air does the body good!" Gage shouts. "Everyone back inside or your friend here gets it!"

Demario struggles, but the clown adjusts his grip on the knife, and from the way Demario grimaces, I imagine the blade has pierced his skin.

I've never hated another person more.

Defeated, Dylan and Taylor make their way back to the house through an area of short shrubs. There's a loud snap of metal and Dylan cries out. He goes down clutching his leg. "Shit!"

I see the metal teeth of a bear trap buried in Dylan's leg.

I have a new golden rule for surviving a murderer: *Watch where the fuck you're stepping.*

Gage gestures to Dylan. "Try to save him. Demario isn't going anywhere."

Demario and I make eye contact. He gives me permission to choose Dylan. "Hold on," I mouth before leaving.

Dylan rocks back, writhing in the grass. I'm afraid to see how bad the damage is, but I can't afford to be squeamish.

"Cheaters never win!" the clown screams as he continues to walk backward with Demario toward the house. "Maybe you can hang out with your old lacrosse buddy Jack in physical therapy. We both know what happened to him was no accident!"

"How do we get this off?" I ask Archer. Dylan's leg is coated with blood. It's not severed, but it's a mutilated mess of gouged flesh and shredded veins and tendons. Taylor kneels next to Dylan, whimpering silently into their hands.

Archer points at the springs on the sides of the trap. "Okay, the way I see it, the springs push up to clamp the teeth together, so we just need to push the springs down to open it."

"Are you sure that's going to work?" I ask.

Dylan groans and pants. "Just fucking do it!"

"Careful now, Mr. Billboard!" Gage shouts, taunting Archer. "Hate to see you play the piano without thumbs."

Taylor reaches for Dylan's hand and squeezes.

"Ready?" I say, ignoring the clown and positioning my hands on one spring.

Archer nods. He counts down and then we push. The teeth fall open and Dylan lifts his mangled leg out. Blood pours from the wounds. In the moonlight, his lips are bluish gray and his skin dangerously pale.

"Wonderful. Job well done, kiddos. Now, what are you waiting for?" Gage yells, his altered voice grating against my skull. "Come inside, let's get back to the party."

Archer and I help Dylan up. He wraps his arms around our shoulders and we struggle the rest of the way to the house.

"We can't keep hiding from this guy," I say. "Eventually he's going to get bored playing this game. We need to stop him. The sooner the better." I'm hit by a moment of clarity, and probably a bit of mania.

"So, what are you saying?" Archer asks.

After everything we've been through tonight, being afraid is pointless and I'm over it. I reach up and straighten my tiara.

"I'm saying that we have to take him out. For real this time," I say. "We become the threat."

CHAPTER 26

"Sometimes dead is better."
—*Pet Sematary* (2019)

It takes us forever to get Dylan's muscle-filled ass inside the house, and he's barely conscious because of the pain when we dump him in the first seat we come to, which happens to be Mom's white Italian leather sofa. Josh leans against the wall next to Taylor, who's sitting on a giant floor pillow, clutching their arm. They wear a terrified expression. The clown doesn't relax his grip on Demario. He watches us from the opposite side of the living room. A thin trickle of blood stains Demario's sweatshirt.

"Everything's going to be okay, Dylan," I say, soothingly.

He nods, not moving his forearm from over his eyes. His skin is a ghastly gray, and his breathing doesn't sound right. I think he's going into shock.

Taylor lets out a long, noisy sigh that transitions into a rasp. They tug on the collar, looking absolutely miserable. "He's going to kill me," they say, quivering.

"Probably," the clown says with a giggle.

"That's not going to happen," I say fiercely. If I want Taylor to believe that they'll make it, I need to believe it too.

I turn to Gage. "You wanted us back inside and we're here. Let Demario go."

"Have it your way." The clown shrugs and shoves Demario forward and he almost trips. Archer and I rush forward and usher him over to the sofa.

Gage smiles. "Hey, hey. Why the long faces? This is supposed to be a party!"

Taylor raises both middle fingers.

"Resuming hide-and-seek tag in three . . . two . . . one." The clown pumps two quick blasts on his horn.

No one moves.

"Oh, you need motivation?" he asks. He storms over to the sofa and we all back up. Gage digs his fingers into Dylan's leg, triggering fresh screams. Blood squirts between the clown's fingers and soaks into his pristine white gloves. I scream at him to stop.

Archer rushes toward Dylan, but the clown points a pen-shaped gadget at Taylor. Of course, he had a backup remote for the shock collar. "Or should I zap them first?"

He clicks the remote and Taylor yelps, clutching their neck.

Archer stops short and backs away, hands raised. "Look, I'm chill, okay? We just want to help him up." After a moment, Archer and I hoist Dylan up. Josh, Demario, and Taylor are already standing across the room. The clown peels off the bloodstained gloves and tosses them aside, revealing a tattoo on his right wrist of a black arrow beneath a multicolored jester hat.

Can't run from the Jester forever.

"S-Silas . . . Silas . . . ," Taylor repeats, staring at Gage. They take a wheezy breath and their lips move again, but no words come out.

Taylor's ex is several inches taller and about twenty pounds heavier than the clown. Gage is definitely not Silas. It must be something about the tattoo that is triggering them, and a gut feeling tells me that something is bad.

Gage makes a tut-tut noise. He raises the horn and pumps two more quick blasts and we shuffle away from him, down the hallway, like two teams in a three-legged race. Gage doesn't follow right away. He raises his hands to his eyes and starts counting, watching us between his splayed fingers.

"One. Two. Three. You can't hide from me," he taunts.

We're moving as fast as we can, which is slightly quicker than a three-toed sloth, and Dylan is leaving a trail of blood on the floor, which will inevitably lead Gage straight to us.

"Four. Five. Six dead pricks!"

"We'll meet you in the bedroom by the garden," I whisper to Demario.

At the end of the hallway, Demario turns left with Taylor and Josh while Archer and I head right with Dylan. We usher Dylan into a half bath and quickly wrap his foot in bath towels to stem the blood flow. I open the bathroom door and peek out. The hallway is quiet, and we shuffle back out, careful to avoid tracking blood on the floor.

"Ready or not, the clown's coming!" Gage yells.

The clacking of the prize wheel echoes throughout the

house. The clown spins it again and again. My heart pounds in my chest. Archer and I are practically dragging Dylan along, racing toward an empty bedroom.

We tumble into the room where Demario, Taylor, and Josh are already waiting. The darkness is suffocating. Dylan grows heavier by the second. He's losing consciousness from shock, blood loss, or a combination of both. We take him to the walk-in closet and help him down in a corner. Archer and Josh wrap fresh towels around his mangled ankle and prop his leg up on a folded duvet. Dylan's breathing is slowing; his chest barely heaves as he powers through the pain. He might be minutes away from passing out. The three of us pack into the closet and huddle. Archer passes Josh his multi-tool to cut the collar from Taylor's neck, but the faux leather is lined with some kind of rip-proof nylon. Josh gives up and hands the tool back to Archer.

"Did y'all see that jester tattoo on his hand?" I say. "That ring a bell for anyone?" I glance at Taylor, but they shrug and don't meet my gaze. No one seems to know about it. But after a moment, Archer tilts his head.

"Remember in tenth grade we learned about the Shakespearean fool in English lit?" Archer says.

The rest of us blink.

"The court jester was a character used for insight and often the only one who dared to speak the truth. In some plays, the jester is the wisest person," Archer explains.

"And sometimes the jester is plain ludicrous," I say, remembering Trinculo from *The Tempest*. But Archer has a point. "You know what? Who's clever enough to coordinate a crazy stunt like this? It has to be someone connected to school for sure. Someone I blocked from Jump Scares."

"So, you kicked him out of your club, he digs up dirt on us and shows up here to murder us?" Archer says.

"Pretty much," I say. "He stalked our socials and he must have hacked my computer to get tonight's guest list. The watch party logs have some info but those are up in my room."

"Then let's go upstairs and check it out," Josh says. He's ready to go, to figure out a new plan. A thin sheen of sweat has broken out across his forehead.

I need all the information I can get. There might be something in the log that'll tell us who Gage really is. If we can distract him long enough to gain the advantage, we just might survive the night.

"Do you think he's going to let us slip outside again?" Josh continues.

"Maybe," I say. Seven of us are dead. He's toying with us, prolonging the torture. But this game of cat and mouse is coming to an end. The next time the clown catches one of us, there won't be a release. We need to be ready.

Archer moves to help Dylan up, but he shakes his head.

"Leave me here," he says between uneasy breaths.

A lump rises in my throat. "No."

He holds up a hand. "Just go. Find what you need to get us out of here." Dylan manages a lopsided grin. "He and I got a score to settle anyway."

I feel bad leaving Dylan behind, but there's no convincing him to come with us. Before we leave the closet, Archer presses his multi-tool into Dylan's hands, and a wordless understanding passes between them.

The house is silent and a few degrees colder now that the fireplace has been extinguished, leaving a lingering scent of ash and soot. I lead the way upstairs with Demario, Archer, Josh, and Taylor behind me. As soon as we reach the top of the stairs, Taylor clutches their stomach and insists on using the bathroom.

I push open the door to my room and point to the bathroom. I pull out an emergency flashlight I keep in the desk drawer.

Taylor freezes in the bathroom doorway.

"What is it?" I say, moving to see for myself.

The tiled floor is littered with dead fish, the ones that were swimming not that long ago in the now-drained tub. Taylor backs away, one hand clamped over their mouth. Taylor swallows their puke. I know they can't stand the sight of raw meat or animal products.

"Ugh, this is sick." I close the door and Demario ushers Taylor to another bathroom down the hall. Josh goes with them.

Archer helps me lift down a set of decorative boxes from a shelf, and I search through the journals until I find what I'm looking for.

"After I launched the horror movie club, I started a new journal. Each horror movie I've featured has an entry, with a small photo of the movie poster, running time, number of log-ins, and statistics to the Jump Scares platform. Then on a separate page,

I make a collage of screenshots of the most memorable comments and reactions left in the chat."

Archer flips through the pages in awe. "This is pretty cool. And you do this every month?"

"Yeah, I like to read through it sometimes," I say, feeling nerdy. I glance up at Archer, but he looks genuinely interested.

I turn to the back of a binder where I have printed lists of all the Jump Scares members and trace my fingers down the list.

"Here." I point at the name @DisturbingJester. "That's him. He started posting cringey comments in the chat. And when I warned him about it, he got nasty, so I blocked him."

"Did he threaten you?" Archer asks.

"No, but he tried to sign up again, from a new account. Luckily, I had already flagged his IP address, so I knew it was him," I say. "That doesn't mean that he didn't sign up from somewhere else, though." A memory unlocks in my mind and I sit up. "Wanna hear something weird? I think I've met him before."

"What? Where?"

I tell Archer about the first day I went to see Dr. Dillard. "There was this guy there, a patient filling out paperwork. I was wearing a *Candyman* T-shirt and we started chatting and I told him about my horror movie club. That night I had over a hundred new subscribers, and I'm sure he was one of them. Here, look," I say, tapping the name again. "He said his name was Wesley, and I've got a Wesley Castle here. I kicked him out of the group for harassing some of the other members. I started getting nasty comments from @DisturbingJester not long after that. It's him."

"Okay. Did you ever see him again?" Archer asks.

"Not since that first time, and I canceled my appointments with Dr. Dillard after I told him about paying my way into the internship. I was just so embarrassed," I say. I take a deep breath, still coming to terms with the discovery. "I think Gage and Wesley are the same person."

Archer sighs. "If you believe it, I believe it. What did we watch the night he joined?"

"*Pet Sematary*," I say, struck by a sudden realization. "Holy shit. The business card Gage gave me tonight had the name Gage Derry. Gage is the name of the son in the movie, and Derry is the fictional town in Maine that appears in many of Stephen King's books." Clearly, we're dealing with a king one percenter.

Archer considers this, then says, "I don't remember Gage having much of a role in the movie."

"That's because we watched the 2019 adaptation. Gage was the villain in the novel and in the 1989 movie. Pennywise from *It* lives in the sewers in Derry." I rub my arms, warding off a shiver. "Gage doesn't know that we know he's Wesley. So let's use it to our advantage."

"So, we confront him, expose him as Wesley, and then what?"

My mouth works faster than my brain when I'm stressed. "We become the threat, remember? Remember when Taylor called him Silas and he laughed? How would he know who Silas is unless he's been stalking us?" I blurt out. The plan is vague, but a final standoff is coming, whether we like it or not.

The bedroom door swings open and I fumble the journal.

Josh walks in, and his gaze flickers from me to Archer to the box of journals between us.

"Where's Taylor and Demario?" I ask.

"Still in the bathroom," he says. He glances behind himself as if expecting someone to burst in any minute. "Listen, we need to talk about Taylor."

A cold rush tingles down my spine. "What about Taylor?"

"Taylor was rambling about being cursed in love. I guess their new almost boyfriend has a jester tattoo just like Silas's," Josh says, sighing.

My jaw drops. "Are you sure?"

Taylor's pretty private about who they're seeing, especially after the whole mess with Silas. "Oh my God . . . Taylor met him in *therapy*," I say.

Archer scrubs his hands down his face. "Not the typical place for a meet-cute. But where are you going with this?"

My heart kicks against my ribs, and I think I'm going to be sick. Taylor referred me to Dr. Dillard. Wesley just happened to be there. And the clown and Taylor's new guy just happen to have matching tattoos? Yeah, that's too coincidental. I press two fingers to my temple to ease the throbbing.

"I need to talk to Taylor right now," I say, pushing the bedroom door wide open.

We step into the hallway to the sounds of a commotion. Fear wedges deep inside my chest like a shard of glass. Demario and the clown are wrestling at the top of the stairs. Gage has the syringe in his hand. I break into a run and call out. Demario and Gage both glance up at the sound of my voice. Demario gets the upper hand. He twists Gage's wrist and turns the syringe on him, driving the needle into Gage's arm. Enraged, Gage gives him a hard shove, sending him tumbling down the stairs. I scream. Demario lands in a crumpled, motionless heap at the bottom of the stairs.

Gage faces me. He's smiling. *Didn't he say the syringe was filled with ketamine? How is he even standing? Leave it to me to rent the only legit superhuman clown in New York.*

"Woooo!" Gage does a little shimmy as he tugs out the needle. He takes a deep breath. "Vitamin B12. Enhances energy and improves cognitive function. I needed that." He tosses the syringe over the stair railing. "Killing a bunch of spoiled brats can really wear you out, you know."

My anger erupts. I rush at Gage, fully intending to shove him down the stairs, but he pulls out a knife, stopping me short. Josh calls to me, but the pounding in my ears drowns him out.

Archer's already behind me, pulling me backward. "We can't help Demario. Not now."

"Your friend Taylor took off. They should know by now that they can't hide from me," the clown says. He reaches for the pen-shaped remote dangling from a lanyard around his neck and presses the clicker on the end.

Taylor's gurgled cries echo from a few rooms away, in the library.

"Better get in there before I zap them again," the clown snarls. He mimics pressing the remote again. "My fingers are getting itchy," he sings.

I pause to think. If Demario is knocked out, Gage won't kill him. He wants his victims to see it coming. Plus, Taylor could give me the answers I need to throw the clown off. And I need to know what that tattoo means. With a groan and another look at Demario sprawled out at the bottom of the stairs, I take off in the direction of the library, tears streaming down my face. I stagger into the room on legs that feel like they belong to someone else.

Moonlight reflects off the gilded book spines of the ceiling-high collection. Taylor is slumped in a corner, hands clawing at their neck.

Before I can ask about the tattoo connection, Archer and Josh burst into the room with Gage behind them. Up close he is even more terrifying. His red lipstick is smeared on his cheeks and his scalp is blistered. Blood trickles from an ugly gash under one eye. He lurches at us with vicious stabbing motions and we back away, putting as much space between us as possible. Josh inches closer to the glass door leading out to the balcony.

"This has gone too far. We get it: we're the worst. Put the knife down. Please. You need to stop this," I say. My voice quakes, devoid of Final Girl energy.

Gage hauls Taylor to their feet and buries his nose in their hair, nuzzling as he inhales deeply. Taylor squirms against the knife, their muffled sobs growing louder. Gage exhales with a guttural, satisfied groan.

"'Tasty, tasty, beautiful fear,'" he says, quoting Pennywise from *It*.

"Did you hurt Dylan?" I ask, already afraid of his answer. I should have tried harder to convince Dylan to come with us.

The clown makes a stabbing motion with the knife and uses his free hand to mimic holding a phone to his ear. "Hi, you've reached Dylan. I'm not available to take your call right now."

I bring my trembling hands to my lips. "You killed him?"

"If he lives, he wins, and I hate to lose," Gage says with a fake shiver.

"Is that where you got that cut under your eye? Did Dylan try to take out your eye with that multi-tool when you were trying to kill him?" I ask, smug. The overwhelming fear I've been feeling subsides, replaced by white-hot anger. Then I remember Demario's broken body is still out there, exposed. I won't let the clown win.

Taylor's legs start to give out, so the clown tugs them up roughly against him. He presses the blade into Taylor's neck again, this time drawing blood.

"Why are you doing this?" I ask. I never should have come back inside the house. Stepping on a live wire in water would have been a smarter death, one that was on my own terms.

The clown cocks his head as if not understanding my question. "Why am *I* doing this? *You* bought the Evil Clown Level 4 Scare package! *You* signed the contract!" He starts to giggle. "And now all your friends are dead."

He turns to Josh, all traces of laughter disappearing from his voice.

"Tie them up."

CHAPTER 27

**"You know me, cutting necks and
cashing checks."**
—Day Shift (2022)

"Wait, what?" I recoil as Josh storms toward me.

"Josh, it was you this whole time?"

Josh smirks. He lunges for me, and I dodge him, slapping at his grabby hands. Archer shoves Josh hard in the chest.

"What the fuck, Josh?" Archer says.

He fooled everyone. Pretending to be our friend this entire time. Hanging out with me and Demario and keeping Elise's secret. Archer even invited him to chill backstage at one of his shows.

The clown makes an exaggerated production of clearing his throat. Taylor whimpers as he presses the knife to their throat again. Archer backs away from Josh, his hands raised.

"No one else needs to get hurt," he says. He might as well be talking to himself because Josh whips out a set of zip ties, eager to carry out the clown's orders.

I'm overcome with intense desperation. Josh and I are friends. Are *supposed* to be friends. I confided in him about how nervous I was about getting into a good film school. He knows how important the internship is to me.

It was Josh. He's Ghostface No. 2. He ties my wrists in front of me, so I'm forced to look at his smug, hateful face the entire time.

"Why, Josh?" I ask, close to tears. Because I'm not as close to Dylan, him betraying me would've hurt less.

"Why what?" he says, expressionless. "Why am I using zip ties instead of cuffs? Why did I choose your party?"

The headache that's been pulsing at the back of my head flares. My mouth opens, but the words evaporate on my lips out of disbelief.

"I hope you know that you're an accomplice to murder," I say, yanking my bound hands away from him. He moves on to tie Archer's wrists, and then he unclips my fanny pack and tosses it aside.

Josh shrugs. "There won't be anyone alive to prove it."

"You're such a piece of shit," Taylor says.

Gage hisses in Taylor's ear, "Shut up or I'll shut you up. I can get way more creative than the glue I used on your pussyhat-wearing friend."

I'm not going out like this. I rush forward to body-check Josh, but the clown sticks a leg out and I trip. Without full use of my hands to break the fall, I land hard on my shoulder, narrowly avoiding hitting the bookcase. My tiara, once secure in my hair, goes flying off my head, bounces and breaks. I flop over on my back, groaning from the pain.

The clown turns to Josh. "Remind me to get the recipe for that chloroform dupe before we kill her."

"It wasn't supposed to end this way," Josh says, almost conciliatory. "We were supposed to be the best of Salford Prep, but you guys really are the worst. Getting in through the back door for an internship, Noelle? You're just like the rest of them."

I glare at him. "Gee, tell us how you really feel, Josh."

Josh scoffs. "It's about all of you getting away with everything." He starts listing on his fingers. "Archer steals from an indie artist and lets his fans destroy her on social media; Taylor brings their friend Chelsea into Silas's toxic mess, leaving her with a criminal record and no friends; Dylan mows down the competition and walks away with a big sports endorsement deal. I could go on and on."

Gage picks up a beige throw cushion from the Victorian jacquard sofa and uses it to clean his blade. He tosses the cushion at me, and I deflect it with my hands.

He scrapes the knife along the back of the dark walnut chair, and I close my eyes at the screech of metal against metal when he reaches the gold detailing.

"We're not the real monsters here," Gage says.

"Doesn't look that way from where I'm sitting," I retort.

Gage chuckles. "You get to play by your own rules, while the rest of us are supposed to work hard and just hope everything works out?" His expression turns scornful. "You run around doing whatever you like, then call Mommy and Daddy to cover up your dirty deeds, but tonight is about consequences."

"What about consequences for you, *Wesley*? You've killed a lot of people tonight," I say.

Gage hesitates but then starts to clap. "Ten points for the girl who buys her way into whatever she wants. Maybe you underestimated yourself," he says. He points the knife at me, leering. "Took you and your trust fund princeling here long enough to figure it out."

Josh glances from me to Archer. "So, you finally stopped with the cringey pining, huh?"

"I've been watching you two lovebirds. We've got a real-life Romeo and Juliet here," Gage says, grinning. His teeth shine yellow in the hazy moonlight. He stops pacing in front of Archer and kicks him in the knee. "You know they both die at the end, right?"

I use the dim light to my advantage, unclenching my fists and turning my wrists inward. I start to work my way out. The ties are tight, but if I can slip my thumbs out, I can free my hands.

"Kelsi was your friend, Josh," I say, still trying to make sense of the situation. "And Demario and Elise. The others. They didn't deserve this—"

"Ughhh!" the clown bellows. "Believe me, they deserved it. Just as you deserve the special reckoning you've got coming."

The blood in my veins goes cold. The ties are cutting into my skin, but I keep working, twisting my fingers. Archer realizes what I'm doing and he's working his hands too.

"Let's be real for a minute. You wanna talk about Kelsi, the queen of urban decay? Washing her hair with bottled water because tap is 'too harsh for her'?" Gage shakes his head. "My grandpa was in that nursing home and ate that fucking fruit-sticker cake."

Josh folds his arms and smirks. He's actually enjoying this. He traded information about us, but in exchange for what? What does he gain from any of this? If Gage hates rich people, then how are they even on the same side? And it still doesn't explain how they know about my internship or what went down with Archer's lawsuit. The clown clicks the pen-shaped remote, but instead of Taylor getting Tasered again, a recording starts. It's a recording of my therapy session with Dr. Dillard, my admitting to how I positioned myself for a spot in Premiere Critic's internship program.

"That was a private conversation!" I shriek. I'm livid. He bugged my therapist's office. Maybe he searched through the patient files too. "You only named half the group. What about the others? What exactly did they do?"

"Demario," Gage says with a wistful expression. "Seemed like a cool dude, but he just really needed to choose his friends better. You are the company you keep and all that. Now, *Elise* was bad news. Do you know that a helicopter produces nine hundred fifty pounds of carbon dioxide an hour? We know she liked her private weekend flights on Elise Air."

"So you're a climate change advocate too?" I say, dryly.

The clown ignores me and continues. "Remember that 420 party?"

"No. I wasn't there. But how do you know about it?" My gaze lands on Josh, but he's fixated on something on the bottom of his loafer.

"I tagged along with a friend." The clown paces, caught up in his story, and I use his distraction to tug against the ties, digging my fingernails into the track of the zip to derail it.

"Elise baked some pot brownies, and next thing I know, I'm in an ambulance headed to the ER," the clown says.

I had heard about the party. Technically, it was Elise's cousin's birthday party and not 420-themed. Elise called me freaking out. Her cousin had talked her into helping make brownies for the party, but they completely messed up the recipe. Eight guests were treated at the hospital that night.

"So, there I am in the hospital, can't feel my face, then some burly dude shows up in a black-on-black suit and shoves a couple hundred-dollar bills in my hand for me to forget where I got the brownies. And I'm not supposed to be mad about it?" Gage says.

I snort. "You've got a real warped sense of ethics." My wrists are on fire and I'm no closer to breaking free of the ties.

"Ethics?" he scoffs. "Vivek builds an entire social networking site and lets the hatemongers put their stamp all over it. Makes you wonder whose side he was on."

"Vivek's platform was supposed to be for small, positive, thoughtful communities," I say, feeling the need to stand up for Vivek. "He had good intentions."

"Simmer is now an existential threat to democracy! Like it needed another blow!" the clown shouts. "And Charlie, your local Xanax-popping crypto king, was ruining lives one day at a time. His BFF Maddie steals a horse and carriage and nearly gets her accomplice killed, but nothing happens. No repercussions. Tell me I don't get to be angry about a bunch of spoiled rich kids getting away with literally everything." The clown paces the small space in front of the bookshelf. "I made one mistake. One! And ended up with court-mandated anger management therapy and a criminal record. Dr. Dillard is a joke."

"I'm sure you can continue your anger management therapy

in prison," I say. "Who made you judge, jury, and executioner?" I feel my own anger surging.

"Your friend Mariana couldn't stop talking about Puerto Rico. She pledged to donate money to the theater arts on the island, but she never did. She talked about doing it *for the culture*, meanwhile she was hooking up with a white girl who puts ketchup on her tacos."

"Mariana made donations. You don't know what you're talking about. And you killed her because Hailey's white? Are you kidding?" I shout. Gage is having his soapbox, horror-movie-villain moment and this shit is wild.

Gage rolls his eyes. "No, I killed her because ketchup on tacos is a hate crime."

If I had to rank Gage among the top movie villains, this rant would be in the top ten. His rage is steeped in antagonistic and cynical attitudes toward wealth and privilege. He's completely lost touch with reality, but he's determined to make tonight about teachable moments. Are we as bad as he thinks, though? There's an underlying truth to what he's saying that stings more than I care to admit.

I think about how desperate I was to get a film internship. How entitled I felt to it because my parents worked hard so I wouldn't have to struggle. And how easy it was to suppress my own guilty conscience. For many here tonight, money and privilege made their problems go away. Is this what Gage sees when he sees us? A bunch of kids living without consequences?

Gage is unhinged, slashing his way through Castle Hill, but it won't help him escape his own reality. His anger and resentment won't magically disappear even if we do.

Gage sighs and picks at one of the few quills still stuck in his face. "Time to move this party along."

"Wait," I say, desperate to keep him talking. I'm this close to slipping one thumb under the zip ties. I need more time.

"I'm sorry about what happened to Bella Sara," Archer blurts out.

Gage sucks his teeth. "Not me you should be apologizing to."

"What about Dylan?" I ask. "What happened to Jack was an accident. We all saw it happen." Josh fidgets. I still can't believe he did this to us . . . to me.

"That noodle shop was a crime hot spot," Josh starts.

I'm lost for a moment, and then I remember the scandal about Dylan getting arrested after being in the wrong place at the wrong time.

"It was a front for drugs, gambling, and trafficking vulnerable teens," Josh says with disgust. "Dylan knew and he still hung out there anyway. Place had the worst noodles too."

"And what did *you* do about it, Josh? Sounds like you looked the other way too," I say.

We both scoff.

Josh isn't finished yet. "Dylan had his head so far up his ass, with his fancy high-rise apartment and sports endorsement deal that he didn't care about anything else. He got pissed at me for talking about the homeless situation in the city when his dad was busy building more empty skyscrapers on Billionaires' Row." Josh is full of rage. He pretended to be our friend when he really hates us. Where does he get off judging us?

"You're right about the lack of affordable housing as a main factor of homelessness, but did Dylan deserve to be terrorized and murdered for that? Do you even hear yourself? You're such a hypocrite. What have you done? What were you thinking, getting mixed up in this . . . ," I say. The skin near my thumb peels away, but I keep working my hands, grimacing through the pain.

Something inside Josh snaps. "Homelessness in the city is at its highest since the Great Depression," he rants. He runs a hand through his hair. "I didn't see it before, but Gage helped me see the truth about who you really are."

The clown laughs, delighted, as Josh slips deeper into the crevices of an alternate reality.

"I have a question, though," I say, turning my attention to the clown.

"Why us and not him?" I ask with a nod to Josh. "If you're so disgusted by our privilege, how come Josh isn't being purged like the rest of us?"

Gage laughs. An actual deep laugh that rumbles. "Because he paid me. Everyone has a price, right? You should know that better than anyone. Josh and I have a shared vision and together, we're going to make everyone believe that this murder fest was entirely your idea."

CHAPTER 28

**"No tears, please. It's a waste of
good suffering."**
—*Hellraiser* (1987)

"How much?" I demand. I want to hear the number, to know how much our lives are worth.

Josh swallows. His Adam's apple bobs, and he looks to Gage, as if for approval to speak, but the clown is just enjoying the show.

"Answer the question!" Archer shouts.

"Two thousand in cash and an NFT artwork from my personal collection that's worth thousands," Josh says.

"Seriously? You traded our literal lives for two grand and a digital asset?"

"Lucrative asset," Josh corrects.

Un-freaking-believable.

"So, Josh has been feeding you information about each of us this whole time?" I ask Gage, forcing a bit of confidence into my voice. "Is that how you know so much?"

The clown throws an arm around Josh's shoulders. "Our mutual connections in the Liberation Bloc run deep."

Taylor gasps and their eyes flick to Gage's tattoo. So this is the connection. The tattoo is a Bloc symbol.

"*You're* with the Liberation Bloc?" Archer asks.

We're in deep shit.

The anti-fascist, anti-capitalist organization is as far left as you can get. The Bloc is all about anarchy and chaos. A real-life scenario like the movie series *The Purge* is at the top of their wish list. I always knew Josh had strong feelings about our political system, but aligning with a group like the Bloc isn't the solution he thinks it is.

"Our society's broken," Josh says. "It's beyond fixing. We need to start anew."

Gage nods. "The only way to counter inequality across the board is to tear systems down and rebuild them. History keeps repeating itself, but you know when things are going to change?" He stomps forward and I instinctively lean away. "When you find the heart of the capitalist machine and rip it out."

"And what does that have to do with any of us?" I scream. "You're holding me hostage in my own house for what? Killing a bunch of teens seems like a pretty small message to send."

"Gotta start somewhere. You're part of the machine. You and your clique call yourselves activists and influencers. Famous for being famous! But you're leading people astray," Gage hisses.

"Forty thousand Instagram followers is hardly famous. Now *Josh*," I say, throwing down his name like a gauntlet, "is the real celebrity here." The pain in my wrists flares, and unless I break a thumb, I might never get free of the ties.

"Perception," Josh mutters, sinking down into the sofa with a sigh. He seems defeated, sad almost. The audacity.

"What's that supposed to mean?" I ask.

Josh doesn't answer, but the clown circles the sofa until he's facing me and just a few feet away. "My dad spent his entire life cleaning up rich-kid messes. Made good money as a fixer. He worked for one of the shadiest lawyers in the city, working behind the scenes to make all his rich clients' problems go away. He brought me in when I was about fourteen, and I saw some fucked-up shit. Fixers know how to clean, but more importantly, they know how to get information. Planting a listening device in Dr. Dillard's office was the easiest hack I've ever done."

"You're such an asshole." I can't believe what I'm hearing. I think about everything I told Dr. Dillard in our sessions. Feelings I never shared with anyone, including my own family. I might as well be sitting on the floor naked, that's how exposed I feel.

I'm furious at Josh, mostly because his betrayal cuts super deep. Were we ever really friends?

"How'd you even end up at Dr. Dillard's in the first place if you come from a family of fixers?" I ask.

"Some things can't be fixed. I'm another casualty of our broken system," Gage says.

He steps closer, until he's hovering right over me. "I'm not the bad guy here." He points at Josh with the knife and giggles. "Sometimes the monster isn't who you expect."

Then he glares at us, as if contemplating who to kill next.

"So, it's party time," Gage says with a leer. He turns away and stalks over to Taylor.

He clicks the remote in Taylor's direction and they scream. Their entire body twitches as their muscles contract. Archer and I shout and plead as Taylor writhes on the floor. Gage leans over them.

"Your friend Chelsea, the one you abandoned, the one you barely visited after she was released from juvy, got stabbed multiple times with a piece of straightened jail fence as a parting gift. She has the scars to prove it."

Gage sets the knife down on a bookshelf and slides a long piece of metal from one of his pant pockets and twirls it between his fingers. The steel glints in the moonlight, distinctly savage. "It looked a lot like this."

Taylor rolls over on their back, gasping and still disoriented from the attack. Josh just sits there on the sofa, unbothered.

I lift my hands above my head and bring them down hard toward my stomach, snapping my elbows together, desperate to break the tie. The hard plastic cuts into my skin and loosens, but it still doesn't break.

With his hands still bound, Archer leaps up and darts across the room. He rams into Gage, throwing him off-balance.

Josh vaults off the sofa and tackles Archer and they both go down.

There's a loud crunch as Josh's fist connects with Archer's jaw. Gage regains his balance and grips Josh by the scruff of his shirt and hauls him off Archer. I push up off the floor and move toward Taylor, but Gage reaches them first. I catch a glimpse of the piece of metal as Gage hauls Taylor up with one hand and buries it into their side.

Taylor cries out, doubling over, but then they come up, hands clenched, and punch Gage in the throat. The clown's head snaps backward, and Taylor staggers away from him. Gage smiles. Then he clicks the remote, activating the shock collar and his smile grows as Taylor's body contorts. They collapse in a jerky heap, while the clown continues clicking with increasing ferocity.

I charge at the clown, but he shoves me aside hard. Taylor isn't moving anymore. I crawl on all fours to them. Their eyes are closed. I try to check for a pulse, but my hands are shaking so bad I can't tell if there is one or not. I say their name over and over, my brain refusing to accept that I've lost another friend.

Archer and Josh are grappling, but Archer's clearly at a disadvantage with his hands still tied. Josh rams Archer into the balcony door, and it flies open in an explosion of shattering glass. Archer goes down hard, and he rolls onto his side, struggling to get up. Gage snatches the knife off the bookshelf.

A light breeze swirls through the library, catching the leaves of the hanging English ivy plant. I'm leaning over Taylor when Josh hooks an arm around my neck in a sleeper hold, crushing my throat. I flail and kick as he drags me up, twisting and pivoting until I break the hold. Josh glares, his neck corded with veins and his nostrils flaring. He lunges at me again. I swing my bound hands hard against his nose and bring my knee up, not quite catching him in the nuts, but it breaks his grip just enough for me to reach up and sink a chipped, jewel-crusted fingernail into his eye. Josh wails like a wildcat at night. I scuttle backward just as the clown hauls him away and shoves him down on the sofa.

Gage stands over me with the knife, glowering, and my soul levitates right out of my body. I lie on the floor in submission.

"Get your asses over there!" the clown shouts at me and Archer, pointing the knife at the bookcase. I contemplate making a run for the door, but I know I won't get very far.

"What the fuck was that?" Gage yells at Josh. "You know she's mine."

His words are like icicles sinking into me. *Mine.* He's saving me for last. Defiance fires up inside me. I belong to no one.

"Stick to the plan," the clown rages at Josh. "I know you didn't flatten her tires like you were supposed to."

"Because that's my ride out of here," Josh says, full of snark.

It's like I'm seeing a different person, a cockier, meaner version of Josh, and that's absolutely chilling.

"Let me tell you about this guy," the clown says. He stands behind the sofa, an unfriendly hand clamped squarely on Josh's shoulder.

"His parents are cutting him off," Gage says, making a sliced-throat gesture with the knife. "All that money, the houses, the cars are gone."

A muscle in Josh's jaw jumps. He looks absolutely furious, not with Gage but with simmering anger at the entire world.

"Josh, what's he talking about?" I ask.

Josh forces a laugh. "My parents decided that passing down a large sum of money would be bad for me. Apparently, I'll be more motivated in life without a trust fund."

"You're not getting an inheritance?" My breath whistles between my lips. Josh had big plans for it.

Josh picks at his cuticles and continues. "They're paying for college, but after that I'm on my own. Dad said the money can serve a bigger and better purpose in the community, that ass-hole."

Even though my parents aren't jumping up and down about my career plans, I know without a doubt that their hard work is building a legacy for me. I've heard enough conversations at home to understand that white kids who grow up rich are more likely to stay wealthy than Black kids from households with similar income levels. So even without a cushy trust fund, Josh's family name and connections alone will knock down doors. He'll be just fine.

"That sucks, Josh" is all I say instead.

"That money? That's supposed to be my legacy," Josh says. He tries to stand, but the clown nudges him back onto the sofa. "How am I supposed to live?"

Without college debt, probably considerably well. Right now, though, it's best I keep my mouth shut.

"But I showed him," Josh says, relaxing into the sofa. "I showed all of you, didn't I? Do you have any idea what it feels like, watching you with the helicopters, apartments, and custom designed this and that? Everything is a flex for Insta. Meanwhile, in the real world, I'm applying for part-time jobs down at the golf club just to afford a ticket to Coachella next year. And Dad is even talking about me paying half of my car insurance." His breath is coming heavy now, as if he's about to spontaneously combust.

"Being mad at us doesn't change your situation," I tell him. Josh is already too far gone, too deep in his own despair and jealousy. Anything I say might be the match that sets off the fireball waiting to let loose.

"Can you be a bit more supportive? Your friend is having a tragic moment," the clown says. He gives Josh a reassuring pat on one shoulder.

"Oh, my bad," I say. "I didn't know *friends* went around conspiring to murder other friends."

My comment bounces off Josh. "Dad backed out of the apartment deal. Now he and Mom are moving to Costa Rica to live on some hippie commune so they can grow lettuce and wear moccasins . . . at least, they were."

"Because your dad got sick?" I ask.

Josh sits back, looking smug.

Gage laughs. "Because he *made* him sick. He's been poisoning his dad for weeks."

"Oh my God, you're insane," I say.

Josh is indignant. "If he's not in the picture, Mom will want to stay in New York. She'll collect his insurance money, share the wealth with her family, and everything will go back to normal."

This sounds like a true crime podcast episode where the wife slowly poisons her husband with drain cleaner or something to get his fortune.

"What kind of person kills their own dad for money?" the clown says. "And I'm the villain here?" He turns on Josh, face red with disgust. When Josh spoke, his eyes were cold and vacant. There's nothing but darkness. Gage must've noticed too.

"You and your podcast are so full of shit. You're an even better actor than Mariana. Your episode about the amount of water it takes to grow avocados was balanced with the perfect amount of righteous indignation. Truth is, I only brought you into the Bloc for the donations. We need people like you to prop up the balance sheet, but then you talked us into buying crypto from your friend and we lost a shitload of money. You might have your brainwashed followers eating out of your hand, but you're more toxic than anything floating around in the Gowanus Canal. And to think I was actually going to let you live tonight," Gage taunts.

The temperature in the room drops a few degrees as the clown's tone shifts. Cold air swirls through the broken door. In seconds, Josh is in a headlock, the knife pressed to his throat. He pounds on the clown's arm, squirming helplessly.

"We had a deal!" Josh shouts, his voice garbled. His sneakers squeak against the polished tiles as he tries to pry the clown's arm away.

"You're everything that's wrong with society, Josh Sullivan. Do you see me walking around feeling bad for being white? You're so busy showing off how woke you are, atoning for your whiteness, that you don't lift a finger to help anyone else," the clown says. He traces the blade along Josh's cheek. "I learned a lot as a kid hanging out in Zuccotti Park with my dad. Occupy Wall Street was just the beginning. The ninety-nine percent are rising up."

The clown leans down and whispers in Josh's ear, "That's why I came to this party tonight, not just for your cowardly little friends . . . but for you, too. I know that's a lot to unpack."

Josh glitches for a moment.

"What the hell, man? Remember what you stand to gain. That NFT is worth over ten grand," Josh blusters.

"*Was* worth ten grand," the clown corrects. "Yesterday while you were busy crying into your gluten-free sparkling water about your lost inheritance, the crypto market crashed. Wanna know how much that NFT is worth now? I couldn't even buy a Happy Meal with it! Now who's the real clown?"

Before Josh can react, Gage yanks his head back and draws the knife clean across his throat, slicing it open. Bright-red blood sprays out. It gushes down the front of Josh's T-shirt, snaking and soaking into the spaces around the raised letters that spell out THE LIBERAL ELITE.

"Killing Josh wasn't necessary," the clown says contemplatively. "But I *really* wanted to do it."

A piercing cry tears out of me. This time, when I channel my inner Final Girl and raise my arms and snap my elbows together, the zip ties finally break, and I bolt for the door.

CHAPTER 29

"Well, hello, Mr. Fancypants. Well, I've got news for you, pal. You ain't leading but two things right now: Jack and shit . . . and Jack left town."
—Army of Darkness (1992)

Gage moves for the door at the same time I do. He's faster and my hands are numb and tingly. I snatch a black marble bookend from the bookcase and fling it at him. He ducks, but he's not so lucky with the brass pineapple doorstop that clocks him in the head. Gage goes down, and his head hits the pointed ear of the life-sized corgi statue on the floor next to the sofa. Mom always jokes that it's the most loyal dog on earth. The clown doesn't get up.

I grab the knife from the floor, my hands trembling. "Did I kill him?" I ask, fumbling as I edge the blade under the zip tie to free Archer's hands.

"No, but he's out," Archer says. The restraint snaps, and Archer massages his wrists. I swallow down the bitter taste at the back of my throat.

"That would be too easy, right? Evil never dies," I say.

It's not lost on me that Archer and I are the last two standing, and I'm determined to keep it that way.

"We should tie him up," I say. Every second counts. "Check him and Josh for cell phones. They had to be communicating somehow."

A deep crease settles between Archer's brows as he stares down at Gage. "Hey, wait. Let me check him out and you search Josh."

"What? . . . You think he's playing possum?" I whisper.

"There's one way to find out," I add. I'm done playing. I grab an amethyst geode paperweight from the writing desk and whack Gage on the head. There's no response. But seconds later, a thin trail of blood leaks out under the hairline of his wig.

"Guess that confirms it?" Archer says.

I let out a shaky breath and move over to Josh. His entire front is soaked with blood. My hands are shaking, but I force myself forward and take a deep breath. *You can do this.* I pat his pockets before angling my hand inside one. I exhale and repeat with the other pocket. I pull out a wallet but no phone.

Archer nudges Gage a few times with one boot before searching his pockets.

"Jackpot," Archer says.

"You found a phone?"

"No, but we can work with this," he says, holding up a zip tie.

"Grab his arms," I say, quickly going over to help him.

We gather his hands behind his back and pull the plastic restraint until it saws into his skin.

Back with Josh, I lift his left hand and examine the smart-watch on his wrist. "It's a fitness tracker," I say. I press the watch stem, but no Emergency SOS button appears. I swipe at the screen a few times, but this thing doesn't even have voice mode. Maybe his parents did cut him off. And Josh really did come prepared to screw us over.

"It has fall detection, though," I say, toggling the button to the On position.

"I can't wrap my head around this . . . and poisoning his dad. All over money," Archer says.

"It's sick. He really had everyone fooled," I say.

I glance at the open balcony door. I can't believe what I'm about to suggest. "Throw Josh over the balcony and wait for the watch to alert emergency services."

Archer's eyes lock with mine. We are actually going to do this. Even though Josh is already dead, it still feels as if we're about to commit murder.

"Grab his legs," Archer says.

It takes us a moment to get coordinated. Josh's head lolls to one side, tethered by nothing but tendons and bone. *Breathe, Noelle. Breathe.*

"Damn, he's heavier than he looks," I say, grunting.

Archer props Josh's torso up against the low railing while I hoist his feet up.

"I hope this works."

"It will," Archer says, and I believe him. Because it has to.

"What's the first thing you're going to do when this is over?" I ask.

Archer grabs a fistful of Josh's shirt and I toss one of Josh's legs over the rail. This isn't as easy as either of us thought it would be. Then again, neither of us has thrown a body off a balcony before.

"The same thing I was planning on doing when I first saw you tonight," he says. He grins. "I'll tell you one day soon."

"Can't wait." I give Josh one final shove and he goes tumbling over the rail. Neither of us bothers to peer over the balcony when his body cracks against the pavement. I wipe my hands on my dress and meet Archer's intense gaze.

We're both so lost in the moment that we don't immediately notice the clown waking up.

"Oh my God, look," I say, pointing at Gage. He's already sitting up, scanning the room in a daze.

"Where'd you put the knife?" Archer whispers.

My head is a cloud of fog as I retrace my steps. "Shit. I think I left it on the bookcase."

Stupid.

We rush back into the library, giving the clown a wide berth. Archer tucks me behind him as we head for the door. Gage staggers up and also heads for the door.

"We have to stop him," I say.

"Wanna see a cool party trick?" the clown says. He raises his bound hands behind his back, and with a sick, contortionist move, wriggles his arms over his head to the front.

"What in the devilment?" I mutter.

"Nope. Noelle, we gotta go," Archer says, urging me forward.

Gage brings his hands to his mouth and begins to gnaw at the zip tie, using his fake teeth as serrated blades.

Archer and I grab books off the shelves and start chucking them at Gage's ass. Collector's editions of *Fledgling* and *The Good House* and *Brown Girl in the Ring* bounce off the clown's nose. Alert now, he rushes at us, but Taylor pops up suddenly like every horror movie killer you *knew* wasn't dead. Somehow, Taylor has enough sense to roll onto their side and swing their foot out, sweeping Gage's legs out from under him. Gage goes down hard.

"Taylor!" I cry out. Relief floods my entire system like a shot of adrenaline. Taylor is alive . . . and kicking ass.

"I am not the one, asshole," Taylor says in a hoarse voice as they lean against the bookcase to stand, continuing to give Sidney Prescott in their now tattered costume. "People keep trying to knock me down, but I won't go easily."

Gage's jaw drops. With one hand clutching their injured side, Taylor rips the lanyard with the shock collar remote from Gage's neck. Archer hooks Taylor's arm across his shoulders and opens the door, ready to rush out of the room. I'm right behind them, but Gage lurches forward and snags my ankle when I'm halfway out the door. Taylor is able to stagger away, melting into the smudgy shadows of the hall.

I cry out and grab onto the doorframe to break my fall. Archer lands a kick in Gage's shoulder, and I yank free. I turn to run, but I don't miss the opportunity to stomp on Gage's outstretched right hand, grinding it into the carpeted floor.

"That's for Elise, asshole," I say. I rear back and stomp on his knee. "And that's for Demario." I turn for the door but double back to drive a kick into his ribs. "And that's for my Birkin!" I reach for Archer's hand, linking our fingers, and we take off.

"You're dead! You hear me?" Gage screams after us.

I wish we had thrown him over the balcony instead of Josh, but I'm not like Gage. I'm no killer.

We swing a sharp left and then a right. I glance over my shoulder, but there's no sign of Gage. Even after the beating I gave him, he took off faster than a subway rat.

"Hold up," I say, tugging on Archer's arm.

"What?" Archer whispers. The desperation in his voice matches my own.

"If he's not behind us, did he go after Taylor? Where the hell is—" My voice dies in my throat as Gage leaps out from an adjacent hallway, cutting off the way to the stairs. A small smile spreads across his face.

I run backward before spinning around and charging back the way we came. A scream is trapped in my throat. My parents' suite is up ahead. The clown clomps behind us, limping, and breathing heavily as he closes in.

Archer and I rush inside my parents' room and barricade the door with a dresser. Archer yanks on the windows, but the jump is way too high. My heartbeat thunders in my ears.

Thud.

Gage slams his body against the door. It's only a matter of time before he forces his way in.

"Bathroom," I say, grabbing Archer's hand. Moonlight spills through the open shades.

Thud.

"There's an oak tree outside the window that hangs over the pool house. We can climb down," I tell Archer. I've never climbed a tree in my life, but I'm not gonna overthink it. The window in the small bathroom is sealed shut too.

"The cops are on the way, asshole!" Archer yells, closing the bathroom door. I really hope Archer is right. *But what if the fall detection alert feature on the watch doesn't work? What if no one comes?*

I rummage around under the sink, desperate for something to break glass. I hand Archer a bottle of bathroom cleaner.

He examines the green bottle. "Grime fighter? What am I supposed to do with this?"

"Aim for the eyes!" I say, still rummaging.

I discover a wrench behind the cleaning supplies and clutch the cool metal tool in my hands like a lifeline. Archer turns the nozzle to Spray and tucks the bottle into the waist of his pants. He flexes one wrist, his fingers slightly swollen. I've got to get us out of here. I spin the wrench in my hands like a racket before attacking the window. Gage continues to ram the bedroom door, grunting loudly and angrily.

I slam the wrench against the windowpane, focusing my frenzied hammering on the lower corner, where the glass is weakest. I don't know if this will work, but I have to try. I smash a hole through the first pane with a panicked sob. Archer wraps a towel around his hand and we break through the second one and clear as many of the glass pieces as we can.

Chilly air blusters into the room.

The dresser tumbles over with an earsplitting crash. Fear snakes down my spine. Is this it?

Archer boosts me up to the window from behind. Glass fragments pierce my palms, but the rush of adrenaline allows me to power through the pain.

"Just get out of here, okay?" he says, a hard rasp to his voice. All of his earlier tenderness is gone. His hands are on my thighs, my back, shoving and pushing. I barely get one leg out the window before he shoves me out the rest of the way. More shards of glass slice into my shoulders and legs as I tumble out. Then Gage barrels into the bathroom.

I should be hauling ass across the rooftop, but I'm frozen at the window. I see the crazed look on the clown's face.

"C'mon, Archer!" I scream. I grab his arm, flinching from the twinge of glass embedding itself into my arms while I tug him through the window. Gage rushes him from behind.

The clown grabs him by the back of the shirt and hauls him back into the bathroom. He slams Archer's head into the wall beneath the window. Archer cries out and wobbles away, dazed, but he's able to reach into his waistband and blast Gage in the face with lemon-scented cleaner.

Gage slaps his hands to his eyes and hollers. His legs bump the toilet bowl, and he fumbles his way to the sink. Archer takes advantage of the moment to land a roundhouse kick in his chest, sending the clown skating across the tiled floor.

"Yes! Beat his ass!" I yell.

Archer makes a mad dash to the window, but Gage is on his feet faster than should be humanly possible. He tackles Archer from behind, and before he can regain his balance, the clown snatches the ceramic toilet lid off the tank and smashes it into the side of Archer's head. Archer goes down again and this time he doesn't move.

"Archer?" I call out.

Gage steps over Archer's unmoving body, his face expressionless as he stalks over to me.

I back away, but too fast. Glass crunches beneath my boots and I skid on the wet rooftop. I attempt to steady myself and manage a few shaky steps, balancing on the sloped roof. A polka-dot-suited leg emerges from the window. I gasp and try to pick up the pace, but the height is disorienting, and I can't shake the image of Archer lying facedown on the tiled floor.

"It's just me and you now, Noelle," the clown says behind me.

I glance over my shoulder and my heart just about stalls. Gage is closing in fast, his steps steady and measured. There's no way I can beat him to the end of the roof or climb down the tree. Not when I'm taking baby steps. Not when one misstep will send me sliding down this roof to my death.

Then I see it. The open skylight greets me like a vision of hope. I turn to face the clown. The wind cuts right through my pink dress. My legs are shaking, but I've made it this far. Against all odds, I'm still here. Still standing.

"I'm so sick of entitled snowflakes like you," the clown spits. He takes a step closer, but I hold my ground. I have to play this right or the game ends for me tonight, forever.

"And then you go and purge your souls to a therapist for six hundred a session and walk out with a clear conscience," he rants. "Guess I should be thankful to Dr. Dillard for giving back to society by taking me on as his one pro bono client a year."

"I bet you hate that, don't you?" I say, taunting him. "Maybe if you actually opened up to Dr. Dillard and let him help you, you wouldn't be a murderer, *Wesley*."

The clown huffs a laugh. "It wasn't supposed to be like this. At first, I just wanted to give you a good scare, teach you shit stains a lesson, but the more I learned about you and your entitled friends, the more I realized that the world would be a better place without people like you in it. And I'm not the only one. The proletariat is tired. The revolution is here."

First I'm a snowflake. Now I'm a shit stain. Meanwhile, he's a whole-ass killer hiding behind a janky clown costume. "So, did you miss all the classes on civil rights? Are you paying attention to the news *today*? Racism is very much alive," I say, shifting to keep my balance. "Black celebrities get harassed all the time—look what they did to LeBron, Serena, freaking Beyoncé. Racists don't care if I move rich because I'll always be Black."

Gage's expression sours. "We're going to tear this system down and the best way to start is with the ones who stand to inherit it. The ones who cheat and drop money to get what they want. The ones ticking the minority box so they can skip the queue. What happened to hard work in this country?"

I'm on the roof but might as well be in the twilight zone. *Inherit the system?* I almost laugh out loud. Black people can't even get reparations.

"Equality feels like oppression for people like you, Wesley. Half the people you murdered tonight didn't have the same privileges as you do! Are you serious? All this talk about meritocracy is bullshit, and you know it. Affirmative action didn't come out of nowhere. You can rationalize it however you want, but the real reason you're here is because someone else got the things you wanted, isn't it?" I ask, knowing that I'm prodding the bear with a hot poker.

"Let's be honest—it's reverse racism," Gage says with a straight face.

"Oh no," I say, rolling my eyes. "It's not on me to teach you about whiteness and its relationship to power. Read a book. Preferably in prison." I take another step backward.

Gage scratches his armpit. Maybe it's the itching powder. "I want to play one last game with you, Noelle. An easy guessing game. How many bones do you reckon you'll break when I throw you off this roof?" he taunts, inching closer. "How many hours will they spend picking up the pieces of your brain when you go splat?"

I ignore the tightness spreading across my chest. Gage cackles as if his lunacy makes sense.

Thick yellowish clouds creep over the moon, making it even harder to see. The skylight is just behind me now, less than five steps away. The clown sniffs the air, reveling in the dizzying petrichor.

"That Larkin poem, it wasn't just about Kelsi's parents, was it? It was about Josh's and yours too," I say. Gage must still be in his teens—he would have been a little kid during Occupy Wall Street. The seeds of what he is now were planted a long time ago over a movement focused on economic inequality, but Gage's resentment of a capitalist system blossomed into such a hateful indictment of wealth and privilege that he found a home with the Liberation Bloc.

"Josh was a delusional egomaniac. He was right about one thing, though. You're not Final Girl material," he says.

My spine stiffens. But I have to keep going. "Hate to break it to you, but I've been surviving. I've lost count of the number of times I've had to force myself to speak up, to take up more space. I've had people who claimed to have my best interests at heart discourage me and tell me I should be less ambitious." I step back until my boot hits the point where the roof shingles meet the glass panel of the skylight. "I've been a Final Girl all along."

Gage finally charges at me, closing the distance between us. I raise a shaky hand and point behind him.

"Oh my God. Archer, you're alive!"

Gage swings around, almost losing his balance, giving me just enough time to sidestep the skylight. I glance over my shoulder.

"My bad. Must've been someone else," I say. I hobble farther away, moving parallel to the skylight.

"Bitch!" Gage yells. He rushes forward with a giant leap and likely the intention of rolling us both off the roof. His entire face changes the moment his foot connects with nothing but air. He tries to propel himself forward but tumbles through the opening instead. He claws at and scrapes against the glass panels, his body dangling perilously. I move around the skylight, well out of his reach, and face him.

"Help me!" he shouts, all aggressive.

I shake my head. "First off, take that bass out your voice if you want something from me."

"Noelle," he pleads. His eyes are wide and his chin trembles in the silvery light. "Things went too far. I heard what you said earlier. I'm listening and learning . . . give me a chance. Please, I can't hold on."

"Then maybe you should let go," I say, softly. I spotted the ring covered in blades on his fingers earlier. I know without a doubt that he would turn them on me in a heartbeat.

His face hardens. "I'll find you. I'll make you suffer, I'll—"

"The electrician's coming tomorrow, so we drained the pool earlier," I say, cutting him off. "Must be empty by now, so you ain't goin' do shit."

His mouth falls open in surprise, and his fingers finally lose their grip. His scream echoes as he plummets into the abyss, landing with a thud that will stay with me forever. The emergency deck lighting is enough for me to make out the dark outline of his body, limbs bent at odd angles. I watch and wait, afraid to turn away in case he pulls another Michael Myers and vanishes. He doesn't.

"Thoughts and prayers, bruh," I say. My legs give out and I sink down and sit, with my head in my hands. I glance over at the bathroom window. Archer's in there, hurt or worse.

The clouds float past the moon, bathing the rooftop in light. Stars peek out, some shining brighter than others. The clown remains motionless at the bottom of the swimming pool, but I stay on edge. I focus on taking one deep breath, then another, concentrating on the glimmer of flashing blue and red lights in the distance, growing brighter on their way to Castle Hill.

CHAPTER 30

"Well, Clarice, have the lambs stopped screaming?"
—*The Silence of the Lambs* (1991)

Fire trucks are parked at chaotic angles in front of my house after pulling the gate off its hinges. Cops string yellow tape around the property and a team of crime scene analysts dressed in white haul their forensic kits through the entryway.

"Noelle?" Archer calls out the moment he emerges from the front door. From a distance, I can see that his head is bandaged and his left hand is wrapped in thick gauze dressing.

I gather the metallic warming blanket around my shoulders and leap out of the ambulance.

"Archer?" I go to him, then pause because I don't want to cause any more pain. But he hugs me tightly anyway, triggering a fresh set of tears.

"Are you okay?" he asks, rubbing my arms. His gaze roams my body, taking me in whole. His eyes settle on the white bandages on my hands and wrists from the zip ties and lacerations from the glass.

I hiccup through my tears.

"Is she okay?" he asks the sympathetic EMT who followed me from the ambulance.

"Yeah, but we should get you both to the hospital to get checked out. You've been through a lot tonight," the EMT says.

Archer and I just nod.

"I was so worried when I woke up," Archer murmurs into my hair. "What happened? Did he do anything else to hurt you?"

I shake my head. "He fell through the skylight before he got the chance," I say, reliving the moment.

"It's over now," Archer says, tugging the metallic emergency blanket tighter around me.

The EMT ushers us both to the ambulance, and we sit on the ledge between the open doors.

More emergency vehicles arrive, and there's a news van parked outside the gate. An animal control officer appears from around the side of the house, wrangling a miniature pony. There's a loud shout as someone disables yet another bear trap. The paramedics who rushed into the house with stretchers are making their way back outside. Demario is wheeled out with an oxygen mask covering his nose and mouth.

"D!"

His head turns when he hears my voice, and he manages a weak thumbs-up as the gurney is hoisted into another ambulance. I've never been more relieved. Taylor is wheeled out next. Their face is almost as white as the sheet covering them. We make eye contact. A small smile spreads across their face. One that seems to say, *We made it.*

Two police officers are marching our way. An officer in a navy blazer and dark pants introduces herself as Detective Rivera and the white uniformed cop as Officer Kowalski.

"Hi, Noelle. Your parents are on the way. They are going to meet us at the hospital and we'll take your statement there," she says.

"Okay, thank you," I say, rubbing my arms under the blanket.

"We've got a team out searching the riverbank for any sign of Elise Thomas," she says. Her expression is grim. "We'll find her."

By then, it'll be too late. As much as I want to hope, in my heart I know that Elise is gone. Demario wouldn't have left her side if there was any chance she was alive. I burst into tears for what feels like the hundredth time tonight.

The officers head into the house, just as the body bags are rolled out. I climb out of the ambulance. Archer tries to nudge me back inside, but I can't look away. I tighten the blanket around myself and walk over to where the convoy of gurneys makes a solemn voyage down the driveway. Friends who walked into my house for a Fright Night party and now they're leaving in body bags. Kelsi and Dylan, Hailey and Mariana, Charlie and Maddie, Vivek and likely Elise. Each one of them, a wound in my heart that will never heal. A weight settles on my shoulders.

"We'll get through this," Archer says. "Together. I'll be wherever you need me."

"I was promised a Mozart sonata," I say, teasing.

Archer turns to me and tilts my chin up to meet his eyes. "I'll play one for you every day if you want me to."

"Something that can make me smile through tears?" I ask.

He presses a kiss to my temple. "Anything. You know, hanging out with my muse might have a few perks."

This gets a laugh out of me, but the intensity of his expression makes my legs do a little wobble.

"Not a bad way to spend the holidays," I say dreamily. It feels good to have something to look forward to.

Archer raises his bandaged wrists. "Bruised but not broken. Can't say the same for the ribs, though."

"OMG, and you're just standing here like it's nothing! C'mon, we should get to the hospital," I say, nudging him along.

"I've been called hardheaded a few times," Archer says, tapping the bandage wrapped around his head.

Laughter dies on my lips when the door to the pool house opens and the last gurney is carted out. I suck in a breath.

One thing is certain. Winter solstice, the longest night of the year, has nothing on this Halloween. "It's finally over," I say, linking my arm through Archer's.

The stretcher jerks to a sudden stop and the body bag shifts and flops to one side. I let out a loud yelp and multiple heads spin in my direction. An EMT reaches down and prods the front wheel of the gurney out of a crack in the driveway.

"Aye, these wheels are tricky, but we good now," he says, repositioning the body.

My face heats up with embarrassment as sympathetic looks are thrown my way. The stretcher gets rolling again, bumping and squeaking down the driveway.

I let out a shaky breath. "Guess the night wouldn't be complete without the most overdone horror cliché, right?"

"What's that?"

"The not-dead-yet," I say, feeling goose bumps pop up every-where.

Archer barks a laugh. "I don't think my head and hands can handle a sequel."

"Absolutely not," I say. What happened tonight is the kind of personal story that could get me into a top film school, but I don't know if I'll ever be ready to relive tonight, not even for a future Jump Scares podcast. Maybe one day I'll get there. Or not. Archer and I make our way back to the ambulance.

"What time is it?" I ask.

"It's 12:22," he says.

I think back to earlier times in the night when Josh said he never loses and I wouldn't make it to midnight in a horror movie situation. Guess there's a first time for everything. The EMT straps us into our seats and closes the double doors. The am-bulance rolls out of Castle Hill. Archer squeezes my hand, and I squeeze back. I stare out the back window of the ambulance, watching the hive of activity around the house. Josh Sullivan was wrong about a lot of things, but especially me. Then again, I'm used to being underestimated.

What can I say?

I win.

JUMP SCARES STARTER PACK
TOP 10 ESSENTIAL BLACK HORROR MOVIES*

1. *Get Out*
2. *Night of the Living Dead*
3. *Us*
4. *Attack the Block*
5. *Candyman*
6. *His House*
7. *The Boy Behind the Door*
8. *Blacula*
9. *Vampire in Brooklyn*
10. *The People Under the Stairs*

*Watch at your own risk.

ACKNOWLEDGMENTS

It really does take a village to publish a book. Thank you to the readers who gave this book a chance. I appreciate your support. To my husband, thanks for answering all my weird and mildly disturbing questions with thoughtfulness and patience, and never doubting as I embarked on this author journey. Thank you for all you do. To my son, thanks for the hugs and candy. To my parents in Barbados, for encouraging me to "keep going with de writing ting" and for celebrating all my wins. Your constant reminder that I could do anything I set my mind to stays with me.

To my agent, Danielle Burby, thank you for always cheering me on, and for all your efforts behind the scenes. Partnering with you has made this maze that is publishing easier to navigate. You are an absolute gem.

To my editor, Bria Ragin, this story has been a dream project. Thank you for your editorial insight, sharp eye, and encouragement. I'm sorry you had to flag so many idioms. Thank you for working your magic on these wild chapters. This book wouldn't exist without you. To the entire team at Delacorte Press and Random House Children's Books, thank you for your enthusiasm. You've made my debut experience a memorable one.

Special thanks to: Wendy Loggia, Beverly Horowitz, Barbara Marcus, designers Ray Shappell and Cathy Bobak, managing editor Tamar Schwartz, Lydia Gregovic, copyeditors Heather Lockwood Hughes, Colleen Fellingham, and Alison Kolani, production manager Shameiza Ally, and my publicist, Joey Ho.

To Betsy Cola for the amazing illustration that captured my vision of Noelle perfectly. The design team delivered an amazing cover and interior that exceeded everything I could have hoped for.

Writing can be a lonely endeavor and having a few people in your corner makes a world of difference. To J.Elle, mentor extraordinaire, thank you for taking me on as a mentee in Author Mentor Match and being so generous with your time and knowledge. I wouldn't be here without your support. Shakirah Bourne, the best hype woman an author could ask for, thank you for your friendship, publishing insight, taking time to read my drafts, and all the brainstorming sessions. Also thank you for introducing me to the rum sour.

To my writing community, thank you to Sophie Li, Danielle Parker, and Jade Adia for reading my early chapters and offering feedback. To Kelis Rowe and Kristen Lee, thank you for keeping my spirits high and motivating me with your stellar books. Shout-out to the ladies of the Queen Squad writing community. I appreciate y'all.

To Cherie Jones, over a decade ago in Barbados we dreamed about publishing books. We said it would happen for us. Our books are now standing next to each other on my bookshelf. Special acknowledgment to the National Independence Festival of Creative Arts in Barbados for providing a platform to showcase the literary arts. It gave me the courage to share my stories, and I've been writing ever since. To anyone with a dream, keep moving forward. Above all else, thanks and praise to God.

ABOUT THE AUTHOR

Lisa Springer is a writer from Barbados currently living in New York with her family. When she's not writing, she's probably reading, dreaming about the beach, or plotting her next dark and twisty story. *There's No Way I'd Die First* is her debut novel.

lisaspringerbooks.com

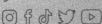